THE DEVIL YOU KNOW

USA TODAY & INTERNATIONAL BESTSELLING AUTHOR

VERONICA EDEN

CONTENTS

ABOUT THE BOOK

FROM USA TODAY AND INTERNATIONAL BESTSELLING AUTHOR, VERONICA EDEN, COMES A STANDALONE NEW ADULT BROTHER'S BEST FRIEND ROMANCE WITH A SPUNKY HEROINE, THE LOCAL THIRST TRAP, AND AN UNORTHODOX TUTORING AGREEMENT.

Tatum Danvers has plans and goals for everything in her life. Whatever she sets out to do, she achieves. There's only one thing she's determined to check off...

I'm all set for my first semester at college.
Dream field of study. Five year plan. Brand new notebooks.

But one thing can't come to campus—my V-card.

Being a virgin isn't the biggest part of my problem.
What I need to prepare for the full college experience is someone to teach me what to do in bed. Though I hate to admit defeat, this is one accolade I can't earn on my own.

I have the perfect tutor in mind: my brother's best friend.

Cooper Vale. Hometown heartthrob, sultry bad boy, and my neighbor since we were kids.

PLAYLIST

Heat Waves — Glass Animals
Forbidden — Maxchalant, Maiah Manser
Dick — StarBoi3, Doja Cat
Watermelon Sugar — Harry Styles
Better — ruelle
Promiscuous Motive — Josiane Lessard
feel something — Bea Miller
Overwhelmed — Ryan Mack
Champagne & Sunshine — PLVTINUM, Tarro
Ocean Avenue — Yellowcard
MONTERO — Lil Nas X
Off Limits — BAYNK, Glades
Hands — Oceans Ahead, Shelley Harland
Skin Talk — Stuck On Planet Earth
Fire — Part-Time Friends
Fuck Up the Friendship — Leah Kate
Heartbeats — Jose Gonzalez
Better — Pink Panda
Stay — The Kid LAROI, Justin Bieber
OUTRUN MYSELF — Jack Kays, Travis Barker
Ghost — Justin Bieber

Moonlight — Chase Atlantic
Infinity — Jaymes Young
When I Don't Have You — Idarose
Alright — Alpines
Sunroof — Nicky Youre, dazy

PART ONE: SUMMER

ONE

TATUM

There's nothing quite like the high of a new notebook haul. Brand spanking new notebooks come out on top to get my heart racing like nothing else, herbal or not.

The plastic crinkles as I rip it off the additions to my collection, then a wide smile overtakes my face. Okay, maybe a slightly manic one, but *notebooks*—blank, fresh, awaiting all my thoughts, dreams, lists, and plans. My heartbeat spikes, dancing around like a puppy about to get its favorite tasty treat. Oh, yup. That's the high kicking in.

Instant serotonin boost.

I lay my bounty on my white quilted bedspread, lovingly tracing the colorful spirals coordinated to the bright citrus fruit patterns on the covers of the 3-pack. A content sigh leaves me.

"Perfection."

Possibility.

My favorite feeling in the world.

Opening the cover to the one with orange slices, a giddy thrill runs through me at the sight of the blank page. I keep notebooks, art journals, and planners for everything in my life. The structured organization has helped me visualize and achieve every goal I've set for myself. It's how I maintained a 4.0 GPA through high school while participating in three different clubs and graduated with honors last month. With college on the horizon at the end of the summer, I have no intention of quitting a good thing when it's working for me.

My attention shifts to the inspiration wall above my bed, the mod peach-pink circle painted on the wall covered in my hopes and dreams. It has saved fortune cookies with encouraging and motivational messages, Polaroids of my accomplishments mixed with memories I love with friends and family, clippings I've kept from postcards that gave me a boost, and my favorite quotes from books I've read.

The corner of my mouth lifts when I survey how far I've come from a girl who used to panic at the amount of tasks on my to-do list, frozen into indecision by how much I wanted to do. A therapist I used to see every other week handed me a notebook to journal in one day as a way to dump my thoughts and it just *clicked*. I never looked back.

Deep laughter and the rhythmic beat of a basketball dribbling against the pavement drifts through my open window, followed by the swish of the net when the ball is dunked. My brother Jackson and his best friend Cooper are shooting hoops in the driveway between our two houses.

The breeze makes my curtains billow as I slip off the bed to peek out the window, inhaling the salty sea air. Everything smells like the ocean and sunshine during summertime in South Bay, California. The quaint coastal town is known for three things: surfing, summer tourism, and South Bay College where I'm starting my freshman year in a couple of months.

Is it possible to be nervous-excited-anxious-impatient all at once? Because that's how I feel every day crossing off the days on my sea turtle-themed calendar.

Cooper Vale snags my focus once more. Jackson passes him the ball. With a crooked grin and a languidness to his limbs that oozes sex appeal, he sinks another shot. My brother whoops and gives Cooper a high-five.

I wet my lips as I drink in the impressive muscles Cooper has on display. Shirtless and rocking cut off cotton joggers, he's god-like perfection with tan skin from hours spent surfing with Jackson. He takes off his baseball cap and ruffles his messy brown hair, laughing at whatever my brother says that I miss because I'm too busy trying to control my heart from swooning like a regency maiden at the dimple that pops out when he smiles.

The second his gaze darts up to my window, I smother a squeak and collapse to my knees. Either he has damn good intuition or I was thinking too loud. Okay, this is super mature. I'm eighteen and hiding from my brother's best friend, the guy who has been my neighbor since I was four.

"Get it together, Danvers." I mumble the words in the way Cooper always teases me when I get stuck in a ramble, imitating his cocky surfer boy drawl.

Crawling on my hands and knees—yes, I haven't fully recovered from the urge to hide, even if he can't see me spying on him anymore —I make it back to my bed, reaching for the basket of my most important journals I keep beneath the bed so Jackson won't poke through them like a nosy jerk.

I grab the one that's a simple black moleskin with silver bold lettering that proclaims *FUCK YES YOU GLORIOUS BITCH* on the cover and flip it open to a floral-patterned page I've looked at so many times, the spine is permanently creased to automatically get there without help.

This list is my most prized one—my ultimate life plan. Not my summer plans or my college packing list for my freshman year at South Bay, but my career path and my most private desires.

All of my meticulous preparations have come together. Check marks fill every box except the one goal that has evaded me, the goal I need to achieve before the summer is over. I'm all set for my first semester at college, a day I've been imagining for so long that's finally almost here.

Dream field of study? Check. Five year plan? Check, check. Brand new notebooks? Checkity-check.

But there is one thing I don't want to bring to campus with my— my V-card.

The box left unticked glares at me in hot pink gel pen on floral-patterned notebook paper. *Have sex.* Seems simple enough, right?

3

Wrong.

Every other goal or dream I've ever put on my list was a cakewalk compared to this one. But I achieve everything I set my mind to, so I will check off that box one way or another. And damn it, I will do it before I enter South Bay College as a freshman.

My V-card isn't on my college packing list. It's not that I'm in some big rush or need to make it special with the right person. I don't buy into either camp of the pressures presented by the social construct. What I hate is feeling unprepared and like something is just outside of my grasp. The FOMO is real and it irritates me.

Releasing a terse sigh, I get up and stride to my mirror. Freckles stand out across the bridge of my nose and my light brown braided pigtails are streaked with blonde from the California sunshine. I squint at my blue-eyed reflection. Short and dainty, with enough bank in my backside to fill out my bleach splattered shorts, I'm not exactly the picture of a pinup people lust after.

I don't have any problem with how I look or want to change anything about myself. Well, besides that one pesky thing. I've never really thought about my looks. School and my aspirations have always come first. So much so that I feel like I'm allowing life to pass me by without embracing it.

Being a virgin isn't the biggest part of my problem. In order to lose it, I'll need someone to help me check that box off. After giving it a lot of thought, I've come up with a plan that's...well, all right, it's this side of crazy. But it's the kind of crazy that will work, and I'm all about results.

All I want is to feel like I'm ready for the full college experience. In order to succeed in this goal, I need someone to teach me everything there is to know about being great in bed. I need a practice run. Someone to let me make mistakes until I figure things out. I just want to know what's ahead of me and be able to enjoy it.

Maybe I've been lying to myself. I am in a bit of a rush. But it's my choice—all I want is to know what I'm doing without having to wade into online dating or suffer through fumbling with guys who might want more than I'm willing to give. I don't want a boyfriend while I'm prepping for the fall semester and working at the Tiki Taco Shack on the beach. This isn't about them, it's about me.

I've been too damn busy meeting every other one of my achievements that I haven't had time to date a lot. Some—I'm not a total prude. But it's been...a while. The last time I went on a date, there might have been chaperones involved. Okay, fine, I barely dated in high school. That's why I'm one of the few people my age in South Bay with hardly any experience past first base.

That's changing this summer, though. Not the boyfriend part, the experience part.

I have the perfect tutor in mind: my brother's best friend.

Cooper Vale. Hometown heartthrob, sultry bad boy, and total player. He's always got a girl with him in his photos on social media. When our group of friends hangs out at the beach, all he has to do is dish out that crooked smile and he has the attention of every girl within sight.

He's everything I need to get through this ordeal and meet my goal before freshman orientation as painlessly as possible. It helps that when I see him he stirs a hot, achy feeling between my legs with his confident grins, sharp jawline, and warm brown eyes that make me want to melt inside.

Attraction won't be a problem. It never has been.

But here's the catch: Cooper has always been off-limits. Duh, he's Jackson's best friend. It's not just because they're almost two years older, but Jacks swore me off his friends a long time ago, same as I did to him. I never had a problem with it when I've been so focused on my studies. It's not like Cooper's ever looked at me the way he looks at the girls that hang off his arm.

He's also the only guy I know who's available after recently breaking up with the girl he's been dating for the last year.

If I'm not allowed to fall for the guy I pick to help me, I won't risk developing feelings. This is purely scientific and in a controlled environment, like the psych studies I'll be conducting for my future doctorate degree.

As if it needs to be stated again—I mean, just look at the guy, with that beach bum tan, windswept hair, and the faded blue baseball cap he wears backwards—but for the record, Cooper is the perfect man for the job.

Better the devil you know, especially to proposition to become your tutor between the sheets.

Nothing could possibly go wrong, right? Cooper is totally the safe option. No way will either of us catch feels.

It's a genius game plan. Smirking, I grab my notebook from the bed and visualize Cooper agreeing once I present the idea to him with a proposal I've been working on for a week. Kidding. Kind of.

Commence Operation: Lose My Virginity.

TWO
COOPER

A lazy half-smile pulls at my mouth with another satisfying *swish* when the ball slips through the net. I'm on fire today, sinking every shot. It feels damn good.

"Dude." Jackson's groan draws a chuckle from me.

I shrug. "What can I say, bro?" I pop one shoulder in a shrug. "Master at work."

"You're killing me today," he complains.

"Nah, I'm just on my game." I put minimal effort into jogging across the driveway between my house and my best friend's to retrieve the ball, tossing it to him one-handed. "We still catching waves later?"

It's hot as hell out, baking my skin, and I'm looking forward to the cool crush of the saltwater on my body.

"Always, man." Jackson shoots me a grin at the prospect of our favorite pastime—surfing.

South Bay has the best surfing beaches within an hour radius. It's one of the reasons people flock here every season. Plus the tourists like to take Instagram pictures in front of the sun-washed pastel bungalows from a bygone era and shit. Live like a local for the Gram. No joke, there's a renovated Airbnb around the corner from here that goes for like a grand a night.

Outsiders see the quintessential California beach town, but all anyone who grew up here sees is the beach, surfing, and the college most of us end up at, South Bay College.

Life is good here. At least it has been for me until Kayla started a fight and dumped my ass at the end of the semester. *Again.*

I grit my teeth and shove her from my mind. We've broken up twice before, but even with our on and off cycle, she's the longest relationship I've ever had. It was kind of nice to have someone who wanted me for more than my body. Someone who wanted to talk to me and lean on me. Or so I thought, but she was only after the same thing every girl I've hooked up wants—my dick and the bragging rights for taking a ride.

Being needed felt good. Made it seem like I was doing something right when everything else was up in the air. It made me realize how much I want that for real, and it's thrown me off my usual game since the start of summer.

Not wanting to think about any of it, I shut down that line of thinking to return later and haunt me when I'm laying in bed buzzed or baked to take the edge off. My advisor said there was time. Until then, my summer is going to be filled with time on my board in the ocean, hanging with my boy Jacks and our friends, and getting up to crazy shit as usual during the tourist season.

Jackson pushes his hand against the back of my head with a playful shove. I get him back by stealing the ball and pivoting before making another beautiful shot. I know it's going in the net before it makes it, and Jacks knows it too, groaning as he slings an arm over my shoulder.

"I'm calling it," he says.

"Aight. I'm heading in for a drink. It's hot as fuck out." He grunts in agreement while stripping out of his stretched out muscle tank. I jerk my thumb toward his kitchen door. "Want anything?"

"I'm good. I've got to shower, anyway. My shift at the Shack starts in an hour."

Adjusting the bill of my favorite baseball cap, I shoot him a smirk. Everyone in our social circle, including his sister, works at the Tiki Taco Shack. The small beachfront shop is a staple in town.

"Later, man." I give Jackson a fist bump.

"Peace and love, brother."

He heads inside first, while I check my phone. No texts from Kayla. I didn't expect any, and yet some part of me keeps hoping because even though she just likes to play games, we were together long enough for me to want it to be more. To be serious.

This is ridiculous. Why the hell am I mooning over her? I'm not a guy who does serious relationships. It's how I got my rep as a player.

Whatever.

Music sounds from the house. The corner of my mouth lifts when I recognize it as one of Tatum Danvers' playlists. I've grown up as their neighbor and Tate loves to play her music loud when she's trying to get in the zone and hype herself up for whatever goal she's chasing. She's someone that always knows what she wants to do, plus the five steps that follow it. I admire that about her.

A familiar but unwarranted warmth fills my chest as I walk toward the door. It's the exact opposite of how I should feel when I think about my best friend's younger sister.

Sure enough, I find her in the kitchen with her phone on the counter blasting her Spotify playlist. She's lingering in the fridge, half hidden and unaware of my presence. Swiping my tongue over my lip, I give in to the urge to peek at her playlist title. This one's called *main character theme music: the soundtrack of a bad bitch*. An amused huff slips out of me.

Tatum gasps as if she's been caught sneaking around, turning a wide-eyed look on me. "Hey."

Damn, she's cute. The only thing that's kept me from resisting her is the fact I'm not allowed to want her.

"'Sup." I nod in greeting with my chin. "Psyching yourself up or something?"

"Or something." The shy smile she offers turns determined, and she rakes her teeth over her lip.

I track the movement, mirroring it absently. Cheeks coloring, she clears her throat and turns away, messing around with her phone while I grab a glass from the cabinet. The cool thing about growing up as next-door neighbors with your best friend is how comfortable you become in each other's house. Jackson is the same when he's at my place.

Without asking, because I don't need to when I know the answer, I get a glass for Tatum, too. I detour to the fridge for ice and the jug of fresh homemade lemonade Mrs. Danvers keeps full throughout the summer. Our glasses sweat from the chilled drink against the heat.

I add a splash of water to hers, because she always complains about lemonade being too sweet without cutting it. Weirdo. My mouth curves affectionately of its own accord.

"Here." I hold the glass over Tatum's shoulder from behind as I pass by, taking a deep, refreshing gulp from my own. "Goddamn, your mom makes the best lemonade."

Her spine stiffens at my proximity, and she whips around, nearly knocking the glass from my hand. I set it down before she spills it and place a steadying hand on her arm.

"Careful."

"I—sorry." Tatum's stare lifts from where I'm touching her to meet my gaze. "Thanks. For the drink."

My thumb strokes her arm. She has nice, soft skin. "No problem."

Those full lips tug into a smile that makes my stomach tighten. If only I could have something with her. We'd be great together. Unlike my other hookups, something with her would be more than physical.

Except that can't ever happen. It's a line I won't cross. Her brother would end me for ever touching her—for even thinking about touching her.

And yeah...I've thought about it.

Who wouldn't? Look at her, with those pouty lips, bright blue eyes like the sea, a tiny waist I'm sure my hands would encompass if I held her, and a sexy little ass that looks great in those shorts. Tatum Danvers is cute as hell.

Okay, maybe I've thought about it a lot.

Maybe I think about it so much because Tatum is forbidden fruit to me. Just one taste of my best friend's sister is all I crave.

"So listen..." Tatum trails off.

I clench a fist and lean casually against the counter, bracing my forearm until my dick behaves in my joggers. Jesus, I'm fucked up.

She's right there and I'm thinking about shit I have no business entertaining in my mind.

Her gaze locks on my bare chest. It's not the first time she's seen me shirtless and blushed, but it's the first time she's been so open about it without averting her gaze and ignoring my physique. I lift a brow, interested in the reason for the change.

Dangerous path. Ah, fuck it. I'm curious.

"Yeah?" I prompt.

She licks her lips, drawing my attention to their fullness.

"Would you, like—" Tatum cuts herself off and curses under her breath. Gathering herself with a fortifying breath, she forges on, pinning me with her piercing gaze. "Would you want to hang out? Tonight, or this weekend if you're busy."

"Jacks is going surfing with me after his shift. You can ride with me if you don't want to ride your bike to the beach."

Her shoulders sag slightly, but she steps closer, putting a small hand over mine where I'm braced against the counter. Damn, her hand is so tiny compared to mine. I bet if she placed her palm against mine, I could curl my fingers over hers and still have room to spare.

Tatum flexes her grip on my hand. "No, uh. I mean hang out just...just you and me."

THREE
TATUM

Just you and me. There. I did it. It's out there.

My breath catches as I wait for Cooper's answer. He's not really paying attention, focusing on my hand over his. Oh crap. Am I being too forward? What's the big deal, guys are forward all the time.

See how shitty social constructs are? No one needs this kind of stress in their life. I'm just a girl trying to ask a boy to—the chorus from *Dick* by StarBoi3 plays in my head because sometimes when I can't sleep I spend way too long stuck in a dissociative endless scroll through TikTok.

Crudely, yes, what I'm doing is asking Cooper to tear up my pussy with his dick and send it to an early grave. Please. Preferably multiple times throughout the summer, because I'm sure this is going to take a few tries for me to learn. Strictly for educational purposes, of course.

Except...

Oh shit. There's no recognition in his gaze. He doesn't get what I'm asking at all, despite how closely we're standing.

Cooper hitches a shoulder and plays with the condensation on his glass, tracing a finger through the path and sucking the gathered moisture from his finger. My mouth drops open at the sight and my mind supplies helpful segues of what else he could do with that mouth, my imagination running wild with sexy fantasies. Oh god. My face heats.

He chases it with a deep drink of his lemonade. I'm fixated on the bob of his throat as he swallows.

"Sure," he says. "We can chill sometime."

The off-limits agreement me and my brother have is really coming back to bite me in the ass if Cooper doesn't see me as anything more than his friend's sister. Damn it. My fingers curl into my palm once I rip it back from resting over top of his.

The weird moment of intimacy between us breaks when he shifts away, stretching his sculpted arms overhead and giving me a tantalizing show of his bare back as his shoulders flex with the movement.

My mouth goes dry. Jesus, does he have to be such a fine specimen? Naturally athletic, he exudes confidence that makes my pulse thrum whenever he's around.

The thing about Cooper is he's hot, but he knows it. He's the type of guy who is totally aware of the effect he has on girls when he shows off his body and doles out those heart-stopping crooked smirks like free candy.

Not only that, he's tactile. Like that thing with my arm a second ago. I believe he thrives on the attention he gets when he flirts like it's a pro sport.

I once watched him score free tickets to a private beach concert for him and Jackson in under five minutes and all he had to do was sweep his gaze over the girl in charge of the event. He probably got me lemonade to distract me with his charm, so he didn't have to spend too much time talking to his best friend's little sister without any buffer.

Made just the way you like it, my helpful inner logic Tate reminds me.

Shut up, bitch. It doesn't mean anything.

Of course he knows how I like my sweet drinks cut with water after growing up with him half-living here with front row seats to my arguments with Jackson about why it tastes better diluted.

My theory is proven when he twists around to shoot me a cocky wink. The dude's got game and that's exactly why he's the ideal candidate for my project.

"Later." He puts his empty glass in the sink and nods to me.

At a loss for what to do when he misses my point, I offer a weak wave. Well, crap. Back to the drawing board.

I didn't even get the chance to do the presentation speech I prepared, the one I worked on for days. Should've gone with that instead of a soft broach. We could've been up in his room by now and my little problem would be taken care of.

The thought of that unchecked box on my list of goals burns in my brain.

"Damn it." The glass of lemonade on the counter is the only witness to my mumble as I trail a fingertip through the condensation.

Face prickling with heat and stomach fluttering, I slowly bring my finger to my mouth and trace my lips with the cool wetness. My eyelids droop and I picture Cooper's mouth brushing mine to chase the taste of lemonade.

Another bout of determination fills me.

This is going to work. This plan *has* to work.

I won't give up that easily.

FOUR
COOPER

Tatum's request to hang out is still stuck in my thoughts a couple of days later. I can't get it out of my head. It's lumped right in with the existential dread that picks the best moments to creep up on me, like now at 2am while I'm sitting up with insomnia.

Doesn't help that she's always occupying a corner of my mind.

My gaze cuts to the open window. The Danvers house is dark. Tate's window is catty-corner to mine. The sound of the waves is faint, but easier to hear this late. Our block isn't far from the coast.

I should've agreed to go to the party with Jackson tonight, but I wasn't feeling it. He rode me about it all day during our shift at the Shack and after, while we sat on our boards waiting for the perfect wave. I haven't been in the mood to play wingman since Kayla dumped me.

Maybe that makes me a shitty friend to skip out on helping him score, but there's been a lot on my mind.

Namely the crumpled up piece of paper sitting on my nightstand I've read a hundred times. The letter from my advisor came at the end of the spring semester about my academic probation. My freshman year was filled with a bit too much partying and not enough hitting the books to keep up with my classes. It claims I need to find direction and turn my GPA around for my sophomore year of college.

A ragged breath leaves me as I sink back onto the rumpled sheets, scrubbing a hand over my face. I don't know. Have no fucking clue what direction I want my life to take.

I'm about to turn twenty, how the shit am I supposed to know what I want to do forever?

Sure, I believe some people know their dreams and aspirations long before college. People like Tatum Danvers, who have it together and can see their life plan clear as day.

But I'm not one of those people. My major is undeclared and I'm still not sure what I should decide on. What if the choice I make isn't the right one? What if I want to change my mind in a year? What if whatever I end up doing is something I wake up five years down the road hating?

Christ, I need to take the edge off before I push myself into a full-blown anxiety attack over this life crap.

All I know is things are easier in the summer, when all I have to worry about is work, surfing, playing ball, and just living day to day instead of looking ahead and planning my future out.

With a groan, I roll out of bed and rustle around in my stash for a joint before heading to lean out the window. I brace my forearms on the windowsill. The first hit has my eyes hooding in relief.

I'm not an idiot. I know I'll have to figure out something.

My parents might be chill as owners of the health and wellness retreat center they founded, but they want me to apply myself. Do the work, that's what they always say.

Maybe I can sign up with a study group or find a tutor. Tate pops into my thoughts and my head jerks with a snort. I mean, yeah, she's a little academic genius with how many honors she had around her neck at her graduation. I've seen her notes spread out on their kitchen island, color coded and everything. As much as I'd like the excuse to hang out with her one-on-one, she'd probably have no interest in helping me resuscitate my grades.

I should at least talk to her about it. I won't get anywhere with this if I don't try to find help.

My phone vibrates, pulling me out of my buzzed late night musings. I figure it's Jackson, drunk off his ass and telling me exactly what I'm missing by passing on the party.

The lazy smirk drops off my face as soon as I see the name. Kayla. Shit, I hate the way part of me considers going down this path again.

Kayla: miss u bbyyyy

My teeth clench. There's a photo of her, glassy-eyed, boobs squeezed together in her low-cut top for my benefit, styled hair messy from dancing at the club she likes in Del Mar. She's wasted.

Bitterness floods through me. This is how it always is with her, how we picked things back up last time. She starts a fight that ends it, then sexts me in the middle of the night. I fell for it twice before because I liked her and I sure as fuck liked getting naked with her, but not this time.

I'm done with girls like Kayla. Done with girls who manipulate me because they want to ride my dick. Yeah, I'm known as a guy who can get a chick into bed easy, but that doesn't mean sex is all I want. I'm a person, not a damn warm-blooded dildo they can grab when they're in the mood.

I leave Kayla on read and take another drag on the joint. Gradually, the tension ebbs from my shoulders, and I finally relax enough to feel drowsy.

My attention slides to Tatum's window before I close mine. Once again, her offer to hang out crosses my mind. Maybe I should take her up on it. It'll give me an opportunity to talk to her about study tips without Jackson breathing down our necks.

I allow my mind to wander into forbidden fantasy territory, imagining our heads bent close together, the excited way she talks when she's explaining a topic she's passionate about, then catching her chin with my fingers and kissing her because I can't resist any longer. It's one of countless little ideas that won't ever happen.

The side of my mouth lifts as I strip to my briefs and climb into bed. Folding my hands behind my head, a sigh leaves me feeling more at ease.

If there's any girl in South Bay who's the opposite of Kayla and her manipulative, dick-obsessed shit, it's Tatum.

FIVE
TATUM

Getting Cooper to give me his dick is harder than I first thought. It seemed like it would be easy from how many girls I've seen him bring home, but of course I'm the one who can't figure out what to do short of holding up a neon sign.

My mouth purses to the side. There's a local artist that does them custom. Maybe if it really comes down to it, I can see if I could afford a small one. But would Cooper be the type to get it if I went more discreet with emojis, like a gravestone and a cat, or do I really have to spell it out for him I'd like a ticket to ride?

Squinting, I track Cooper's movements through the Tiki Taco Shack. Our shift is almost over and a pair of girls in his section keep ordering drink refills so he'll linger while they flirt. A coil of heat tightens low in my gut at the inviting smile he offers them, his head tipped forward so his messy brown hair falls over his forehead.

They make it look so simple.

He's been hard to pin down in the last few days, but tonight he's giving me a ride home since we're both closing. I'm asking him straight out when we're alone in his Jeep. The direct approach has to be the key to making him understand what I want his help with.

I blow out a breath and prop my hands on my hips. Damn,

maybe it's a blessing I was too busy doing everything else I wanted so I never knew what a challenge it could be to secure a virginity-obliterating hook up.

"Order up," Marco announces from the kitchen. "Last call."

A flurry of stragglers on our wooden swing seats at the bar hold up hands to put in their last orders while I deliver the basket of tacos to one of my tables. A cool breeze blows in off the beach through the open air tiki-themed restaurant, sending a shiver down my spine.

"You good?" Cooper asks when he joins me at the spot the employees chill when things are slow.

I rub my arms. "Yeah. Just the breeze."

He hums absently, half his focus on refilling napkin dispensers. I take the opportunity to study his profile, admiring the sharp angle of his jaw, the build of his broad shoulders and arms. Our colorful uniform t-shirts with leis stretches across his chest snuggly, offering a front row show to the outlines of the sculpted abs and pecs beneath.

I'm startled out of my poorly concealed thirsting when he shuffles by and puts his zip up hoodie over my shoulders, smoothing his big hands down my arms. We have outdoor space heaters I could stand by, but he still gave me his hoodie.

The soft material envelops me in a musky scent mixed with the ocean and a hint of patchouli. My teeth sink into my lip to contain the embarrassing noise threatening to escape me.

Jesus, am I a swooning maiden? I've grown up with this guy. Why am I battling butterflies?

"Uh, thanks?" I mumble.

"Gotta keep an eye out for you. Warm up, T." Cooper shoots me a cocksure wink that hits me right in the chest.

God, he's so smooth. He's got his charmer skills down pat. I make sure he's no longer looking before slipping my arms into the sleeves that are like sweater paws on me.

Surrounded by Cooper's scent, I coach myself until work is over, going over what I'll say on the ride home.

Once the restaurant closes, I follow him to his blue Jeep. He twirls his keyring on his finger and has a natural swagger in his step.

The inside of his ride smells the same as his hoodie and the beeswax of his surfboard wax. It's familiar, yet new. I've never focused so much on this stuff, despite catching plenty of rides with him.

Before I can get a word in, a text distracts him. He checks his phone, then frowns, his shoulders tensing.

"Is everything okay?" I ask.

"Yeah." He glances at me and dumps his phone in the cup holder, jaw working. "It's nothing."

As he pulls out of the lot, another text lights up his screen. I don't mean to look, but it catches my eye. It's from his girlfriend. *Ex*-girlfriend, I thought. Doubt swirls through my stomach, twisting it in a knot. They broke up. For like the third or fourth time. I've lost track. But they're over, right?

He catches sight of the texts at a red light. Three more have come in. He grumbles under his breath and flips the phone around dismissively. It reassures me I'm not in danger of coming on to someone who isn't available.

Cooper pulls down our block before I've said what I need to. Damn the short distance from the beach.

My heart thumps against my ribs as if it's ready to cliff dive into the ocean. I curl my fingers in the material of his zip up hoodie, throwing a surreptitious glance at him. He's totally unaware of my dilemma, one elbow leaning on the door and his hand resting over the wheel, fingers drumming along to the song playing low on the radio.

The words I've been practicing leave me in the dust.

We reach his driveway. My time is running out.

Screw it. I've just gotta do it. The words spill from me in a rush.

"I need to lose my virginity before college starts and I want it to be you."

The Jeep jolts, tires screeching to a halt when Cooper slams down on the brakes. I grab hold of the oh shit bar on instinct, bracing against the rough stop. He grips the wheel with both hands in a white knuckled grip, staring ahead.

There's a long moment of silence before he finally responds.

"*What?*"

Slowly, Cooper angles his head to gape at me. My stomach erupts in a riot of nerves. In my head it sounded way more logical, but he's looking at me like I'm insane.

"I want to learn what to do in bed before I get to college. Like, at a proficient level," I say. "Ergo, I need to have sex. With you."

My calm, clinical tone doesn't help. Cooper chokes the wheel hard enough that it creaks. He rips his gaze away from me, only to swing back a beat later. It's dim in the car, but I can just make out the intent way his brown eyes roam over me.

My cheeks prickle with heat. He's never looked at me like that before—not outside of my own imagination. Like I'm desirable. Someone he wants to unwrap and discover in every wicked way. I shift in my seat, rubbing my thighs together.

"What the fuck?" Cooper's tone is strained, no longer easygoing.

The way his voice becomes kind of gravelly makes me swallow as a warm ache builds between my legs.

"I feel like I was pretty clear. Is there a problem? Are you not into me?"

The way he sneaks glances at me, only to avert his eyes a second later says otherwise.

"You've lost your damn mind." Cooper forces out a breath and scrubs a hand over his face. A laugh punches out of him. "It's a joke, right? You and Jackson have a weird sense of humor. I'll get you both—"

My brow wrinkles. "I'm not kidding around with you. It's pretty straightforward. You like to fool around with girls, and I want to figure out what I'm doing with someone I can trust."

Shaking his head, Cooper throws open the driver's side door and gets out without answering me.

"Hey! Coop, wait!"

I scramble out of the Jeep to catch him. I collide right into his arms as he grabs me, pushing me against the back of his ride, practically pinning me. Fighting off a rush of heart-pounding desire, I meet his stony gaze beneath the amber glow from the streetlight. This is nothing like the Cooper I've grown up with—the carefree, confident surfer boy replaced with someone even hotter who gets my blood racing.

The arousal intensifies. I like this version of Cooper. Is this who he is with all his girlfriends?

He's not holding me hard enough to hurt me, but he uses his strength to keep me in place. Our bodies brush together. A muscle in his clenched jaw jumps.

"No." It's firm and final. Almost angry.

"No?" I repeat. "Why?"

"Just—no, Tate." He rakes his gaze over me. "Jackson would fucking kill me if I ever touched you."

I scoff. "You're touching me now." His grip flexes, like he needs the extra proof. I put a hand on his chest, enjoying the twitch of his muscles beneath my touch. "Come on, rail me, dude. I know you can do it—I've heard those girls scream when you bring them home. Do that, but to me."

Another ragged breath hisses out of him with a muttered curse. His attention falls to my lips, a crease appearing between his brows. A battle of warring emotions flickers over his handsome features. I run my hand down his chest, and his stomach clenches beneath my fingers. A sexy rumble vibrates within him.

"So." I drag the word out. "Your bed? Or the back of the Jeep? I'd prefer a bed, I think, but my room is out—we can't risk my brother or—"

"No," he growls as he presses closer to me to tower over me. My pulse thrums in my core at his commanding tone. "No fucking way."

It takes a second for his refusal to register when I'm so wrapped up in how hot he is. I blink.

"Wait—seriously?"

"As a goddamn heart attack, T." He grasps my jaw, tilting my head up. His thumb caresses my chin, edging close to my lip without touching. "I can't. I'm sorry."

Before I press him further, he's gone, leaving me alone as he stalks inside his house and slams the door. I'm still wearing his hoodie, wrapped in his scent like the ghost of his strong arms hugging me. I sag against the Jeep, closing my eyes. My body hasn't gotten the memo of how hard we crashed and burned.

Maybe he's not into me. But...that's not the vibe I got. I might not be experienced, but Cooper was looking, no matter how much he tried not to.

If he wants me, then what's the damn problem with taking my virginity?

SIX
COOPER

It's official. Tatum Danvers has lost her goddamn mind. And I'm right behind her, because I was so close to saying yes last night.

Everything in me wanted to agree and take her up to my bed. Peel her shorts down. Leave her in nothing but my hoodie while I took her apart.

While I made her *mine*.

The beach is my favorite place in the world, but even being out here surfing with Jackson and our boys isn't enough to distract me from my fantasies becoming a reality.

Tatum wants me to...

Shit, it's been running through my thoughts nonstop since she sprung it on me after I pulled into the driveway. I barely slept, and when I did my dreams were full of torturous fantasies of Tatum naked and crying out my name while I did everything I've always wanted to her.

"Coop!"

Jackson's shout makes me jerk on my board and nearly lose my balance. Rookie move shit. I clear my throat, thinking of anything to get rid of the thoughts of his sister making me hard.

"Dude, if you're going to space out, go back to shore." Jackson splashes me. "I'm not saving your ass from drifting."

"Thanks, dick." I splash him too, then swipe my wet hair back as I scan the horizon. "Yeah, I'm heading in. I think the good ones are done for the morning. The wind is running interference."

He grunts in agreement. "Bummer."

"We've got the whole summer ahead of us still before classes start back up."

I lean down on my board and swing around to paddle back to shore. Jackson follows my lead. My arms cut through the water with ease gained from surfing any chance we got as soon as we learned how to balance on our boards. It's second nature to be out on the water, watching the swells for the right moment to capture the thrill of riding a good wave. Out here, I can let go of everything and just be.

It doesn't take long for Tatum's words to steal my focus again.

I want it to be you.

Christ, it's like she was in my head, aware of every thought I've ever had about her. The ones I tried and failed to kill before they took root.

What guy wouldn't want a girl like Tatum saying those words to them? Shit, it was sexy as hell, even if the rest of her request threw me. Being told you're wanted is a heady thing you grow addicted to.

But as much as my ego and my dick like the idea of Tatum being into me, it stings to know she's not like I thought. She's just like everyone else who doesn't see past my body. I believed she was different, but it's all girls see when they look at me—muscles, a cocky smile that makes them drop their panties, and a good time. That's it. Nothing deeper. More important than body talk.

It doesn't matter. She's someone I can't ever have.

"Bro," Jackson says from behind me. "Are you listening?"

"What?" I twist to peer over my shoulder at his concerned expression.

"I asked you a question."

I want it to be you.

Shaking my head, I fight off the guilt twisting my stomach. I made Jackson a promise.

"Sorry, man. Weird night, I didn't sleep a lot."

It feels like crap to lie to him, but there's no way I'm telling him what his sister did last night.

"There's a bonfire out at Mariner's Cove this weekend. We hitting it up?"

"Sounds good."

Maybe a party is what I need to wipe this strange week from my mind. Distract myself with a good time.

Once we're back on the beach, we draw the attention of chicks out early to get their tan on as the pair of us swipe droplets of salt-water from our faces. Jackson peels his wetsuit down to his waist and I spy a few phones going up. I snort, shaking my head wryly. They all think they're discreet, but I know a thirst photo on the fly when I see one.

I scrub a hand through my damp hair, raking it back from my eyes as we reach my Jeep. While Jackson gets our boards on the rack up top, I check my phone. The text from Kayla I delete immediately, but the string of messages from Tatum makes my stomach clench.

Tatum: If you're sure you can't help me, then I'll have to compromise on doing it with someone I trust. At least help me find the right candidate who isn't going to sell my kidneys on the black market after. There has to be someone willing out there I can make it work with. I didn't want to do it this way, but at least I can secure a hook up. What about this guy?

Tatum: Or this one says he benches 220, claims he knows the secret to making a girl squirt, and requests not to meet the parents in his profile. Promising.

Tatum: Only 5 miles away. Looks like he'd smash my virginity to pieces. [smirk emoji] [eggplant emoji] [fire emoji]

Each of the texts is broken up by a screenshot of Tinder profiles. First of all, why the fuck does Tate have a Tinder account? Second of all, absolutely fucking not.

A rush of jealousy crashes over me while I scroll through the fuckboys she picked out, followed swiftly by a possessiveness I have no right to feel over her. She's not mine. And yet the thought of these guys touching her, undressing her, makes my blood boil. My knuckles turn white from how hard I grip my phone and my teeth grind together.

Another text comes in. I almost drop my phone reading it, my brows creeping higher on my forehead with each word.

Tatum: Does it really hurt the first time? I was just reading an article on a sex positive forum about how incorporating lots of fore-play can help relax a girl before penetrative sex. Who was the first girl you had sex with and what did she think, did it hurt her? I've seen your dick print in your basketball shorts and sweats. You're not what I'd call small.

"Jesus," I choke out.

"What?" Jackson pokes his head around the side of the Jeep.

"Uh—nothing," I say in a strained rush.

"Is it Kayla? Or another hottie blowing up your phone?" He waggles his eyebrows suggestively. "See if she has any friends that want to go to the bonfire this weekend."

"It's not." But I can't tell him who it is. If he saw Tate's messages, he'd lose his shit. "I'm done with girls like Kayla."

He shrugs it off and leaves me to it. While he sits in the back and cracks open a bottle of water, I turn around and stab my fingers over the touchscreen keyboard.

Cooper: NO.

Her response is immediate.

Tatum: No...? No to Mr. 8-pack gym bro, or no to the first time pain? Elaborate, please.

At the mention of the second guy, a low growl vibrates in my throat. My fingers fly over the keyboard before I can think logically.

Cooper: Don't swipe for him. Don't message him. I'm never letting him touch you. Same goes for ANY of those guys.

Tatum: Just like you won't touch me?

Cooper: That's different.

Tatum: Look, if I could gain all the experience I'm looking for with a couple of sex toys on my own, I'd lock myself in my room for the weekend and go ham. But that won't help me when I'm at SBC. This isn't a time for silicone replicas. I need real life schooling here, dude.

Cooper: No. You're not hooking up with someone on Tinder. Guys on there are only after one thing.

Tatum: Sounds perfect because that's what I'm after too. You know how to stop me if you want a say in this, otherwise I don't really need your permission. Did you change your mind? I made a pros/cons list last night if you're still on the fence that might inform your decision.

Tate and her damn lists.

A hand clamps on my shoulder and I tense, caught out. Jackson shakes me. "Ready? I'm starving. Let's stop at the Waffle Wagon truck on our way back. I'm craving a bacon-stuffed pancake cone."

My shoulders relax. He didn't see the texts. "Yeah, man."

Shoving my phone away without answering his sister, I finish changing out of my wetsuit and get behind the wheel. As I drive away from the beach, my mind is a mess of thoughts.

The worst part about all of this is how much I want to give in. Since last night, the thought of being Tatum's first plagues me.

I can't stop picturing how her thighs would feel wrapped around me, the sounds she might make, whether she'd be sweet or if she'd want to be adventurous.

But I can't. I'll never know. Jackson would be so pissed if he found out she even asked me to fuck her.

My teeth sink into the inside of my cheek as my head swims with thoughts of the first time I ever checked Tatum out when I realized she wasn't a kid anymore. She's only a year and a half younger, but growing up with your friend's siblings, you just file them under the friend category.

It was a pool party when she was fourteen. Jackson was dating her friend Simone's sister. I'd seen her in a bikini plenty of times, but something about the blue suit with watermelon slices made me take notice that Tatum was growing up and I liked her shy smile when she caught my eye.

That was when Jackson made me promise I wouldn't try anything with her. It's a promise I've kept for four years, but my resolve is crumbling. It makes me feel like the world's worst best friend.

"We'll get you back out there at the bonfire, so quit your brooding." Jackson taps my arm with the back of his hand. "That's what you need. Get the master back in his element. A hot chick to make you forget all about Kayla. She's got you so messed up you didn't even stop and flirt with any girls at the beach."

"Right." I lock my jaw.

Forgetting. I wish. That's out of the question when I live next to Tatum and see her all the damn time.

There's only one girl I can think about right now, and she's the only one I can't have.

Fuck. My. Life.

SEVEN

TATUM

Cooper refused me, but he also turned down every guy I thought could be another solution to my virginity problem. He can't have it both ways, and he doesn't get control over my body.

Harnessing my determination, I roll off my bed and tuck my notebook away. I have the pros/cons list I made memorized at this point from staring at it all day. With one last look in the mirror, I zip up the borrowed hoodie over my bra and a pair of terry cloth lounge shorts. I check my house is quiet before slipping out, crossing the wide double driveway that separates my house from Cooper's, peering up at his window. The light is on, the low bass beat of music muffled.

I test the sturdiness of the trellis leading up the side of his house to the roof before hoisting myself up. This is probably the crazy route, but it's the most direct, and maximizes my chances of being heard out instead of Cooper remaining stubborn and turning me away without listening.

Once I'm up, I carefully crawl across the roof to his window. For a moment, I'm lost in watching him. Usually he's all lazy smiles and cocky winks, but right now something is clearly weighing on him.

He paces the room, cracking his neck from side to side as he palms a basketball. The black v-neck t-shirt stretches across his chest and a pair of gray sweatpants sit low on his hips. Collapsing heavily on the edge of the bed, he adjusts his faded blue backwards cap and his shoulders sag with his exhale. Picking the ball up again, he passes it back and forth between his hands a few times before spinning it and balancing it on his fingers, hollow gaze transfixed on the blur.

I touch my fingertips to the window, wishing I could hug him or do something to help relieve the burden of whatever is stressing him out. I'll part with one of my unused notebooks for him if I can convince him how therapeutic the release is of dumping all your thoughts on the page to keep them from cluttering your head.

I knock on the window.

The sound startles him. He whips his attention to the window and his brows flatten before he stalks over to throw it open.

"Jesus fucking christ, woman. You're killing me," Cooper mutters. "How did you get up here?"

"Climbed the trellis." At his look of disbelief, I lift my brows. "What?"

"Why didn't you text me to come down?"

"Would that have worked?" He sighs and I nod. "See. Come out."

Cooper seems to debate the invite for a moment, but he gives in, nudging me out of the way before he fits himself through the opening.

"Come here. Don't sit so close to the edge. You're not falling on my watch."

He takes my wrist and tugs me near so I'm sitting beside him, close enough that he could put his arm around me like this is a sweet date. As if he's reading my mind, his arm hovers behind me, but he lets it fall to his lap.

The thought of his hands pinning me to his Jeep last night makes me bite my lip.

Bolstered by the way his actions don't match his refusal, I forge ahead with my case. "So... Tinder has a lot to wade through, but I found some other possibles."

Cooper grabs my shoulder to twist me toward him. "What? T, the guys on that app are only after one thing."

I lift my brows pointedly. "Uh, duh. The exact thing I'm after. Seems to add up."

He pushes out a breath, swiping a hand over his mouth. "No. I meant what I said earlier. Don't."

"You think you can keep me from it? Make decisions about my body for me?" I set my jaw, lifting it in defiance. "Not cool, dude. I won't stand for that."

"If it protects you? Fuck yeah, I am." His jaw is locked, too. We're a pair of stubborn peas in a pod. "Why are you so set on this? Why does it matter?"

Before I answer, a lump forms in my throat, twinging sharply. I take a moment to breathe through it.

"I put all my focus on my other goals. Graduate with honors, get accepted to the Psychology degree program I wanted to study, broadening my horizons. And I don't regret doing any of it. I'm proud of the work I've put in. There's nothing like checking a goal off."

Cooper makes a noise of agreement.

"But the thing is, I feel...behind. It's a feeling I hate. I'm great at managing my time between studying and my extra curricular club activities, but I can't help this sense that I'm under prepared for college life. Not the course work, but what happens between all that." I bite my lip, peeking at him from the corner of my eye. "I don't want to fumble through learning something new in cramped dorm beds."

I pause. He clenches his hand into a tight fist and his jaw works.

"Look." I shift to face him. "If you help me with this, I'll do anything you want." My hand goes to the zipper on the hoodie, lowering it partially. "I came prepared. I'm only wearing lingerie under your hoodie. Name your price."

"Holy fuck," he mutters under his breath, avoiding looking at me.

"I'd rather figure this stuff out with a tutor I can trust, but if you're not down that isn't stopping me, Coop."

I'm proud of myself for getting it out without my voice wavering. He remains quiet. A breeze moves through my hair, tickling the back of my neck. I shiver, glad for his hoodie.

He messes with his baseball cap while studying me. "You're cold. C'mon, let's go inside."

I wrangle the hope blooming in my chest and nod. Cooper grasps my arm and offers support I don't need as he helps me climb through his window under his watchful gaze. He follows me in, a wall of heat at my back as he towers over me, his body just barely brushing against mine.

All at once it feels real.

He cups my shoulders and moves by me, going to turn off his music. A flutter moves through my stomach as I peer around. I've been in here before, a few years ago when he was sick and I was delivering school work he missed because Jackson had practice after school. It's not much different, the walls covered in surfing and basketball fan paraphernalia.

The cluster of Instax photos stuck to the wall by his desk draws me closer. Cooper's social life is way more thriving than mine—friends, parties, surfing, basketball games, girls. A photo from a pool party catches my eye. I'm in it. Jackson is on one side, I'm in the middle, and Cooper is on my other side, his arm around me. A rush of warmth fills my chest.

"I still don't get it," Cooper says behind me. I spin around and find him frowning at me. "Can't you just put on some porn and figure it out? There's no getting good at it, you just do it."

"You think I haven't thought of that?" I roll my eyes. It was the first thing I tried. "I'm a learn by doing kind of person. As in doing it with someone, but I don't trust anyone else."

His eyes narrow and he slides his lips together. "Have you ever been kissed?"

My heart skips a beat at the intent way he watches me. "I-I've been kissed before. Definitely."

"That deer in headlights look you're hitting me with says otherwise."

"I'm not lying. It was...um..."

"Spit it out, Danvers."

It's so unfair how my body reacts when he calls me Danvers. The slight growling demand in his tone makes it really hard to concentrate and remain level-headed.

I squeeze my eyes shut, and the confession spills from my lips in one breath. "It was in the ninth grade, okay? On a group date."

Not long after that pool party photo was taken. When he's silent, I open my eyes.

Cooper stares at me for another beat. "A what?"

"A group date. You know, like a bunch of couples. Except my friend Tara was the one who had a boyfriend. She wasn't allowed out with him alone, so she brought friends and so did he."

"Okay, like a group of friends." The arch of his eyebrow is skeptical.

It's also unfairly sexy and makes my insides flutter.

I huff and flap a hand. "A group of friends on a date together. Everyone else was making out, so he kissed me." I grimace at the memory. "There was...a lot of outside of the mouth tongue action."

He snorts. "Probably like kissing a fish."

It's not far off base.

He eyes me up and down, absently tracing his lower lip with the tip of this tongue. The slow perusal makes my stomach tighten and dip in excitement.

"So no real experience doing anything?"

The truth pierces me, but I stand taller, rolling my shoulders back. "That's why I need your help."

Cooper's head cocks to the side as his gaze roves over me again. This time it's not angry, but a hot drag as he takes his time. Heat blooms in my face and my nipples tighten. The corner of his mouth kicks up in a devastating smirk at whatever he sees flit across my face.

This is the Cooper Vale I was expecting—the bad boy player, master of his craft.

"You really want this, T?" The seductive rasp of his deep voice sends a shudder through me.

"Yes." It comes out as a breathy whisper.

"You're sure?"

He takes a step, then another, crowding me until my back hits the wall by his desk. The photo of the three of us is right by my shoulder.

His brown eyes burn into me as he plants a hand on the wall. The ache I felt when we were in this position before throbs between my legs. Swallowing, I nod, not trusting myself to speak and give away the effect he's having on me.

"Yeah?" Cooper touches my jaw, guiding my face up. He lowers his head, hovering his mouth over mine. My heart beats a million miles a minute at the sensation of his breath ghosting over my lips. "Why me, baby?"

EIGHT
COOPER

The promise I made is far from my mind right now. All I'm able to focus on is the hitch in Tatum's breath, the sweet coconut and lime scent from her favorite shampoo, my hoodie engulfing her, the way her blue eyes widen and fall to my mouth at my husky words while I crowd her.

She's so responsive and I haven't even done anything to her yet. Every thought running through my head is hot and filthy. I give in to touching her a little, caressing her neck lightly. It makes her lashes flutter and I eat up her reaction, fixated on the bloom of color in her cheeks.

I want it to be you.

Those words still won't leave my head. I have to know.

"Why me?" I repeat while dragging my knuckles back up her neck.

"Because I trust you," she murmurs. It stirs pride in me. She lifts a hand, hesitating for a moment before placing it on my chest, right over my heart. "And you're...experienced. You know what you're doing."

A laugh puffs out of me. She isn't wrong, I guess.

The things I want to do to her...

Every fantasy I've ever secretly had starring her now has the chance to become a reality.

If I'm going to have a taste of the girl who's always been off-limits, I'm not wasting it. I'll savor it. Take it slow.

Leaning back to give Tatum room to breathe, I rub my jaw. She sways toward me, confusion clouding her pretty features.

"I've never been anyone's first," I admit.

Surprise overtakes her confusion when her lips part. "Seriously? I'm shocked. There are always girls around you. I thought..."

I shrug. "Doesn't mean I'm some virginity killer."

A laugh bubbles out of her. She tucks her hair behind her ear and rakes her teeth over her lip.

"If I'm agreeing to this crazy plan, I've got some ground rules."

"Okay." Her eyes go wide, lighting up with triumph. "How do you want to do this?" She toys with the zipper of the hoodie again— my hoodie. I like the look of her in my clothes. "Should we take our clothes off now?"

So eager. My hand flexes to keep from grabbing her. Her eyes flare with desire at the pop of veins in my forearm and the back of my hand.

The idea of being her first is driving me wild. First to touch her, first to see what makes her gasp and arch her back, first to taste her pussy. Shit, my cock is hard as steel picturing all the ways to make her come apart for me.

Always bold, Tatum skirts around me, making sure my attention is all hers as she backs towards the bed. The zipper drags down in a torturously slow tease until it reveals a line of skin from her collar bone to the elastic waistband of her sleep shorts interrupted by a glimpse of her purple lace bra. My throat bobs with my thick swallow.

This is definitely one of my fantasies come to life, her wearing my hoodie and not much else, stripping for me. Need burns through me to find out what kind of panties she has on, whether they're a thong or the kind that offer an enticing peek of ass.

She sits on the bed, gaze darting away from mine to see my erection tenting my sweatpants. A flicker of nerves has her rolling her lips between her teeth. "How do you want me?"

I won't jump straight into sex. "We're not doing anything tonight."

"What?" She frowns, checking my groin again as if she's making sure it's not an illusion. "You seem ready. I'm ready. I want to get it over with so we can get to learning the good stuff."

"That's exactly why we aren't rushing this. It's part of learning." I scratch at the shadow of stubble on my jaw as I sit next to her, trying not to think about marking her thighs with stubble burn if I buried my head between her legs. "I want you to feel good about it. All of it."

"Oh." She looks at her lap.

Reaching over, I zip the hoodie back up and take her hand, rubbing her knuckles soothingly with my thumb.

"So ground rules," I say. "First one, we're taking this slow. No stripping down and rushing anything."

She nods, though I can see she's frustrated. Her eagerness is sexy as hell and my other brain is pitching a fit that my dick isn't inside her right now. But the sooner we have sex, the sooner this ends. She wants to be ready for college. I only have the rest of the summer.

"You said you'd do what I wanted." My gaze shifts over her shoulder to the crumpled letter from my advisor. I did plan to ask her for studying tips, so this works out. "Help me get my GPA up when the semester starts. You're smart and good at studying."

"Easy." The edge of her mouth curls in a mischievous smirk. "And a good excuse to get you alone."

My grin spreads slowly and I adjust my cap. "True. Good point. Rule two, keep an open mind. This takes time. No one's instantly good at it overnight."

"Practice makes perfect." Tatum's attention is on my mouth.

I hum in agreement, brushing a knuckle over her bare thigh just below where her terry cloth sleep shorts end. The simple touch isn't tantalizing or intimate, but she shivers in pleasure all the same.

Barely knows how to kiss, hasn't dated... Tatum is a blank canvas and I plan to paint a fucking masterpiece.

My finger explores beneath the hem of her shorts, stroking her skin with light brushes.

"Coop," she breathes.

I drag in a sharp inhale through my nose. I will make her say my name like that when I'm inside her.

"Rule three is the big one." I grasp her chin between my thumb and finger to make sure she understands. "We keep this a secret. Especially from Jackson. He can never know."

"Obviously." She circles her fingers around my wrist. "We have a no friends rule. If he suspects us, we can tell him I'm tutoring you. "

"I wasn't kidding the other night. He'd kill me just for thinking about you, and if he finds out I touched you, fucked you—"

"You think about me?" Tatum stares at me as if that's a possibility that never entered her mind.

Ah, shit.

I offer her a crooked smirk and distract her by running my fingers through her hair. She can't know how often she crosses my mind. It's only for the summer. We're not boyfriend and girlfriend, not exchanging promise rings. This isn't real.

"I'm a guy, babe. Of course you've popped into my head while I've jacked it."

"Coop!" She smacks my arm, a scandalized laugh escaping her as she turns bright pink. "Oh my god. I can't believe you just told me that."

Good. It worked. She doesn't see how forced my expression is, believing the mask I slip on.

"Do you have any rules you want to add?"

She shakes her head. "Your terms are logical and reasonable."

I huff, fighting back a smile. "Love it when you talk nerd. We might have to incorporate that into a lesson on dirty talking and how it—" Dragging my teeth over my lip, I flick my eyes over her. "—enhances things."

Her blush is so cute. It's refreshing after so many hookups with girls who know more sexually adventurous shit than I do with positions, toys, kinks—the internet is a beautiful and educative thing.

"There's a bonfire coming up this weekend at Mariner's Cove. You're going."

"Am I?" She raises an eyebrow, a hint of her stubbornness coming back out to play. "What if I had other plans?"

"You forget that I know you, T. I want you there. You need to learn to relax first if this is going to work."

"I'm relaxed," she argues.

"Nah, like in tune with your body." To illustrate my point, I stretch out on the bed, folding one arm behind my head while the other skims my stomach where my t-shirt has ridden up. I'm still half-hard, the bulge obvious in my pants. She checks me out without hiding she's doing it and satisfaction flares through me. "Comfortable in your own skin."

"Fine. You're the master. I'll do this your way."

This is really happening. My resolve buckled and I agreed to Tatum's wild proposition, unable to resist her. Things I've never entertained outside of my fantasies will become a reality. I'll have to be careful so Jackson never finds out I broke the promise I made him.

"I'll pick you up for the bonfire." My mouth tugs into a lazy curve and I slide my hand lower to my waistband. "Now get the fuck out of here so I can jerk off."

NINE
TATUM

The minute Cooper finally agreed, my inner voice dropped to a low pitch as I thought *I'm in* like I've cracked an encrypted code. I've hacked losing my virginity at last.

Except... I'm still rocking the V-card.

Okay, I need to reel it in. Cooper might be the biggest player in South Bay, but he's doing what he thinks is best. Baby steps, that's what this is about. I should be more appreciative that Coop is so considerate and didn't just bend me over the nearest horizontal surface and take me to pound town.

Not that I would have minded that, either. It's the fantasy I had in my head when I returned to my room last night after he sent me off so he could rub one out. I joined him. In spirit, from the comfort of my own bed, body hot and achy all over while I imagined him doing the same thing next-door. Best orgasm I've had all week, but I'm ready for the main event when someone else makes me shudder and gasp.

Maybe that was his plan when he said I needed to go to the bonfire at the cove. Loosen up a little, and then it'll be time to bow chicka wow wow.

"Oh my god," I mumble before covering my face with a hand.

"What?" Jackson grunts from his seat at the kitchen island, hunched over his phone while he scrolls through TikTok.

I finish pouring lemonade and shake my head. He so doesn't need to know what an absolute dork I am, even in the confines of my thoughts. "Nothing."

"Check this one out." He angles his phone so I can watch. It's the new dance trend of the week. "Looks easy enough to learn. Do it with me?"

My nose wrinkles. "Nope. Negative. I am not learning TikTok dances with you."

He groans, pushing the phone more insistently in my direction. "Come on, this one needs two people. Wear a mask or something."

"No way. I worked my ass off to get into my psych program, there's nothing that I'll do to jeopardize my shot by going viral on TikTok for shaking my ass. Employers go after all your online social media presences these days. Not in my five year plan. I've got it written down if you want to see."

"I've seen your damn notebooks," he grumbles.

I take a pointed sip of my drink and lift my brows. "Get your bestie to do it with you."

If there's anyone who loves to make TikTok content, it's Cooper Vale. And with his handsome looks and sultry smile, he has no problem embracing his thirst trap status to lure his followers in hook, line, and sinker. I might be guilty of leaving my favorite videos of his on loop. The thought of the most recent one I saved makes me subtly rub my thighs together.

Jackson shrugs, only half paying attention. "He said he's busy today."

"Aww," I coo with a big fake pout. "Your friend can't come out to play?"

My brother rolls his eyes and shoves away from the island. "Eat a dick, Tate."

While I watch him saunter off into our house, I purse my lips. I'd love to, but my lessons haven't started yet.

I spend a few minutes scrolling through my phone, leaning a hip against the counter while I finish my lemonade. A new pop up market by the beach catches my interest on social media. I don't have plans today and I hate feeling like I'm sitting around. Standing still isn't great for me. I start to get agitated, guilty for not being productive and craving something to throw myself into. Checking out the pop up event will be perfect.

"I'm going out," I call.

Jackson doesn't answer, but I know he heard me since there isn't music blasting from his room. I grab my big crochet purse in case I find something I like while browsing and shove my wallet and keys in it.

I pull up short once I step outside, nearly running into Cooper's chest. Literally, since he has on a faded green muscle tank with wide arm holes and a low neckline that gives a peek at his tan skin. His hair curls around his ears beneath his backwards cap. He smirks, dropping his raised hand that was poised to knock.

Since when has Cooper knocked on our door? He usually lets himself in.

"Oh—hey." My eyes go wide and my cheeks blaze with heat as what went down last night flashes through my head. I awkwardly thumb over my shoulder. "Jackson is inside."

"Cool. But I'm not here for your brother today. I'm here for you, T."

"Me?" That squeak was a whole new octave for me. "Now?"

Cooper ducks his head and his mouth curls into his signature swoonworthy smile, the dimple popping out to mess with my fluttering insides. It's exacerbated when he gives me an intent once over, something bright and warm flaring in his eyes as he catalogs every inch of me.

"Yep." He pops the *p*. "You. Now."

My stomach dips as a shallow breath rushes out of me. Now. *Now.* In my head, the *it's happening* GIF from The Office plays on repeat. There's no way to stay calm in this moment.

"Get in."

I blink out of my shock. Cooper has moved to brace against the open door of his Jeep, watching me over the rim of his sunglasses. My lips part and he offers me a cocky grin, nodding to his ride.

"Where are we going?" I ask.

He swings his keyring around his finger. "For burgers."

"Oh." Surprise colors my tone.

"What?" The smooth, rich sound of his chuckle coils around me as we climb into his Jeep. "You said you wanted to hang out, right? Just me and you."

He's teasing me, but the hot flush spreading over my skin feels too good for me to care. I will my prickling cheeks to not be red and stare at my lap while he backs out of the wide driveway between our houses. I'm not paying close attention to the direction we're headed, too absorbed in shooting him surreptitious glances.

Like everything else, Cooper looks confident and relaxed right now, one hand resting over the wheel, wind from the open window moving the messy hair sticking out beneath his hat. Taking a girl out for burgers is no big deal to him. It's probably been a weekly thing for him since he started dating. To go out with him without Jackson as a buffer is a pretty big first for me. I never made time for boys, and I'm anxious about not knowing what to anticipate.

"Quit thinking so hard over there."

"I wasn't," I protest.

The corner of his mouth lifts. "Liar." Switching to grip the bottom of the wheel, he reaches over to tap my temple. "This is always going. You gotta turn it off if this is going to work."

I scrape my teeth over my lip. I want this to work. It needs to, so I'll be prepared for anything in college.

"You're the master."

"Mm, I like the sound of that."

The flattening of his mouth doesn't match his cocky words or his smoky tone. Before I can ask what's wrong, we're pulling into the drive-thru at In-N-Out.

Cooper adjusts his backwards cap and hooks his arm over the open window on his side of the Jeep to place our order. "Can I get a 3x3, animal style, two orders of fries, a chocolate shake, and a double-double—" I open my mouth, leaning forward to make sure he gets mine without onion, but he's already on it. "—without onions."

He shoots me a quick glance. "Want Coke or pink lemonade?"

Why me, baby?

"P-pink lemonade," I stammer embarrassingly, distracted by another memory from last night of Cooper pressing me against the wall, hot breath fanning over my skin while he murmured to me.

He winks and returns to finishing our order. This is kind of...intimate. If Jackson were here, I'd think nothing of it. The three of us have grabbed In-N-Out plenty of times together. But with just me and Coop? He knows my order by heart. He pays, turning me down when I offer to chip in for my meal. It's a little boyfriend-y.

All of it stokes a warm ember in my chest.

Why him? More like who else but him. He's so suave and sure of himself, it gives him an unbeatable allure.

With a guy like him, I can get out of my head and stop over-analyzing, let myself feel in the moment.

He passes over the bag of food and pulls into a spot at the front of the lot, facing out on the skinny palm tree-lined road that curves down to the beach. Once we divvy up our food, we settle in to eat. While he tears into his burger, I debate bringing up his GPA to find out what I'm working with and what areas he needs to focus on, but something stops me.

All I ever do is talk about academics and goals, but that's not all I am. I like being outdoors, watching the sun rise, and handmade art I discover at craft fairs. I secretly want to go to an escape room with friends because I think I'd be good at figuring out the clues, and a good song can choke me up. But I don't share that side of myself often. It's like I've trained myself over the years of being so goal oriented to only be keeping up a continuous report of my progress, like I'm some overachieving super bot who doesn't have emotions.

The salty fry feels like bland cardboard in my mouth.

I want Cooper to know the real me—to see all the parts he's never found. Not because he's going to be my first, but because he's granting me an intimate part of himself to help me, so I want to give him the same by offering a genuine piece of myself in return.

But how am I supposed to act right now? Is this one of our lessons, and does it start now, or did it begin the minute I opened the door?

The questions swirl through my head while we eat in silence.

The curiosity burns. Damn, I should've watched another YouTube vlog on what to expect on a first date so I'd be more prepared when the time came.

At a certain point, it gets depressing watching tweens telling me how to navigate this at eighteen. While other people my age bumbled their way through this stage of life, I was too busy with my nose in my books. I don't regret that I worked hard to achieve the goals I set for myself, yet I can't help feeling left behind when everyone else is miles ahead of me.

I'm always going to remain behind if I don't dive in.

"So..." I gather my courage after trailing off and forge ahead, pretending this conversation is one of my goals. Visualize it, I coach myself.

"Hmm?" Cooper pops the lid of his chocolate shake and offers it to me.

I swallow. He's doing it again. He did make a point of just how well he knows me from living next-door. I dip a fry in his milkshake and shove it in my mouth. My brother and his best friend always let me dip my fries in their shakes, but I never order one for myself. He might be aware of my habits, but there are pieces of me left for him to discover.

"Are we just hanging out, or is this your prerequisite to the main event?" I push it all out in one rushed babble of words, stomach quivering with nervous energy.

Cooper is quiet for a beat, studying me from the corner of his eye.

He reaches over and I go still. His thumb wipes the corner of my mouth, coming back messy with spread from the fry I stole from his meal. Heat arrows through me while he holds my gaze and licks it off his tongue, captivating me.

"Are you relaxed?" he rumbles.

Oh, hello. Cooper Vale in the house. Not my next-door neighbor, but the smooth motherfucker with the thirst trap reputation. Flirty mode: ON.

"Super relaxed?" It comes out like a question I don't know the answer to.

The corner of his mouth kicks up. He leans in, brushing my lips with his thumb. My stomach dips when he presses into my mouth. There we are, sitting in his Jeep with the windows down at the In-N-Out while he mimics a blowjob with his thumb.

"Hungry for something else, babe?"

No amount of planning or practicing conversations in the shower could prepare me for this.

Instead of answering, I think about diving in and watch for his reaction when I curl my tongue around his thumb. He blinks, the amused flirtatious expression dropping. Those warm brown eyes darken and he presses down on my tongue with the barest amount of pressure. It makes a rush of hot and cold tingles race over my skin.

Overwhelmed by my impulsiveness, I pull away. The second I do, he chuckles and leans back, patting my leg.

"You're not ready yet." He sticks a trio of fries in his mouth and steals my pink lemonade to wash it down like what we did was nothing. For him it probably is. Suggestive but tame.

Once again I face the sense I'm miles behind everyone else.

"I am," I insist.

I just didn't know what to do next.

"Nah. But this is good." Cooper flashes me a reassuring smile and squeezes my knee. His big hand encompasses my leg. "I'm figuring out where you're at."

I can respect that. Still, I'm put out this isn't resulting in any dick riding.

"Don't look like that."

I find him studying me with a soft smile. "Like what?"

His eyes drop to my mouth and he traces his lower lip with his thumb. "You've got this cute pout, and it's tempting me to make it all better."

Our gazes meet and this time when he leans in, my lips part. He cups my jaw, the touch light as he moves slowly like he doesn't want to fluster me again. This time he really is going to kiss me, his intent unmistakable in his eyes.

A husky hum leaves him as he brushes his nose against mine,

angling his head. My heart skips a beat at the sweep of his thick lashes when his eyes close.

This is it—my first real kiss.

The loud bang of an engine muffler startles both of us, bringing us back to reality.

"Shit." Coop laughs, swiping a hand over his face.

A cherry red classic muscle car rolls by, leaving a rumble in its wake long after it rounds the bend.

"You done eating?"

"Yeah." Unsure how to get the moment back, I fold up my wrapper in a neat square and collect my trash.

He starts the car and braces a hand on my headrest while backing out of the parking spot. "I'll take you home. I'm supposed to go to campus for a meeting with my advisor for next semester."

"Actually, before you came, I was going to go down to the beach. There's a pop up market I want to check out. Drop me off there?"

He nods. "Need me to pick you up later so you don't have to walk back? My meeting shouldn't be that long."

There he goes again. His hoodie, knowing my order, watching out for me. It's probably best if I don't read into his inclination to take care of me.

"It's cool. Jackson already said he would."

"Aight." His focus is on the road instead of the internal dilemma I'm facing.

Cooper might be on board with the plan now, but I can't let myself forget the most important part of our arrangement. This thing between us isn't real. He's doing it all because he's my sex tutor. That's it.

I can't catch feels for my brother's best friend.

But it might be too late.

TEN
COOPER

Mariner's Cove is already popping when we roll up after dusk. A peek in Tatum's direction sends a burst of amusement through me. She's leaning forward, eyes wide, taking in the bonfire and the people dancing around it.

"You cool?" I check.

"Totally. Yes. Of course."

I bite my lip to hide a smile. Reaching over, I touch the back of her neck. "You've been to parties before?"

"Birthday parties. Family holiday parties. School functions," she mumbles. Her gaze skates to me and she points at herself. "Lame social life, remember?"

It was right to bring her. This small party is nothing compared to the parties on campus. I need to help her find a comfort zone.

My knuckles brush her nape and I enjoy the way it makes her shiver. "You'll be fine. You've got me here as buffer. Try not to think too hard. This is all about learning to relax. If you want to do something, do it."

"Do it." She nods firmly, like she's psyching herself up.

My lips twitch. It's adorable.

"I've got you, T."

She snaps her attention to me at my warm, steady tone, and the air thickens between us. My fingertips skate down her cheek to hold her chin. The desire to kiss her rises so fast it leaves me lightheaded. I came so close to tasting her before. Holding out is killing me when all I want is to devour her. Not yet, though.

It's too risky to do anything here, anyway. Jackson should be here if he isn't already.

"Best way to do it is to dive in. No skirting around the edges waiting for your moment."

She nods, fixated on my advice like it's the most important thing she's ever heard. Smirking, I tilt my head in the direction of the bonfire in silent invitation. We get out of the Jeep and she pauses, glancing down at the denim overall dress she has on over a tight black t-shirt. My gaze moves between her and the other chicks at the party. They're all dressed in low-cut tops, short skirts, and pants so tight they look painted on.

"You look good." I give Tatum an appreciative once over. "Don't worry."

"Yeah?" She smooths her hands over the bottom of the dress. "I don't know."

Making sure no one's watching, I step into her space and tug on one of the straps. She makes this cute little squeak that has me grinning.

"Babe, believe me. You could wear a brown paper bag and still look hot."

Hot enough to eat up. I wish I could walk her to the edge of the party, past the glow of the bonfire and show her just how much I like her outfit. But this isn't about me, it's about her.

She sucks on her bottom lip and peers up at me with those big blue eyes. Freckles from time in the sun dot her button nose. When I nod again, brushing hair away from her face, she grins wide enough for me to see the crooked tooth from when she fell off Jackson's bike. I love the quirky imperfection. Makes her seem more real than any of the girls I've been with who would freak over something like that.

I take her shoulders and steer her toward the party. As we approach, everyone recognizes me. I get back slaps and nods. Girls smile, guys pass me a drink. I don't really know most of them, but I

see them all at parties, and everyone makes a point of knowing me—
or at least pretending to.

Tatum shrinks into my side and avoids the curious looks she gets
from people. I won't push her, but any attempts I make to include her
in conversations are short lived.

Once I finally get us away from the people crowding us, I take
Tatum over to the fire.

"First step of relaxing? Letting go of any worries about what
people think. What you wear doesn't matter."

"If you say so."

"That's the secret to confidence."

She eyes me up and down. "No arguments here. You've got that
in spades."

I motion to the keg in an offer to get her a drink. "People flock to
anyone who's sure of themselves. I didn't do anything to build myself
up, I just did my own thing."

"It's because people are drawn to what they want," she says as I
hand over the plastic cup. "They can believe they're capable of
ditching their own self doubts if they see it in others."

Smirking, I press my lips to her ear when the music gets louder.
"Like that. Keep talking nerd. It's your thing and it's hot when you
explain that psychological stuff."

She laughs and swats at my chest with the back of her hand. "So,
can we dance? I need something to keep me busy, or I'm going to end
up standing in the cove equivalent of the corner."

"Not can we. You're still overthinking. Tell me what you want to
do, woman."

Tate purses her lips. "Fine. Come on, party bud. It's time to
shake our asses."

"That's more like it." I grin and follow her.

I catch sight of Jackson talking to some friends we surf with and
nod at him when he spots me. Confusion crosses his face when his
attention shifts to his sister.

The breeze coming off the ocean is cool, but the flames of the
bonfire are warm. Tatum finds us an open spot and throws herself
into dancing before she can think her way out of it.

Pride and warmth fill me, along with a possessive feeling. I'm the one who gets to teach her this—the first to touch her, to show her how good I can make her feel. I swipe my tongue over my lips and my fingers curl into my palm to keep from pulling her closer.

She sways back and forth, lifting her drink and closing her eyes as she moves to the music, oblivious to my thoughts. I'm not ruining a good night by being laid out by my best friend's fist for touching his sister. Instead, I keep a respectable distance between our bodies and hype her up when she gets into it.

"This is pretty great," she says breathlessly as we jump to a fast-paced song.

The whole crowd is doing it, connecting us all in the moment for this shared experience. The look on Tatum's face is priceless when she beams at a couple next to us bouncing in time with the beat. Her hands shoot into the air and some of her drink sloshes over.

"I'm having so much fun, Coop."

"Good."

When the song ends, she leans into me with a weary gasp. "Okay. Enough dancing for a bit. Need water."

"Come on." Chuckling, I slip my hand into hers and lead her through the crowd.

She holds on tight. Resisting her while we danced was too much. We're playing with fire doing this lesson while Jackson is here. But if he comes at me, I'll just say I didn't want to lose her in the crowd. The cove is packed for the party.

We stop at a cooler filled with water bottles. I grab two and give one to her.

"Thanks." She cracks the cap and takes a deep pull, throat working.

I freeze with my bottle halfway to my lips, captivated by the sight.

"Hey!" A girl's voice behind us startles me out of my trance and I slosh some of the water on my shirt.

"Simone!" Tatum's eyes go wide and a hint of regret creeps into her voice. "Hey. You're here."

Her friend moves a thick braid of shiny black hair over her bare shoulders and cants her hip to the side.

Simone lifts her eyebrows, peering between the two of us. "Coop."

I offer a nod in greeting. She turns back to Tatum.

"I didn't know you'd be here. When I talked about the party earlier this week you didn't say anything."

"Oh, yeah." Tatum shrugs. The movement is stiff, but she plows on. "It was last minute. Jackson already left by the time I decided to go. Cooper gave me a ride. Otherwise I totally would've texted you."

Her brush off appeases her friend. The pair of them couldn't look any more different—Tatum's hair down and Simone's braided in an intricate style, Tatum's face free of makeup while Simone has a smokey cat eye thing going on, and Tatum's overall dress compared to Simone's off-the-shoulder crop top and mini skirt. Yet they've always been close friends. Simone hooks her arm through Tatum's and grins, shaking her cup.

"I'm just glad you're here, girl. I've been trying to get you out to a party for years."

"I know." Tatum offers a pretty smile. "No point dwelling, though. I'm here now."

"Here's to new leaves and living it up." Simone taps her plastic cup against Tatum's water bottle.

"I'll drink to that," I chime in.

"Did your housing assignment come this week?" Simone asks.

"This morning finally!" Tatum grins and the brightness of it hits me square in the chest. "Huntington Hall, what about you?"

"Yes! Me too. Hopefully we'll be on the same floor, but at least we'll be neighbors."

They perform a complicated fist bump-handshake combo that they probably learned from TikTok. I squint in confusion.

"Why don't you request each other for roommates? Then you don't get stuck with someone you don't mesh with."

Tatum shakes her head. "We both agreed. We want to do it up right when we go to college. We'll have plenty of time to spend together."

"Plus, we'd probably drive each other crazy if we roomed together," Simone adds. "Happened to my sister when she was at college. She and one of her best friends got a room together and ended up breaking up as friends by the end of the first semester."

"Harsh," I say.

"Girls have a totally different social structure," Tatum says. "Let me guess, you'd have to really hate your roommate to stop being his friend."

"I mean, if he did some shady shit, I guess."

"You walk in on him jerking off in one of your socks," Tatum offers.

"He leaves all his dirty underwear on your side of the room," Simone says. "All these little things that seem annoying at first build up."

I frown. "I'd talk to him first."

The girls share a look and shrug before laughing. They start talking about their majors and a crooked smile curves my mouth while listening to Tatum's enthusiasm for the courses she picked for the fall semester. Someone who overhears joins us and they hit it off when they find out they'll have a class together. Her earlier nerves have faded away and she's relaxed with the party atmosphere.

"I'm going to grab another drink. You want anything?"

Tatum pauses her conversation with the girl who joined us and shakes her head, shooting me another bright smile. "I'm good. I'll be here."

"Okay. I'll be back."

Simone watches me for a moment as I amble through the party, glancing back to watch Tatum. I duck my head when I catch her gaze tracking me. The last thing I need is for her to suspect anything. It'll be hard enough to keep Jackson in the dark without adding Tate's friend to the mix.

I'm able to watch without being caught while I get a fresh drink. My attention lingers on Tatum and I can't help checking her out again. The girls have formed their own dance party separate from everyone else, and I'm hooked on every dip and sway of Tatum's body.

She's too damn tempting. I still can't believe she hasn't had guys all over her. She's definitely caught the eye of several tonight, but she hasn't noticed.

I have though.

And when I see another one inching his way closer to shoot his shot, I start walking.

"Yo."

Jackson's greeting almost makes me choke when I've nearly reached the girls. Clearing my throat, I nod to him. "'Sup bro?"

He glances from me to the girls his sister is dancing with. "Which one are you looking at? Not Simone?"

The sharp addition has me lifting my brows and staring into my plastic cup. I'm not touching that one. But I need to cover, because I can't tell him who I was actually watching.

"Nah. Not my type."

"Bullshit." He laughs and slaps me on the back. "Every girl is your type if they mean you get your dick wet."

I hide a grimace and jerk my chin at the girl Tatum and Simone made friends with. "The chick with the rack in the pink shirt."

"Nice," Jackson says appreciatively.

I didn't realize how close we were, but Tatum freezes, whipping her head in our direction. A look of hurt flashes for the briefest second over her features before she shuts it down.

Shit. I didn't mean for her to overhear that.

If she was my girlfriend, my balls would be toast. But that's the thing. Tatum isn't my girlfriend. The kind of relationship and connection I want won't ever be in the cards for us.

I don't have to linger on the crappy guilt for long. A shout behind us steals everyone's attention.

ELEVEN
TATUM

"Beer pong tourney! Let's go, bitches!" The guy running through the party shouts at the top of his lungs before crashing into my brother and Cooper, almost knocking them both over.

"Harris, dude." Jackson laughs.

"You're wasted," Cooper says in an amused tone.

I push down the hurt I have no right to carry. Of course I'm not Cooper's type. He only said I looked good in this overall dress to make me feel better. It was just part of his lesson on believing in myself so I could relax.

This is exactly what I was thinking about when we got burgers. I need to stick to the plan because nothing real is even feasible between us. We're too different.

"C'mon," Harris insists. "They're starting now. You gotta go."

Cooper and Jackson share a look. A competitive smile curves Jackson's mouth. The way he tells it, they're undefeated champs.

"Aight, let's do it," Jackson says.

"I'm going to go. I see my friends." Jenny takes my hand with an excited grin. "But give me your number first. We can sit together when our class starts!"

For the briefest moment, jealousy arrows through me. This is Cooper's type, straight from his mouth. As soon as the thought crosses my mind, I smother it. Girls have enough problems to deal with navigating our relationships with each other and the way the world treats us to add extra crap on top. I don't need to be jealous of her if Coop likes her. He's not mine.

"Sure." I put my number in her phone and she texts me.

I avoid Cooper's eye as we all walk over to the group surrounding a table set up for beer pong. They play the first match against Harris and another guy I've seen around the Tiki Taco Shack.

"You want to play the winner with me?" The quiet guy who followed our group stands close to me.

"I've never played," I say.

"Yeah?" He grins and ducks his head. "I'll teach you."

This is an actual boy talking to me. Flirting with me, I'm pretty sure. But I shift my gaze to Cooper. His eyes are on us while Jackson shoots into the other team's cups. In the flickering orange light from the bonfire it's difficult to tell what's on his mind. Jackson sinks his shot and Cooper slaps his back.

"I'm Tatum, by the way." After hesitating for a second to consider what's acceptable, I stick my hand out.

"Carson." He shakes my hand with an entertained expression, looking at Simone.

"Simone," she offers. Instead of shaking hands, they nod to each other. "Are you at SBC?"

"Yeah, I'm about to be in my third year. What about you?"

"Entering freshman," I say.

"Cool. We should hook up when the semester starts." He inches closer, brushing against my side when his arm slips over my shoulders. "I can show you around. It's a big campus. I was lost as hell my first semester there."

I bite my lip and point at Jackson and Cooper. "I've been to campus. My brother and his best friend are sophomores there. It works out for me because I'm a total planner. I'd definitely stress out if I didn't already know the campus."

"Oh." Carson meets Cooper's intense gaze and stiffens before stepping away. "I'm going to grab a drink, but I'll be back for our game. You'll be a pro by the end of the night. I'll show you my fail-safe technique. It's all in the wrist."

"Okay."

"Dude." Simone hooks her arm through mine and murmurs in my ear. "That guy is into you."

"Yeah?" A weird sensation coils in my stomach, but I don't think it has anything to do with Carson.

"But what's up with Coop? He hasn't taken his eyes off you all night. Look, he can't focus on the game at all. He actually missed a few shots when Carson was talking to you."

She nudges me. Reluctantly, I lift my gaze and find his attention on me once more. The odd sensation repeats, twisting my insides.

"It's nothing," I lie. "When he gave me a ride to the party, he promised to keep an eye on me. He's just keeping his word."

Simone squints at me. "Uh huh."

"For real."

"Whatever you say." She turns back to watching the game.

Carson doesn't come back by the time Jackson and Cooper win. The people who all seem to know Cooper crowd around him, cheering. Jackson tugs him out of the circle and makes his way over to me and Simone.

"Bro, tell me why I had to cover for your ass? You never miss. I don't know what's up with you," Jackson says.

"I dunno, just off my game tonight." Cooper's eyes flick to me, then cut away. He pulls off his hat and scrubs at his scalp, messing his hair up. "Too tired after my shift today I guess."

"Did you see my last shot?" Jackson asks us with a big grin. "It sailed right in."

"It was pretty cool," I say.

Jackson tugs me against his side with a laugh and puts an arm over my shoulder. "I'm about ready to roll out. Come on, Simone. I'll give you a ride back." He bumps his fist against Cooper's. "You hanging longer or heading out?"

Cooper doesn't answer right away, glancing at me. "I might chill for another hour."

I roll my lips between my teeth and allow my brother to steer me to the car. Right. Cooper is the party guy. He could have his pick of any girl here to keep his bed warm tonight. It's not like he has to go because I'm leaving. This isn't a date.

Despite saying he's staying, he follows us out to the lot where everyone parked.

"I had fun tonight," I say.

Cooper grunts, offering a tight smile. "Good."

"Next time there's a party, don't say no and change your mind last minute," Simone says. "We want you to come out."

Jackson makes a noise of agreement while he digs his keys out of his pocket. Simone and Jackson get in the car, but I pause with the door open. Cooper shoves his hands in his pockets, watching me. Our eyes meet. Without him, I really wouldn't have come to this party. I mouth *thank you* and get in the car.

As we leave Mariner's Cove behind, Simone watches TikToks on her phone in the back seat. Jackson fiddles with the bluetooth connection to his Spotify.

"You could've told me you wanted to go to the party. I wouldn't have left you home."

I shrug, unsure how to navigate my cover story with my brother. "It's fine. You already left, I didn't want to call you back. Cooper happened to be heading out when I decided I wanted to go."

"You hung out with him a lot. Dancing."

"I didn't really know anyone, and he didn't want to leave me alone. He promised to watch out for me. Then we ran into Simone."

He swipes a hand over his mouth and lets it go.

Simone leans into the passenger window when we reach her house and gives me a kiss on the cheek. "See you, babe. Glad you were there tonight!"

I laugh at the shimmying dance she does as she backs away from the car to get to the porch of her bungalow-style house.

Jackson doesn't stop giving me the side-eye after we drop Simone off. I pretend not to notice, because my brother wouldn't know subtle if it was a huge wave crashing over him. We make it all the way home with his eyes shifting to me every twenty seconds. Before the car comes to a stop, I throw open my door.

"Tate—wait a minute," he huffs.

"Gotta pee!" Classic excuse to run inside and shut myself in the bathroom until something distracts him.

Once I'm through the door, I halt. Mom stands at the island mixing a fresh batch of her homemade lemonade.

"Mom. Hey."

She smiles and I lose some of the anxious edge I'm balanced on. "Did you go out?"

"Yes." My eyes widen. "With Jackson. He was there."

Mom hums in approval and nods. "That's good. I'm glad he watches out for you."

"Sorry I didn't tell you."

"It's okay, as long as you have someone with you."

The door opens and Jackson comes in, less shocked than I am to run into Mom. He grabs a glass and takes over stirring. While she's distracted, his attention cuts to me.

"Thought you had to take a piss," Jackson mutters.

I shrug. What is with everyone giving me the third degree for going out? I'm eighteen. It's healthy to socialize. Surprisingly, Mom's the only one who seems cool. But she also doesn't know what Jackson and Simone do—that I was hanging out with Coop most of the night.

"Where did you go?" Mom asks. "I heard about a concert happening."

"Mariner's Cove." Jackson pours lemonade into his glass and his mouth curves in appreciation. "It was a bonfire party. Nothing major."

I hold my breath, waiting for him to say I showed up without telling him I'd be there. He doesn't. Sibling code kicks in—my brother's got my back. It only makes me feel worse for kind of breaking our promise to stay away from friends.

My phone vibrates in my hand and I clasp it to my chest so Jackson and Mom won't see. It might not be...but just in case it's from Coop, I won't give us away. My heart thuds.

"Night," I say.

"Goodnight, sweetie. I'm glad you had a good time." Mom kisses my head. "It's nice to see you getting out more."

"Yup. It's great."

I skirt around them and head for the stairs, avoiding Jackson's eye. His nosy gaze bores into my back as I hurry up the steps to get to the safety of my room.

With a relieved breath when I reach my goal, I lean back against my closed door and slowly peek at my phone. I bite my lip at the notification—a text from Cooper. It says one thing, but it's enough to make my stomach dip.

Cooper: Tomorrow night, 9pm study session.

Heat throbs between my legs. This won't be a cram session with books and notes. Pressing the back of my hand to my flushed cheeks, I cross the room and take out my notebook. The unchecked *lose virginity* line stands out against the floral-patterned page. My fingers shake as I send back a response to say I'll be there.

TWELVE
COOPER

This time I wait for Tatum outside, watching from the shadows by my door as she sneaks out. She startles once she makes out my form in the dark, clutching her chest.

"Jesus," she hisses.

I grin. "I am the ni—"

"If you're about to make a Batman joke right now, I can't even with you." Tatum elbows past me, hesitating only a moment before awkwardly letting herself into my house.

It stirs a funny sensation in my chest. I'm comfortable at the Danvers' place, and Jackson half-lives at mine, but Tatum isn't used to my house. I like the idea of her letting herself in without thinking.

She doesn't speak again until we make it to my bedroom, too busy pausing at corners and tiptoeing around while I follow. She's so cute, it's difficult not to laugh. I've never felt this—never been almost jittery to touch a girl.

Tonight she's rocking a light pink long sleeve t-shirt and the same terry cloth sleep shorts from before. I scrape my teeth over my lip at the thought of peeling them down her legs.

"So, is study session going to be our code word?" Tatum asks while I lock the door.

"Does Jackson snoop through your texts?"

"No, but it's not like he never sees my phone. It's a good cover."
She grins. "Should we actually study? I'll need to assess where
you're at to know how to help at some point for our little deal. I
brought a fresh notebook so we can organize everything into
categories."

With a rumble, I pull her closer, effectively shutting her up.
"We're going to do a different kind of studying tonight."

"Oh." It puffs out of her on a soft breath.

The corner of my mouth tugs up in a lopsided grin. She feels
good in my arms. Her body is the perfect size to fit against me as if we
belong like this. A tremor runs down her spine, and I chase it,
rubbing her back in soothing circles. She might claim to be ready to
go all reverse cowgirl, but I can read her.

Before we get to what I have planned, we're going to do a warm
up to help her unwind. Knowing her, I'm betting she's never tried
what I'm planning to make her do. Not for someone else since she's
never dated, and probably never considered what a confidence
booster it is to do it for herself.

If I'm going to coach Tatum, I'm going to be thorough as fuck.
She came to me about this, so I'll do it right. She wants the player
everyone knows me as.

Tatum tips her head back to peer up at me. "Do we have a word
for go? How do I know when and where to start?"

A husky laugh leaves me and I take her hand, pulling her over to
the mirror hanging from my closet door. I put her in front of me and
trace my fingertips up and down her arms. Her lashes flutter.

"Foreplay?" she asks.

"Something like that. I want you to start with some sexy selfies.
Not nudes," I add when her eyes bug out. "I just want you to get
familiar with how hot you are."

"You think so?"

Tatum's voice turns shy. I bite the inside of my cheek. She has no
idea what goes through my head every time I look at her.

"Do you want to use my phone or yours?"

"Yours," she decides after a moment of serious debate that almost
makes me laugh. "I don't care if you keep them. You can compare

them to your other booty calls and let me know what I can improve on later."

My mouth pops open and I swipe a hand over it. This is exactly why I need her to get out of her head. She'll never let go of her tight control if she keeps analyzing everything.

"Here." I hand over my phone and back up a few steps to give her room, dropping to my bed to watch. "Take your time. I've got all night."

Tatum peeks at me over her shoulder. After a few seconds, she mumbles, "I've, um. I've never really done this."

Called it.

"It's okay." I lean back on an elbow and tug the hem of my t-shirt up to give her an example. "Follow your instincts. I can put on some music if you want. Remember what I said at the bonfire? Just dive in."

She gives me her undivided attention like I'm giving her the answers to the universe. Christ, when she looks at me like that, I want... No, I need to shut that line of thinking down.

"Those shorts make your ass look great, so maybe that's a good place to start."

She laughs, the sound stirring a pleasant sensation in my chest. I watch with a hooded gaze while she scrolls through my music and selects a song. At first I can tell she's thinking too much. I'm about to jump in again and direct her how to pose for the camera when something clicks. She arches her back and pouts at the mirror and the air in my lungs punches out of me. I mentally mark that one to save for myself when I look back through my camera roll.

Tatum goes slow, but little by little she gains confidence by spending one-on-one time with herself and my mirror. Her fingers slip beneath her shirt to caress her stomach while she bites her lip. The head tilt is killer—my kryptonite.

Watching her like this, heat pulls into my groin. I shift around, subtly adjusting my erection. After another ten minutes and probably forty more selfies, I can't take anymore.

"Okay," I rasp. "I think you're relaxed enough for what I really have planned."

Tatum blinks, her eyelids heavy. Shit. She's turned on, too.

"How'd I do?"

"Good."

Her lashes flutter and she drops her gaze. With a soft smile, she hands my phone over. I trace my lower lip with the tip of my tongue.

"Did you enjoy it?"

"Yeah. It was kinda fun."

Smirking, I take her hand and grab a pillow from my bed. "We're just getting started. That was your warm up."

A soft laugh leaves her. "So what's next, hot shot?"

"Lay down."

"Isn't the bed more comfortable?" She peers between my bed and the pillow I set on the floor.

"Trust me."

Tatum purses her lips like she wants to challenge me. I grin and tug her against me, fitting my palm to the small of her back. My lips find her ear and she leans into me.

"You'll like it. Promise."

"You're the master," she breathes.

"Bet. Now lay down."

Once she's settled, I pull out a strip of fabric from the pocket of my sweatpants. It's a silky dark blue scarf I borrowed from the back of my mom's closet.

"Isn't jumping right to tying me up a little bit, I don't know, in the deep end?"

"Relax." I chuckle, dragging it over her legs. "It's to blindfold you. And I'd never do something you weren't comfortable with. This is just another way to get you out of your head, so you focus on what feels good. So unless you're saying you want to be tied up..."

She bites her lip. I'm intrigued by the way her pupils darken. Interesting. I file that away for later and continue skimming the soft material over any inch of skin showing. She hums, closing her eyes.

"Okay."

My mouth curves. "Good girl."

Tatum releases a tiny sound that goes right to my cock. Jesus, she has no idea how sexy she is.

I make quick work of securing the blindfold. Once I'm satisfied she can't see, I trace the inside of her wrist.

"Oh." She sighs. "That feels nice. I thought you'd go right for the money."

"Nah. It's better this way." I keep going for small touches to erogenous zones—the side of her neck, the curve of her lip, the patch of skin above her hip where her shirt rides up. "With the blindfold on, you don't know what's coming."

To illustrate, I lean down and press a kiss to her jaw and skim the waistband of her shorts. Her breath hitches.

"Can I take these off?" I dip a finger beneath the elastic band.

She nods. "Please."

The plea is soft and tinged with eagerness.

I swallow back a groan. When I do fuck her, I'm going to have to jack off at least twice beforehand to pregame, or I won't last with her begging me all pretty like that.

I slide both hands up her sides to push her shirt high enough to expose her tan stomach. I spend a minute caressing her skin, tracing random patterns. Her stomach concaves when I find a ticklish spot by her hip I'm dying to kiss until I leave a hickey to prove I was there.

"I thought you were taking off my shorts."

"Getting there, baby. Patience. I want to explore you some more."

"Oh. That's... Okay, yeah."

"You like that?" There's no way to hide the hint of smugness in my tone.

She swats at me. I capture her hands and pin them to the floor, dragging my nose along her jaw.

"Tell me you like it."

"I do. It's...hot."

I reward her with a line of kisses down her neck that leaves her breathless and arching. My teeth graze her pulse point.

"Coop," Tatum whispers in a hazy tone.

Before I get carried away and forget my plan, I hook my fingers in her shorts and peel them off. It takes me a second to think, what's left of my brainpower rushing south because *fuck*.

Tatum rubs her thighs together. The bikini cut thong is white cotton with purple and pink stripes. Transfixed, I slip a finger beneath the thin sides and slide the material back and forth. The sight of her pink shirt rucked up and her sexy panties is better than any thirsty nude pic I've ever received.

I almost forget the plan again. The idea behind the blindfold is to get her used to being touched until she's comfortable.

Dragging my fingertips along the edge of the thong, I inhale, wishing I could skip the plan and bury my face between her goddamn legs. That is definitely happening at some point—I want to eat her pussy until she's so oversensitive from coming she has to shove me away.

"You're killing me," Tatum mumbles. She rubs her thighs together again and shifts restlessly. "I'm all tingly from getting worked up."

"Back at you." I scrape my teeth over my lip. "Because damn, babe. You look so good writhing on my floor. I haven't even done anything yet."

A husky laugh bubbles out of her. I like it when a girl can laugh at moments like this.

I cover her hand with mine and thread my fingers through hers. Guiding her, I make her skim her stomach, teasing close to her panties before redirecting.

"What are you doing now?"

"Starting our study session. You're going to touch yourself, but I'm going to show you where."

Her chest moves with the catch in her breath. Good, she likes this, too.

We're quiet for a few moments while I concentrate on moving her hand where I want to tease her. Our joined hands move under her shirt, grazing the underside of her tits. She's not wearing a bra and her hard nipples show through her shirt. My mouth waters with the need to close my mouth around them and suck until her shirt is soaked through.

I move her hand down to the inside of her thigh, dipping low and changing directions before we reach the apex between her legs.

She huffs out a little breath that makes me smirk, but doesn't protest when I drag her hand back up her stomach. This time we cover her breast, my knuckles brushing a nipple. She bites her lip and presses into the touch.

"Squeeze," I murmur. "Touch yourself for me, Tate."

Licking her lips, she follows my directions and massages her tit. Her head tips toward me and I pet her hair.

"Play with your nipple. It's begging for your attention."

A sound of pleasure sticks in her throat while she rolls the pebbled bud between her fingers. When she's squirming, I move her hand to her other tit. Once I'm sure her breasts ache, I guide her hand down her stomach.

Lower. A groan rumbles in my chest. Lower. Tatum presses into our joined hands, seeking pressure where her body is begging for it. *Lower.*

"Touch your pussy, Tatum."

Both of us force out twin breaths as our hands slip inside her underwear.

"Don't stop until you make yourself come."

THIRTEEN
TATUM

Don't stop until you make yourself come.

God, my entire body is on fire. With the blindfold, everything feels heightened—*more*. Parts of me I had no idea were so sensitive sing, even the skin between my fingers where Cooper's are threaded between mine as he guides me to touch myself. I might come from the first stroke of my fingers as he pushes my hand between my legs.

This is the most erotic thing I've ever experienced.

Sliding over my mound to touch where I'm aching for release steals my breath. Cooper makes a low groaning noise. It's detached in the darkness I'm swimming in behind the blindfold. His big hand squeezes mine encouragingly until I give in to instinct.

At first I just tease my fingertips over my folds, going slow. His breathing turns ragged, but he doesn't push me. It feels so good. Every caress sends an intense wave of tingles across my skin. I shiver, my hips rocking of their own accord in anticipation of more.

"You feeling good from petting yourself?" He puts the barest amount of pressure on my hand to mimic the movements I've been doing, but more firmly. He makes me cup myself, but it's like *him* cupping between my legs. "You like teasing yourself to the edge?"

Rolling my lips between my teeth, I nod. A hot flush spreads over my body, leaving my skin sensitive when he leans down to breathe over my throat. His lips barely brush where my collar bone peeks out from the neckline of my shirt.

"Keep going." His low order against my skin makes me shudder. "I want to see you come, Tate."

"Yes," I whisper.

He lets me take the lead again and I continue rubbing myself in the way I like, circling my clit. I sink my teeth into my lip and choke on a sound of pleasure. In the dark of the blindfold, every one of my nerve endings sings, my whole body hyper aware of the orgasm building.

"Fuck, you must be wet. I feel it on my knuckles," Cooper rumbles.

Arousal thrums through me, pulsing in my clit. I've played with myself plenty of times, but this is unlike anything I've felt before. Even in my hottest masturbation session, I've never been dripping like this.

It's still my own touch, but he's controlling it. Somehow, it makes it ten times hotter. I don't know when he'll interrupt me, reminding me I'm not alone, that he's watching, that this is for him as much as it's for me. I can't see anything, but I imagine the way he's looking at me while he makes me touch myself.

"Goddamn, baby. Put your fingers inside. I need you to fuck yourself with them so I can feel more." His grip flexes and he nudges our joined hands lower. "I want you grinding against your hand."

A moan tears free before I can smother it.

Swallowing, I do as he says. My fingers glide through my folds from how slick I am. It takes nothing to push one inside. I gasp, clenching around it. He curses and encourages me to move by tightening his hold on my hand and making me thrust deeper. I let him, too turned on by the idea of him fingering me with my own fingers.

"Fuck, that's hot," Cooper rasps. "Look at you. So sexy, baby."

My free hand scrabbles for something to hold on to while my core turns into liquid heat. I grab the leg of his bed right as Cooper presses the heel of my hand against my clit.

"Can you take another finger?"

Whimpering, I nod. He must bend over again, because I feel the grin he presses against my throat.

"Good girl. Do it."

When I obey, he hums next to my ear, flicking his tongue out to taste it. I shudder as pleasure ripples through me like an echo chamber from every sensation I'm experiencing without my sense of sight.

"That's it."

Everything is hazy in my mind, all of my focus consumed by how good this is. I feel free.

I won't last much longer. My legs tremble with each roll of my hips as I do exactly as Cooper directed, grinding into my hand while I finger myself. His breaths fan over my neck. I picture him alternating between watching intently as our joined hands move inside my panties and leaving torturous, sultry kisses along my neck and jaw.

"You ready to come?"

My nod is driven by urgency as my movements quicken. "Close."

"Yeah? You teetering right on that edge? Bet it won't take much more to tip over. It'll feel so good, T. So good." He nibbles on my ear, tracing the shell of my lobe with his tongue. A rough groan from him makes me gasp. "God, I wish it was my cock inside you right now instead of your fingers, but you look so fucking hot about to come."

His dirty talk does it, along with the way he presses down on my hand at the precise moment to shatter me. The ripple of pleasure bursts out from my center in a wave of ecstasy. I moan as he takes over for me, keeping my fingers going.

"That's it. Good girl, making yourself come," he rumbles against my throat.

I float in the aftermath of my orgasm, barely aware of the light kiss Cooper places on my cheek as he pulls our hands free. I slide my legs together, humming at the little aftershocks tingling across my skin.

He brings my hand to his mouth and closes his lips around them, sucking. I gasp, struggling into a seated position. I still can't see, but I feel his tongue winding around my knuckles, mapping every inch.

"What are you doing?" I breathe.

"Tasting you," Cooper mutters before putting his mouth back on me.

My cheeks prickle with a flush. It's so obscene and dirty, but that's what makes it even hotter.

"You, um," I stammer. "You like doing that?"

He hums in response, lapping at my fingers. "Fuckin' love it. Can't wait to get my mouth on you for real."

Cooper has stolen my breath multiple times tonight, but this time it wheezes out of me as I go lightheaded. Will we do that next? The throb of desire between my legs is hopeful.

I nudge the blindfold off and almost squeak at the sight of him. He's staring at me with hooded eyes, nibbling my fingertips. There's an impressive erection tenting his sweatpants. That full dick print makes my mouth water.

"What now?" I ask when he finally relinquishes me.

He drags a hand through his hair. Without his signature ball cap to keep it in place, the ends curl around his ears and over his fore-head. He tips his head back and blows out a breath.

"Let's call it a night there. That was a good start."

"Wait, what?"

My shoulders slump as my gaze falls to his lap. He's definitely into everything we did. Why would we stop before he gets to finish, too?

"You're hard. I thought—"

"We've got plenty of time. I just wanted to focus on you tonight."

He gets up and adjusts his dick so it's not as obvious. I avert my eyes, then feel silly for it. We just had both our hands down my underwear, touching my pussy. He licked my come off his fingers. Besides, he doesn't seem too shy about reaching into his own pants with me right there.

"Okay." I drag out the syllables and climb to my feet. Without the distraction to leave me feeling free, my thoughts churn once more. "So, uh..."

Cooper grabs his phone and swipes through some of the photos I took. The corner of his mouth lifts at some of them. He gives me a smile.

"I'm giving you homework."

"Wow, you're really taking this whole sex tutor thing seriously," I sass.

"I want you to go home and take a sexy selfie every day to keep getting more comfortable in your own body." He dips his head, peering at me through his lashes. "Send them to me so I know you're doing it."

I slide my lips together and nod. "When's our next lesson?"

"Soon. I'll text you for a study session."

"Okay." I bite my lip and find my shorts. I motion to his door. "So should I...?"

"Hold on." His voice is a rough growl that startles me. "I can't wait. I need one more taste."

He closes the distance between us and takes me by surprise with a kiss. I drop my shorts and part my lips with a shocked gasp. He makes another jagged sound and grabs my ass, hauling me against him as he deepens the kiss. The swipe of his tongue against mine makes me groan, and I hold on tight to him. We stumble as he herds me against the wall and nudges his knee between mine while his hands massage my ass.

Another noise tears from my throat as he encourages me to move on his thigh. It feels just as good as his hand over mine, and I grind on his muscled leg as we make out.

The kiss is a tidal wave that traps me in a riptide I never want to leave.

My breath hitches and a cry lodges in my throat as I shudder against him, coming again. He tenses, fingers digging into my ass.

"Wait," he says when he ends the kiss.

"What?" I cling to him, still quivering.

"If we don't stop, I'm going to take everything from you right fucking now, T."

My heart thuds. I swallow. "What's the problem with that? That's the point."

He leans back far enough to give me room to breathe, but his hands still squeeze my ass. His gaze is dark and blazing as he takes me in with a piercing sweep of his eyes.

"Rule one." Cooper's voice is wrecked.

It's all he says. I sway and his grip on me flexes. I nod, then he mirrors the movement.

"Rule one," I repeat hoarsely.

Our reminder of the rule we both agreed to—taking this slow.

* * *

Once I step through the door to my house, I lean against it, filled with a happy glow. The secret pleased smile is impossible to wipe off my face as I think about what just happened with Cooper.

I head upstairs. Every inch of my body feels alive and free.

"Where were you?"

Jackson's voice through his open door jolts me out of my thoughts. I pause and lean in his door, nodding to him in greeting.

He glances up from his laptop and narrows his eyes. "And what were you doing that's got you smiling like that?"

Guilt washes over me. The worst part of this whole plan is that I'm lying to my brother. I hate doing that.

And it's not just me—Cooper's lying to him, too. His sister and his best friend.

I'll have to be careful. I won't break Cooper's rules, and I can't slip up and let Jackson find out what we're doing.

"Oh, uh." I wave a hand, struggling to find a cover story. Can he see it all over my face? "Simone was craving a milkshake and fries. Period stuff. I rode with her."

Just as I hoped, at the mention of her period, Jackson loses interest. He seems to buy it readily. Good thing, because once I've committed to the story, I realize I don't have any food with me.

"You didn't bring me anything?" A relieved breath leaves me. He's more focused on the unspoken agreement to always bring each other food if we're picking something up. "Jeez, what did I do to you that you'd snub me like that?"

"Sorry. I wasn't feeling anything. I'll get you next time," I offer.

He smirks, appeased. His attention returns to his laptop.

"Are you watching a movie?"

"Nah, checking the open seats in the classes I need to register for."

My brows shoot up. "Wow, you're actually early this year."

Jackson's chest expands with a laugh. "Yeah. I almost missed out on a required course for my core curriculum freshman year, so I'm more on my game this time."

Crossing the room, I knock on his skull. He grunts and wrestles me off, flicking my thigh.

"There's a brain in there capable of rational thought after all," I tease.

"Get out of here. You're so annoying."

The bite in his tone is fabricated. It's a universal sibling language to love and be annoyed by each other in the same breath.

We wrestle playfully for a few more moments, each getting cheap shots in that leave us evenly matched. Swallowing back my laughter, I back up with my palms in front of me.

"Okay, okay. Truce." He grumbles, but nods. I circle to the other side of his bed to see his screen. "What classes are you registering for?"

"A statistics class and economics. The statistics one is going to make me regret majoring in business."

I grin. "Sounds fun."

"Nerd. Did you register yet?"

"Duh. The minute they opened up." I smirk in triumph. "Got everything I wanted. My fall semester schedule is perfection, if I do say so myself."

Jackson rolls his eyes. "Probably all 8am classes."

"Three."

He gives me a lopsided smile and shakes his head. "Did you schedule in time for fun, too? You don't have to be all about school all the time."

I bite the inside of my lip. That's exactly why I have Cooper tutoring me. Because more than anything, I want the full experience.

The unforgettable memories people make in college. I don't want to look back and regret that I never lived.

"I know." I pluck at the hem of my sleep shorts.

Jackson picks up on the shift in my tone and bumps my shoulder lightly with his knuckles. "Relax. It's nothing like high school. You'll like it. At first it's a lot, but once you start putting yourself out there and making friends, it all feels chill. Just don't be me and sleep through all the morning classes you sign up for."

I snort and knock my shoulder against his. "My classes are the last thing I'm worried about. More like, how do I make sure I get along with my roommate, and have enough time for everything I want to pack into my days."

His shoulders shake with an amused huff. "Yeah. I don't know why I even worried."

"Night." I pop off his bed and head for the door.

"Later."

When I reach my room, everything comes flooding back. I press a hand to my belly—the same hand Cooper used to guide me in touching myself. My teeth sink into my lip as a flutter moves through my core and my thighs clench.

How soon is his promise of next time?

Even after coming multiple times with him, I'm too wired to sleep. I hop into the shower. My nipples tighten at the hot rush of water and an exhale flies out of me. The heat gradually builds again, but I only brush teasing touches over my skin, holding off to make the pleasurable ache in my core last.

As I'm slipping into another pair of shorts and a flowing tank top, my gaze snags on my phone. I wonder what he did after I left. Did he take care of himself?

Cooper did give me homework. A sexy selfie every day. And I pride myself on being an excellent student.

Licking my lips, I swipe my phone from the charger and move to stand in front of my mirror. I test out some of the angles I liked best when I was in his room. The shorts are thin enough to see my purple panties through them. He liked my ass in the other shorts, so I start there again.

I allow the tank to fall off my shoulder on one side and lift a knee to my bed for balance while I twist around to snap a photo of my ass.

The result is a sultry pose that highlights the curves. My ass is plump, but my breasts aren't big. Yet the photo looks good. I really like how I look in it, like a gorgeous woman. I'm peeking through the hair spilling over my shoulder, back arched.

Butterflies fill my stomach after I take a few more shots. I pick the one I like best—the first one.

The corners of my mouth tilt up as I open Instagram and start a DM message with Cooper. I don't need anyone accidentally figuring out what we're doing by seeing our texts.

Tatum: Sooo, my homework assignment. Should I do them like this?

I pick a photo and send it, then decide on impulse to also send him my other favorite—the closeup cropped shot that shows my lips parted and a peek of sideboob through the loose armholes of my tank top.

Tatum: Is this good?

His response comes a few minutes later while I'm distracting myself by looking up guides and tips on Pinterest, saving them to a secret board.

Cooper: Fuck. [fire emoji]

A breathy laugh leaves me. Smirking, I pick another photo to send. It's the saucy one where I shimmied my shorts down low enough to show a tantalizing peek of underwear and dipped my fingers inside in an imitation of what we did tonight.

Tatum: In case you need some spank bank material over there. Could've had all this in your bed tonight.

Talking like this gives me a burst of confidence. I feel normal, less like I'm behind. It feels natural to teasingly flirt with him like this.

A photo from him comes through and I nearly drop my phone. He matched the last one I sent. He doesn't have the sweatpants on anymore, sprawled on his bed with his hand in his boxers, fist wrapped around an obvious bulge.

Oh my god. Is he—? Right now?

Another message pops up in our chat.

Cooper: You're making me regret sending you away, baby girl.

Part of me wants to sneak back out of the house and go back to his room next-door. My body is certainly partial to the idea. But his ragged murmur of rule one when we kissed stops me from suggesting it.

We have time.

Tatum: Night [kissing emoji]

Cooper: Night

Another smile crosses my face as I set my phone on my night-stand. I rifle through my notebook stash and pick one to make a record of our study sessions. This one has a dark cover with blush roses. Opening to the first blank page, my smile stretches into a grin.

Session one, I write. Then I fill the pages with a detailed account of every sensation, every dirty murmur, and the way it made me feel.

Excited anticipation fills me. This is working out. My body thrums with the thought of next time.

I look at the photo he sent back, biting my lip. *Damn boy*. It's mouthwatering, filling my head with dirty fantasies. I still haven't seen his dick, but I imagine it's as perfect and sexy as every other part of his body.

If I can affect a guy like Cooper, things aren't hopeless. Check mark to the one box I want to nail, here I come.

FOURTEEN
COOPER

I last two days before I text her our code word for another study session. My thin self-control almost snapped the other night when I had her in my room, grinding on my thigh while I pinned her to the wall and kissed the shit out of her. Every second since she walked out has been an acute form of torture.

And I'm the genius who gave her the homework assignment. Tatum does exactly as I instructed, sending hot as fuck selfies. Twice a day, because she's always going to be an overachiever.

Screw past me, that guy's a dick.

My phone vibrates and when I check it, I press the heel of my palm to my groin. Tatum sent another photo through the Instagram DM thread where we've been doing this to keep it on the down-low. She's supposed to come over for tonight's lesson.

See you soon, it promises.

She's wrapped in a short towel, wet hair falling around her face and shoulders in darkened tangles. Her tan skin is flushed from the shower, and she's leaning forward slightly to offer a tease of cleavage. The more she sends, the more confident she grows with them.

"Fuck," I drag out in a low mutter. "You're so paying for these when you get here."

I held back the first time, but tonight I'm taking her apart.

Last time I only had a taste. Tonight I'm going to feast until I taste nothing but her on my tongue for days.

The thought makes my dick throb. Gritting my teeth, I debate if I have time to rub one out again before she gets here. I opt not to, trying to kill my boner by looking up the South Bay College course registration site to check if the class I need has opened up a new time slot yet.

Twenty minutes later, Tatum lets me know she's heading over. I go downstairs to meet her. My parents left this morning for a health and wellness retreat they're speaking at, so we have the place to ourselves. It's a good thing, too.

Tonight I plan to make Tatum scream for me.

I won't stop until I take her apart.

When I open the door, I peer around the shared driveway, looking for her. Frowning, I check my phone. Did she get caught sneaking out, and had to make up a cover story?

"Tate?" I keep my voice low.

A blur of movement rushes me from my left, and I have a fucking heart attack until her sweet coconut lime scent hits me. I grab her shoulders and haul her inside.

"Jesus, you little demon. Are you trying to get us caught?"

Tatum's laugh is warm and honeyed. She leans into me for support. "Oh my god, your face. Consider that payback for giving me a jump scare the other night."

"The only one serving up payback tonight is me, baby," I promise. She shivers at the heat in my tone. I chase it, mouthing at her throat. "You've been driving me crazy with those hot pics."

Now that I have her in my arms again, I'm about to haul her cute little ass over my shoulder and take her upstairs. She makes it hard to keep my cool.

"You're just saying that."

"For real."

"Yeah?" She leans back with a shy smile and I lead her upstairs. "So you'd say I'm passing Sexy Selfie 101?"

"Thirst pic game strong, T. I couldn't wait another minute to get you back for our next study session."

It's the honest truth. I've been rocking a half chub for two days whenever I think about those photos.

When we reach my bedroom, her eyes hood and she peers around. I watch her gaze land on the spot where I had her blindfolded and writhing for me.

"We have the house to ourselves." I stand behind her, ghosting my fingers over her hips.

"Oh? Where are your parents?"

"Retreat." I nuzzle into her neck, darting my tongue out to taste her skin. Her hair is still damp from showering. "Know what that means?"

"What?"

Damn, I love the way her voice gets all breathy when I'm affecting her with my touch.

With a grin, I push my hand beneath her t-shirt and stroke the warm skin of her stomach. "It means you don't have to hold back. For tonight's session, I want you to let go completely. You can be as loud as you want."

She sucks in a breath and her belly concaves beneath my palm. "That's assuming I'm a screamer. I don't know if I am."

"Oh, baby." Smugness fills my tone. "You're gonna scream. I know it."

"Cocky." Tatum angles her head to see me better.

"Experienced," I counter in a gravelly rumble.

Her pupils dilate and her gaze falls to my mouth. I lean in, capturing her lips in a languid kiss that has her swaying back against me. She grabs my arm for balance. I feed her my tongue, then suck on her lip until she whimpers.

"Get on the bed," I murmur against her lips.

"Are we—?" Tatum spins to face me.

"You'll see." Taking hold of her hips again, I guide her back until her legs hit the mattress. "Get comfortable."

Licking her lips, she follows my directions. It gives me a thrill that she trusts me with all of this.

"No blindfold tonight." I reach behind my head and tug off my shirt. Her gaze roams my body. Grinning, I tilt my head. "I want you to see everything this time."

Tatum swallows, her throat convulsing. She doesn't take her eyes off me, tracking me as I shuck off my basketball shorts. I leave my boxers on. If I don't, I'm the one likely to forget rule one once my head buries between her thighs.

I love eating pussy. Most guys do it because they want to make their girl come or for fairness, stopping once she finishes. But I legit *love* it. If they don't stop me, I keep going. Tate's about to find out first hand how much pleasure it gives me to get a girl off with my mouth.

"You're definitely ready to go." Her attention is on the bulge barely contained in my boxers.

Smirking, I give it an absent rub. "With you? Always." I climb across the bed, braced over her. "You're overdressed."

Boldness burns away her nerves and with an enticing little smile that shows off the crooked tooth I love so much, she peels her t-shirt off, revealing she skipped a bra. As she goes for the button of her shorts, I dip my head to take one of her breasts into my mouth.

She moans, arching up, abandoning her shorts to sink her fingers into my hair to hold me there while I suck on her nipple. I circle it with teasing flicks of my tongue, then move to the other one. She hooks a leg around mine and grinds her pelvis against my abs.

I tug on her shorts. "Off. Now."

"Yes," she breathes. "Please, keep—*ah!*"

Before her plea for more is past her lips, I resume, latching on to her tits with a graze of teeth that has her bucking beneath me with a strangled cry. Together, we manage to get her shorts undone. I help her by pulling them down her legs, discarding them off the side of the bed. Then I meet her eyes and settle into position on my stomach between her legs.

Her lips part. "What are you doing?"

"Getting ready to make you scream." I toy with the waistband of her panties. Tonight they're a dark green with lace sides.

Usually I'd spend time teasing her some more, soak her through her panties before I stripped them off, but just being between her legs is enough to make me impatient. I hook my fingers in the sides and take them off.

The other night I didn't get to fully appreciate the view. My mouth fucking waters and I dip my head, closing the distance between me and her pussy. Her body tenses the closer I get. I pause, playing it off like I'm readjusting my position.

"Remember, anything you don't like, you tell me. I'll stop."

"Are you sure, though? I mean, you don't have to."

"Tate." Sternness creeps into my tone. "First of all, fuck any guy who doesn't want to give you head."

The second the words leave my mouth, I battle a wave of jealousy. No way in hell would I let her near a dickhead like that. The thought of other guys with her drives me insane.

"Okay. But seriously, if you don't want—"

"I *want* to, baby. I'm dying to get my mouth on you."

"Oh." Her eyes widen. "Um, well, okay."

"I love doing this." At her confused look, I place a kiss on her inner thigh. She widens her legs to give me access, then closes them like she realizes how much she's presenting her gorgeous body to me. "I do. And I want to make you feel good. There's a lesson to it, too. One, I want you to let go, like I said. Don't hold back any sounds. Two, you need to know what feels good for you so you can tell the person you're with."

"That makes sense."

I muffle a laugh into her hip. Always with the logical thoughts.

"We cool?"

She hums, settling back on the bed. Her body loses some of the tension, but I can tell she's not all the way there. It's been a long time, but I get it's nerve racking to bare your intimate parts with someone.

I go slowly, starting with soft kisses across her skin. Each brush of lips brings me closer to her folds. She sighs when I hit a particularly sensitive spot near the top of her inner thigh. Glancing up the length of her body, I wait until her focus is on me.

"There's only one rule, T," I rasp. "Eyes on me."

I swear her eyes darken with desire. She nods. *Thank fuck.*

My mouth covers her. God, it's even better than I imagined. The first swipe of my tongue makes her gasp. I groan, sucking and laving her pussy. Shoving my hands beneath her, I squeeze her ass, using the grip as leverage to bring her even closer to my mouth.

Tatum is so fucking responsive. My dick swells, throbbing as I grind against the mattress, my entire body moving in tandem as I feast on her sweet sinful taste. She clamps her thighs around my ears when I circle her clit with my tongue and I grin against her slick folds. I keep that motion up, the sounds of her cries music to my ears.

She never stopped to silence herself. Shyness went out the door as soon as my mouth was on her.

Her hips rock. She's close to the edge. I invite her there with sure swipes of my tongue and suck with the amount of pressure that makes her tremble.

When she comes, she releases the loudest moan yet mingled with delirious curses, chasing the sensation with slow rolls over her hips. I ease back, returning to soft kisses so I don't overwhelm her right off the bat.

"Holy shit," she mumbles. Her hands cover her face. "That was..."

"That was just the first one."

"What?" She spreads her fingers to peek through them.

"We're just getting started. I'm not done with my meal yet. Not even close." I shift her leg over my shoulder and lick a stripe through her pussy. "Mm, you taste so fucking good, baby girl."

"I—you—that's—"

Her stammering cuts off with a choked off sound when I lower my head and suck on her clit. Shit, I love this, love hearing these sounds, but with her it's like the first time I discovered how much I like this all over again. Each time her pleasure crests, arousal rockets through me. I can feel the damp patch in my boxers from my cock leaking pre each time I rub against the mattress for some relief.

With a grin, I add fingers to the mix. Tatum likes that, coming so fast once I sink two fingers inside her while licking her clit that it surprises me. Her body clenches around my fingers, and I tongue the edges of her entrance.

Flicking my gaze up, I find her head thrown back. I stroke her hip, pulling my mouth away.

"Why'd you stop?" she cries.

I smirk. "Keep those eyes on me."

"O-oh."

Tatum's hips press up and I hold them down. She squirms, giving me a pleading look.

"Tell me the rule and I'll keep going."

"Watch you."

"Watch me what, baby?" Now I'm just toying with her, holding myself back from devouring her once more.

It takes her a second to work up the courage to respond. "Watch you while you eat me out."

"Good girl."

That gorgeous flush tinges her cheeks a shade darker. I hold her gaze as I dip my head between her legs, watching every flicker of pleasure across her face. She fights against closing her eyes when she comes for me again. *Good girl.*

Her orgasms blur together. I don't keep track of time. My focus is consumed by eating her pussy. When she feebly nudges at my head with a hoarse whimper, I growl and continue.

"Coop, oh my god," Tatum hisses. "Fuck, fuck, oh god."

Another rumble from me vibrates against her dripping pussy. She's so wet her thighs and the lower half of my face are coated with arousal. The room smells like sex and her.

She sucks in shuddery breaths, her body shaking all over. "Please. Please."

It takes her pulling on my hair to finally push me away. I still want to keep going, but when I sit back, pride swells in my chest. It's primal, almost feral. Wiping my mouth and chin with the back of my hand, I drink the sight of her in.

Her chest heaves and her legs sprawl, no longer self-conscious. She's completely undone because I did that to her. Possessiveness crashes over me, locking me in the barrel roll. I was the first to taste her. First to have my tongue inside her. I'll always be who she thinks of.

Shit, I want to be the only one to ever do that to her.

My cock is rock hard. More than it's ever been after eating pussy.

Tatum is still out of it when I rip down the waistband of my boxers and squeeze my dick. The throbbing heat coils tight in my groin. Her lashes flutter and she catches my eye, watching me jerk off. Groaning, I keep stroking my length, putting on a show for her.

It only takes a couple of minutes before my orgasm rushes up. The look on her face pushes me over, the desire brimming in her eyes and the way she licks her lips. I still taste her on my tongue. With a bitten off noise, I come on her lower stomach.

Blood rushes through my head. When the orgasm fades, I lose my balance, bracing a hand to catch myself. I gasp for breath, staring at Tatum, naked and drowsy in my bed. I want nothing more than to tuck her against me and pass out.

The spell breaks when she glances down at the mess I made on her.

"Ah, shit." Control over my limbs hasn't returned yet as blood returns to my brain. "Sorry. I didn't even ask. I'll clean you up."

"It's fine." She shoots me a sleepy smile. "It was hot."

When I can move, I go to the bathroom and wet a washcloth with warm water. She watches me from beneath her lashes as I swipe it over her skin to wipe up my come.

"I wish I didn't have to leave," Tatum groans, stretching her arms overhead. It pushes her tits out in a tantalizing way. "I'm so comfortable right now. I feel like I could fall asleep."

I wish she didn't have to go, either.

Telling her to stay is on the tip of my tongue. My phone vibrates against the lamp on the nightstand. With a sigh, I lean over and check it.

It's her brother.

FIFTEEN
COOPER

The Saturday lunch shift at Tiki Taco Shack is always busy. South Bay bustles with tourists through the summer, and on a perfect day like this one, they flock to the beach. Jackson works the same section with me. Tatum has the afternoon shift that overlaps ours, but she's not here yet.

Our Insta DMs continue. For every two homework selfies she sends me, I give her one back. It's a dangerous game, but I can't stop. Not since I tasted her. Fuck, I want to again. It hasn't been twenty-four hours, and I'm craving her again.

Once Jackson texted me last night, Tatum caught sight of the screen and swore, scrambling up from my bed to leave. I still wish she could've stayed. Even if it's a crazy risk—one that would get us caught for sure.

I'm wiping the bar as things begin to die down. Jackson stacks glasses at the other end.

"Another round?" I ask the out of town guys chilling on the bar swings.

"Sure thing," one of them drawls in a Southern accent. He has an Atlanta Braves ball cap on. "Hey, you're local, right?"

I nod. The three guys look around mine and Jackson's age. I don't recognize them from South Bay's campus. They must be hitting SoCal for their summer break from college.

"Any good parties going on tonight? We've only got a couple days left." His friend nudges him and he grins. "Lookin' to spend some time hangin' out where the ladies are."

This used to be me. The guy everyone sees me as, the one who parties and hooks up. Even my SBC advisor has heard of my reputation around South Bay.

I offer a lopsided smile in return and shrug. "Tinder? I don't know what to tell you, man. There aren't any I've heard of going on tonight."

Jackson overhears and shoots me a confused look. "What are you talking about? I told you there was another bonfire night at the Cove this weekend." He ambles over and leans his forearms across the lacquered bar top. "Mariner's Cove. Just hop on Ocean Drive and follow it, you can't miss it. See you there."

While he gives them directions, I refill their drinks.

"Thanks," the guy in the ball cap says.

I jerk my chin in a nod.

"Whoa," mumbles the guy's other friend, staring past my shoulder into the Tiki Taco Shack.

Tatum's arrival distracts me, too. I track her as she moves through the restaurant with a big smile, waving to some recognizable regulars while she ties the short work apron around her waist.

The Braves fan grins and keeps his leer on Tatum. "She's cute as hell. Will she be there?"

"Nah." I can't help the frosty edge of dismissal.

His eyes flick to me in assessment. It's the universal look guys give each other when they're trying to feel out whether he just insulted me by pissing on my territory by asking after Tatum. I hate shit like this because she isn't territory—she's her own person. But fuck if I'm not still immediately struggling to quell the protectiveness welling in my chest.

It would be easier to tell him she's my girl, but Jackson is barely two feet away.

"There's also a club not far from here. Tons of chicks from around here go there." I pull up the Instagram page for the club in Del Mar Kayla and her friends always hit up. "Trust me, you'll find plenty of girls there to make some travel memories with."

They take a photo of my phone and talk amongst themselves. I blow out a breath and move away. The need to seek Tate out is strong, but I follow Jackson to the spot the staff hang out at when things are slow. I rub at my chest, swallowing roughly.

It doesn't have to mean anything. I grew up with her following us around the neighborhood. I helped her learn how to ride a bike without training wheels. I've guarded her shell and rock collections at the beach. I'd protect her no matter what. That's all.

A whisper at the back of my mind calls me a big fucking liar.

Tatum passes by and pulls a goofy face at us. A faint smile tugs at my lips.

Jackson grabs the dish towel from his apron and messes around with it, snapping it at me. I grunt under my breath when he catches my leg.

"Dick."

"Don't zone out then." He grins, unrepentant. "That chick from last night got you daydreaming? I don't blame you, bro. The girl I met at the beach yesterday is burned into my brain—sucked my soul out through my balls, I swear to god."

"Nice." I smirk, laughing along with him.

Jackson pauses, raising his brows. "And?"

"What?"

"Dude. Don't play it like that with me. You've got nothing to say?"

I lick my lips, skating my gaze to the side. I shake my head. Jackson snorts and elbows me. We've never faced this before. We have no problem telling each other this stuff. Obviously, if I tell him I was with his sister, I'm a dead man.

"Come on, what are you hiding it for? I know I heard a girl riding the Cooper Vale pleasure train last night when I got home."

My stomach sinks. That nickname sends a wave of displeasure

through me. When he says it that way, all I picture is how used it makes me feel. Any guy I know would call me an idiot and question my masculinity for not wanting to get off as much as possible, but fucking sue me for wanting more than to just get my dick wet without feeling like I can talk to a girl about my day after the transaction is over.

It never used to bother me this much, but it casts the memory of all the ways I had Tatum crying out last night in an awful, harsh light.

"It wasn't what you think. I didn't know my porn was connected to the bluetooth speaker system. Parents are out of town for the weekend, you know how it is."

He frowns at me for evading his question, eyes narrowed in suspicion. I'm saved from his pestering when the sound of Tatum's uncomfortable laugh by the bar catches his attention. We both swing around and move at the same time.

Those out of town guys looking to party are bothering her. The one in the Braves hat has come around to lean in her space while the other two grin at her flirtatiously.

"The Shady Palm. You know it?" One of them asks, swirling his fingers through condensation on the bar close to her.

"Of course." The curve of Tatum's mouth is friendly enough, but her body language is tense. She uses a serving tray to guard herself, hugging it tight against her body. "I live here. I pass it on my way to work."

"When's your shift over, sweetheart?" Braves hat guy asks. He's clearly the ringleader of his friends. "You should come hang out tonight."

"Thanks for the invite, boys, but I have plans."

"We're only here for a couple more nights. Come on." The guy in her personal space traces his knuckle down her arm.

I release a feral sound beneath my breath and cross the Tiki Taco Shack in record time. Jackson presses between them, nudging his sister behind him. It directs her right into my chest as I come to a stop at her back.

"Is there a problem, Tate?" Jackson's voice is hard.

It matches the protectiveness that has roared back to life inside me. My fingers twitch at my side with the desire to curl around her hip and pull her into my arms. I ball my hand into a fist instead, casting a fierce look at the two guys seated at the bar.

"No, I had it covered," she says with a sigh.

"Now you're extra covered. You know we've always got your back, T," I mutter. "These guys bothering you?"

She angles her head to peer at me from the corner of her eye. I choke back a curse at the desire in her eyes and the subtle hitch in her breathing. Her words say one thing, but she leans into me a little.

"We just wanted to invite her out. No harm." One of the guys at the bar lifts his hands.

"She turned you down," I say.

The Braves fan meets my eyes. With my chest pressed into Tatum's back, looming over her and glaring at him, there's no mistaking it. What he questioned earlier is true. She's not available for him.

Even though I'm only supposed to be her temporary tutor to help her hook up with guys.

I clench my jaw at that thought and fight the primal urge to wrap my arm around her waist for good measure.

The angry disdain in Jackson's eyes when he swings around to study her with a quick sweep stops me, sending me crashing back to reality. I might be able to get away with protecting Tatum like she's my blood, but I would hate to see my best friend turn that look on me if he found out about what I've been doing to his sister.

"Sorry, sweetheart. We didn't know," Braves guy croons, watching me from the corner of his eye. "Could've just said you had a boyfriend."

She huffs, the offended and stubborn sound yanking on my heart-strings. I step back an inch with a smirk curling the corners of my mouth.

"I'm not your sweetheart, so you can cut that out. And actually, whether I'm attached to a partner or not doesn't matter." She hands the serving tray to her brother and props her hands on her hips. All three of them widen their eyes, exchanging quick glances. "I'm my own person, and I'm not interested in hanging out. Like I said, I have plans. And if I didn't, I don't think you're the kind of person I enjoy hanging out with."

With that, she spins on her heel and breezes away. I grin after her, the tip of my tongue poking between my teeth. Jackson snorts and shakes his head at his sister. She can stand up on her own, but we'll always be there for her whether she needs us or not.

I turn back to the tourists. "You about done, then? I'll get your bill so you can close out your tab." They mumble an agreement. Once they pay, I hold on to the credit card and lean across the bar. "You probably shouldn't come back here again. Enjoy your stay in South Bay."

They leave quickly at the steely edge in my tone. I heave a sigh and search for Tatum. She laughs in the corner with one of the older regulars, serving up a basket of fish tacos. My heartbeat thumps at the sight of her bright smile.

Licking my lips, I untie the apron around my waist and bump fists with Jackson. Our shift ended a few minutes before we stopped the tourists from bothering his sister.

"Want to come with me to grab supplies for the party?" he asks.

Tatum squeezes past us, brushing against me. A hint of coconut and lime tickles my nose. "Move, guys. You're blocking the door to the kitchen."

The Shack is easily the most popular spot for people to eat out of all the beachfront options. We get tourists, college kids, surfers, and locals. It never crossed my mind to worry about Tatum getting hit on at work, but what if this wasn't the first time?

My shift might be over, but I can't leave yet.

We shuffle to the side. I clear my throat and grab fresh utensils from the galvanized tins in a cupboard against the wall.

"I'm gonna eat first. I'll catch you later."

Jackson shrugs. "See you. Later, Tate."

He messes with Tatum's bun as she comes back through the door.

She automatically kicks at him in retaliation without losing her balance.

I wait until he's gone before I sit down at an open table in the corner. It has a good vantage point of the whole place, so I can keep an eye on anyone who's dumb enough to make Tatum uncomfortable.

SIXTEEN
COOPER

After two of our *study sessions*, my dick is already trained to take notice when Tatum's in my room. Tonight we're actually studying, books and the blank notebooks she brought for me spread across my desk.

"It takes some getting used to, but when you use it to track your weekly tasks, I think it'll help you stay on top of your assignments throughout the semester." She waves her hands as she talks, explaining the concept of bullet journaling to me. There were YouTube videos and an Instagram hashtag involved. "Of course, I don't recommend setting it up like mine unless you're super committed to this level of habit tracking."

I chew on the inside of my lip, flicking my gaze to her face. My head is propped against my hand and I listen better to her talking passionately about utilizing notebooks than I manage to pay attention to any of my professors. If she taught all my classes, I'd have no problem passing. She explains everything in a succinct, straightforward way that's much easier for my brain to grasp than the dull drone of most of my professors.

"What?" Tatum's cheeks flush. "What's that look for?"

"Nothing." I give her a crooked smile. "You really take this seriously. Thanks. I feel like I can do this with your help. Turn my grades around, not screw up, you know."

"Of course you can, Coop." Her smile makes my chest ache. "You're really smart. I have complete faith in you. From what I can tell by going over your papers from freshman year, you understand the material, you just absorb it differently than most people. There's nothing wrong with that. Everyone processes differently. School systems just end up going with what works for the majority, but that doesn't leave a lot of leeway for students who are more drawn to other forms of learning."

This girl. I swallow roughly and cover up the way I want to kiss her by flipping through the template pages she set up in a plain black journal. It's not like any of the ones she collects, no distinct patterns, sassy messages, or pops of color. But it was brand new. She picked it out for me.

"Why write it down when I have the syllabus, the online portal, and my phone calendar?" That was how I handled my assignments due before, with a million reminders.

High school wasn't so bad, I was able to coast through. I wasn't at the top of my class, but I wasn't flunking either. For some reason, freshman year of college really threw me off. It's how I ended up in academic jeopardy, to the point my advisor had to send me the letter shoved into the back of my desk drawer.

"This is a psychological trick. You're more likely to remember a task when you physically write it down."

I nod along, absently twirling a spare pen between my fingers. She talks about her goals so regularly that I'm used to her slipping psychological tid bits into conversation. Part of me wishes I could find that same thing that makes me give a damn about my academics the same as it has for her.

The only thing I can safely say comes anywhere close to her level of passion and dedication is my love of surfing. But I'm not good enough to compete. Three Olympic surfers have come out of our regional area. They're still in the prime of their careers. If I'd started thinking about it sooner, maybe I could've trained more, but the thought of traveling around from competition to competition isn't as appealing as the waves I catch here.

She shoots me a sly smirk. "How about I give you some home-work this time?"

I match her expression, adjusting my backwards cap. "What do you have in mind?"

"This week, use the system. You can track your shifts at work and the tide for the best surfing." She leans into me and sinks her teeth into her plump lower lip. The freckles scattered across the bridge of her nose stand out from the sun she got today. "If you make it through the whole week, then you get to teach me how to suck you off."

I choke on the shocked laugh I bark out. "What?"

"You heard me," she sasses.

I definitely did. And so did my cock. A hot throb in my groin begs me to pull her onto my lap.

I glide the tip of my tongue across my bottom lip. "Why does it sound like it's a reward for you instead of a gold star for me?"

"You seemed to enjoy it when you did it to me." She shrugs, playing it off. I see through the nonchalant act to the curiosity beneath her words. "I want to know what all the fuss is about. And if you're thinking about the potential positive reinforcement for completing the work, your brain will be primed to commit to a new habit."

I lean back in my chair, reaching behind my head to squeeze the brim of my hat between my hands. "Okay, T. I'll do the journal tracker."

She grins, then drops her voice to the one she uses to imitate guys. "Bet."

Another laugh leaves me. "How do you make that sound so wrong and yet so hot coming from you at the same time?"

"It's all in the confidence." She winks. "It sells it."

My lips twitch. She's feeding my own words of wisdom back to me.

Tatum rearranges the notebooks, college textbooks, and old

assignments to clear my desk. A thoughtful look settles on her face. She peeks at me through her lashes.

"So intro to humanities, statistics, and physics." She taps her pen on the spine of the top book in the stack. "And bio this semester."

I nod. "Most of them are basic core requirements for most degrees. Seemed like a good place to start."

"Do you know what you want to do?"

I hitch a shoulder, working my jaw. This isn't a conversation I enjoy having. My parents haven't pressured me about it, but they do expect me to put effort in. I can't coast through college without some kind of trajectory in mind.

Tatum tilts her head and hums as she studies me. "What do you like doing?" At the quirk of my brows, she adds, "I mean like what sort of things interest you when you think of what you want to do with your life."

Shit. I can't tell her I have no idea. But I also realize I can at least answer.

Raking my teeth over my lip, I blow out a breath. "Sports and moving around. Athletic type stuff. Surfing."

Surfing is the big one, the thing I dedicate most of my time to. I swallow against the feeling of self-consciousness while telling this to the overachieving has-goals-and-makes-them-happen Tatum Danvers. The girl who has known what she's wanted to do with her life since she was a kid.

Even my parents followed their passion into their health and wellness business with the yoga studio.

I'm afraid I've screwed up my life by not knowing yet. All the aptitude and career testing the school system put me through makes it seem like you need to pick something, but by the time I graduated from high school I hadn't. I know at some point I have to choose.

Tatum keeps watching me. There's no judgment or a hint that she thinks I should be more realistic with my career path like everyone else. It makes something unravel in my chest, the tension bleeding out of me.

"Surfing. Body-focused things. Okay." She rummages through the pile and opens up one of the other notebooks to a fresh page. "So that could be physical therapy, working in surfboard design, or an instructor teaching techniques or classes."

I watch as she writes *surfing* at the top of the page, then doodles some designs to make the heading stand out. I think the blobs with spikes are supposed to be surfboards. My chest hurts. Zero judgment, and she immediately picked up on what I didn't say. My throat is thick when I swallow.

"There are plenty of options." Tate meets my gaze and reaches over to squeeze my knee comfortingly. "We'll figure it out."

"Thank you." I give in to the urge and wrap my arms around her in a tight hug.

She leans into me, brushing her lips over my throat in a quick kiss. "Of course."

Slipping out of my grasp, she turns her focus to her phone, researching. Each time she finds a new career path option, she makes an inquisitive sound and jots it down. Within ten minutes, she has a list of potential choices.

She's incredible.

I rub at my chest to ease the insistent drum of my heartbeat. "You're really good at that. Better than my advisor."

I'm glad I have her in my corner. My advisor has only focused on my academics. Every time we've met, he's never done something like this.

The corner of her mouth lifts while she writes down another related field. "When I first started setting goals, I failed them. I got choked up by the crushing weight of overwhelm. I learned to break it down. Career is too broad of an idea to tackle, so we need to break it off in manageable chunks. I can help you research these. You don't have to decide now, you have time."

I sling my arm over the back of her chair. It knocks me on my ass how easily she reads me, how fast she figured out my hang ups and worries.

"Okay," she says when she puts her phone aside. "New thing to add to your tracker. Start with this list and each day you should do some googling to look for anything else to add."

"Sounds good."

"Then once we have an exhaustive list, we can start researching how to get into these careers, what you'd need to focus on and the kind of classes to take, and start eliminating anything that you're not interested in."

I'm quiet long enough for her to lift her head from explaining where to add it to the bullet journal. Her lips part at the molten heat in my eyes.

Holding her gaze, I take her chin between my thumb and finger, then dip my head to kiss her. I put everything I don't have the words for into it.

Thank you. You're amazing. I want you.

All of it's true.

SEVENTEEN
TATUM

A week ago, this seemed like the best idea ever in my head. After Cooper shattered my world with his amazing mouth, I want to do the same to him.

"You don't have to do anything you don't want to do, T," Cooper soothes. "I'd never make you if you're uncomfortable."

"What? No, I'm fine. We're doing this. Lesson plan: blowjob."

He lifts his brows and cocks his head. I raise mine, mirroring him. His lips twitch with the urge to grin.

"Pants off, junk out, Coop."

"Well, when you sweet talk me like that, babe..." He loses the battle and gives me a crooked smile, backing toward his bed.

Okay, so I'm being way less sexy than he was when he went down on me, but nervous energy has plagued me all day. I threw down the gauntlet, challenging him to use the bullet journal set up I made for him. Now it's time to put my...well, my mouth where it's going.

On Cooper Vale's dick.

A flutter moves through my stomach. I had a dream about this exact scenario once. Except instead of his bedroom, we were by the pool. The same one he has a photo of stuck to his wall, with me, him, and my brother in it. The dream started out sexy, but then I realized

Jackson and everyone from the pool party were watching us. Total mood killer.

Drawing in a breath, I pluck a hair tie from my wrist and scrape my hair into a high ponytail to keep it out of the way.

"For real, T. If you're not ready, we don't have to do this. Rule one, right? Slow and steady."

My attention snaps to him. "I'm ready."

The tip of his tongue swipes across his lower lip. Holding my gaze, he lowers the waistband of his boxer briefs, then sits on the edge of his bed.

Oh. Holy. Hell.

My stomach bottoms out. I've never looked at a dick and thought, yeah, let me put that in my mouth. But now? I get it. I absolutely want to drive Cooper wild by sucking him off.

I was so out of it during our last study session that I didn't have the chance to fully appreciate it. Liquid heat builds in my belly and I bite my lip, dragging my gaze along the trail of hair leading down from his abs to his erection.

Absently, I realize I'm licking my lips as he circles his fingers around the length, pumping lazily.

"We good, Tate?" he rasps.

"Yeah," I whisper. "More than good."

The corner of his mouth quirks up into that smile that twists my insides into hot knots. "Take it at your pace."

Harnessing my courage, I step between his knees, pushing them apart with my hands before I sink to the floor before him. A breath gusts out of him and his fist flexes around his dick.

"What do you like?" I tilt my head. "If I go by porn standards, I should basically hold my breath and ignore my gag reflex while I choke on it, right?"

He rumbles out a chuckle. "I like it deep, but don't push your-self." With his free hand, he cups my face, brushing his thumb over my cheek. His charismatic brown eyes burn with desire. "No matter what you do, I'm going to like it. The thought of your mouth on me alone is driving me fucking crazy, baby."

My stomach dips again, and I rake my teeth over my lip. He's so good with his words. Every time he speaks to me during our *study sessions*, I have to remind myself he's just getting me ready for what things will be like with anyone I take to bed when I'm at college. He doesn't really mean what he says to me. Still, it's a confidence booster to believe that the idea of me giving him head really arouses him the same way it arouses me.

The longer I sit here and analyze, the more I'll psych myself out. Instead, I lean over and lick the tip. Cooper tenses, releasing a rough grunt. That won't do. He had me riding wave after wave of pleasure to the point I had to push him off me before I melted into a puddle. I want to do that to him. I close my lips around the velvety tip and suck.

"Fuck," he grits out.

My lashes flutter and I smirk around the mouthful of his erection. That's better. This isn't as hard as I thought. Exploring my limits, I take him deeper, enjoying the low groan that escapes him. I quickly find I'm only able to fit half of his dick in my mouth, but I don't let it stop me. He doesn't seem to be complaining in the slightest, muttering encouragement when I gain confidence that I'm making him feel good.

His knees fall open wider and he braces his hands on the mattress, fisting the sheets. As I slowly bob my head, a thrill sparks along my skin at the thought of his hands gripping my hair like that.

It turns out, giving a blowjob is pretty intuitive. I start to enjoy myself as I find different ways to pull a reaction from him. If I press my tongue to the thick vein that runs along the underside, his breath rushes out. If I cup his balls and stroke the base of his cock while sucking as much of him into my mouth as I can, his powerful thighs flex like he's holding back from taking my head and using my mouth to fuck how he wants.

I'm proud of the tremor in his legs when I manage to suck him deep enough without gagging, though he's so big that there's no way I could fit the whole thing without actually taking him *down* my throat.

The thought of it's tantalizing, though.

I get so wrapped up in the rhythm that I don't realize how messy it is. The sound of me sucking him is downright obscene. Saliva drips down my chin, but I don't stop to wipe. He didn't when his mouth was on me, not until he finished.

And I get why he was so into it. This is exciting. Each new technique I try earns a new sound of pleasure. I'm doing that to him.

"Shit, T," Cooper rumbles. "Your mouth feels so damn good."

There's no way to respond with a mouth full of his cock, so I hum. That earns another delicious tortured noise from him that makes me ache between my legs, moaning.

"Can you look at me?" His voice is full of gravel. I lift my eyes, and another pulse of arousal shoots through me at the inferno blazing in his eyes. He threads his fingers into my hair, tugging it free of the hair tie, caressing it. "Yeah, like that. Good girl."

My nipples tighten at the praise and heat prickles in a rush across my skin, leaving me shivering. He holds my gaze and encourages me to go faster. The sensation of his fingers tightening in my hair has me squirming, rubbing my thighs together to stave off the throbbing in my clit.

"Sucking my cock get you hot, baby? Keep looking at me. I want to see it in your eyes."

Shuddering, I peer up through my lashes. *God*, the look on his face is pure sin. His lips are parted and his eyes are hooded.

My tongue teases the sensitive vein and he bites out another curse. He holds me in place, rocking his hips, fucking my mouth with shallow thrusts.

"Oh shit—coming, T, I'm coming." For a moment he tries to pull away, but I release a fierce little growl and keep sucking, following his lead when he didn't stop because I was coming. "Jesus, you're perfect."

Cooper's dick twitches, surprising me before the first spurt of come hits my tongue. Despite my intentions to swallow, I splutter in my effort to figure out *how* to swallow on the fly. The last of his come ends up at the corner of my mouth. I blink up in surprise and burst out laughing at his dopey expression. He joins in, cradling the back of my head and swiping the stray mess from my mouth. It feels good to laugh while we're doing sexy stuff, like I can let go without judgment.

Another burst of determination fills me. Before he can wipe it off, I grasp his wrist and kneel up, bringing his thumb to my mouth to lick it clean.

Cooper rakes his teeth over his lip. "Damn, baby. How am I supposed to believe that was your first time doing that?"

"So it was good?"

"Fuck yeah."

I duck my head as a bubble of pride expands inside me. It feels good to know I'm not lagging far behind everyone else my age. I'm not defective for still being a virgin.

It helps that I'm learning from someone I trust to navigate me through the unknown until I have a good handle on this stuff.

"How do you feel? Do you need water or anything?" He traces my face again, as if his touch is magnetized to my skin and he can't help himself.

I lean my cheek into his palm, enjoying the warmth. "I'm good. My knees are starting to twinge, though. Next time we need a pillow."

He scoops me up like I weigh nothing, pulling me onto the bed with him. He watches me with hooded eyes while he massages my jaw. It is a little sore, but I didn't say anything. I bite down on a shy smile and rest my head on his shoulder. His dick might be hanging out, softening against his thigh, but I like this quiet lull after his lessons.

"What else are you doing today?"

"Waiting for Jackson to get off work." Cooper's fingers sift through my hair. "It's a couple of hours until then. Want to nap?"

"Mm," I agree drowsily.

Lips brush against my head in a soft kiss before he scoots back on the bed, pulling my leg half over him. My cheeks heat at the feel of his dick, still half hard, grinding into my thigh with a lazy rock of his hips.

I feel overdressed in my teal booty shorts and thin camisole, but I'm too comfortable snuggled against his side to move. My eyelids grow heavy and I drift off to the feeling of him caressing my skin and petting my hair.

* * *

I get back to my room late in the afternoon. I wish I didn't have to leave the comfort of Cooper's bed, but he roused me from an epic nap with low chuckles and kisses to my shoulders.

My brother's door opens and closes down the hall. He's home from work, which means he's heading out with Cooper in a few minutes.

I hit the lock on my door. My lips are still swollen from earlier. It didn't help that Cooper wouldn't let me leave without kissing me so thoroughly I almost climbed him like a tree and begged him to fuck me then and there.

Tracing my lips with my fingertips, I park myself at my desk to do my August spreads in my bullet journal with doodles, stickers, and photos I print off from my phone. I lose myself in the creative organizational process for twenty minutes, ignoring the knock on the door from Jackson to tell me he's going out for the night.

When the spreads are done, I set the journal aside. The August headline is a glaring reminder that my freshman semester at South Bay College will start soon.

I dig out my sex journal, the one I've been using to keep track of my progress under Cooper's tutelage. The checklist isn't as complete as I hoped it would be by now. I run a sparkly red gel pen down the list to check off oral.

Virginity remains unchecked.

Cooper's style of teaching me this stuff is good. Too good, sometimes. Enough to make me forget the lines we've drawn with our rules. The nap today might not have been hot and heavy territory, but my heart still gives a pathetic little wobble when I remember how *not real* cuddling with Cooper is.

It means nothing.

We're just friends. Well, he's my brother's friend. Without Jackson to connect us, we'd be nothing at all. Just neighbors.

Except he's not quite the notorious bad boy, or as much of a playboy as I always believed. The cocky vibe he's always given off is nonexistent around me now that I've gotten to know him better.

And since he's gotten to know me. He's learned my body, and all the ways to make me shatter.

A text distracts me from my musings. I wipe the besotted smile off my face and read a message from Simone.

Simone: Bestie SOS. Bored out of my skull.

Tatum: Milkshakes, universal fixer of everything?

Simone: Whoa, I didn't realize the situation was dire enough to call for milkshakes. What other problems are we slaying today?

I bite my lip, debating whether to come clean to her and admit what I've been doing with my brother's best friend.

Fuck it, I decide after a minute. I need someone like her who is impartial to the situation, and if anyone will reel me back in from diving off a feelings cliff for Cooper Vale, it's her.

Once I type it all out and text her back, my stomach clenches with nerves. I keep an eye on the dancing three dots, organizing my notebook stack on my desk to be perfectly color coordinated and meticulously lined up as I wait for her reply.

Simone: Only you would come up with such a wild plan [laughing emoji]

Tatum: Constructive and helpful opinions only please.

Simone: Everything makes so much sense now. Why he was watching you at the party. My advice? Have a fucking blast, babe! This is an ideal FWB situation.

Tatum: And if I catch feels? I need to protect myself. He's too swoony to resist sometimes.

Simone: [GIF of a swooning maiden]

Simone: It's chill. I've got your back. Send me an SOS anytime and I'm there.

A laugh bursts out of me. Shaking my head, I get changed into black cut off shorts, a tank top, and throw on a distressed denim jacket while I wait for her to pick me up for milkshakes. The uneasy weight lifts from my shoulders.

My head is back in the V-card losing game.

EIGHTEEN
TATUM

It's a perfect beach day. I turn my smile into the sun while Simone braids my hair into dutch braids. I'm glad I let her talk me into spending the day at the beach instead of going through my textbooks for my courses a third time since they arrived.

"This is the best," Simone declares. "Working on our tans while we're entertained."

She gestures to the guys in the ocean. I can't deny that it's enjoyable to watch the surfers. Usually we rate them all, but Cooper's the only one I'm able to focus on.

My brother goes down, bailing from his board to cannonball into the wave as it crests, and Cooper pulls an impressive trick that whips the nose of his board up the wave, then back down, muscular arms in position to maintain his balance. Even with the wetsuit covering his body, it's clear his broad frame is built.

"I said it before and I'll say it again. You're living your best main character life," Simone murmurs in my ear, giving my shoulders a teasing shake. I can hear the smile in her tone. She sighs dramatically. "It's hard to see people living your dream, you know?"

"Stop." Laughing, I bump her. "You know what the deal is."

Still, it's impossible to stop watching him. I bite my lip as the guys come in from surfing, wading through the shallow surf. Cooper has his board tucked beneath his arm and swipes his wet hair back from his face. He grins at Jackson and their buddies, busting each other's balls. My heart skips a beat when his gaze cuts across the beach to meet mine.

I can't look away as he closes the distance, my heart rate kicking up in an excited thrum when the corner of his mouth lifts to give me a crooked grin, his dimple popping out. My teeth sink into my lip, and even Simone's husky chuckle doesn't snap me out of this strange trance.

It's been like this since we got to the beach and set up our spot. Every time my eyes meet Cooper's, a thrill shoots through me. There's a magnetic pull between us today that neither of us can ignore.

It makes keeping our agreement on the down low a challenge., fighting against the burning urge to taste his smile and feel his body against mine.

"Better wipe that drool before your brother sees," Simone teases.

"Shut up." Rolling my eyes, I subtly brush the side of my mouth.

The guys return to our blanket and collapse in the warm sand. Jackson and Harris sprawl out with easy grins.

"Anyone need a drink?" Cooper shoots me a smirk, eyes hooded. "It's hot out today."

A flush fills my cheeks while he opens the cooler. These flirty remarks he keeps directing toward me make my skin break out in hot and cold tingles despite the heat baking us.

"Beer me," Jackson says.

Cooper pulls out two Coronas and winks at me on his way to hand off Jackson's drink. I squirm against the flutter in my stomach. Glancing at Simone, she waggles her brows. Now that she knows, she's been observant all day.

"I can't believe summer is almost over already." She leans back on her elbows to tan her front. "Soon the semester will start."

The reminder that my time with Cooper is running out makes me bite my lip. I peek at him and find his attention already on me. He doesn't look away when I catch him. Instead, he drags his eyes down my body, checking out my purple floral bikini. The way he looks at me sparks a throb of heat in my core. It's brazen with our friends right here.

Harris groans. "Don't remind me. I'd rather surf and sleep and party."

My brother and Cooper laugh at him. Ty, their other buddy, shakes his head, running a hand over his closely cropped hair.

"I'm with you, man," he laments. "But I'm doing a semester abroad in the spring. I'm trying to go somewhere with bomb ass waves."

"Hell yeah." Jackson raises his drink in toast to that.

"Sounds killer." Cooper's tone is genuinely happy for his friend, but his smile doesn't quite reach his eyes. "I should've thought about that sooner."

His gaze flicks to me. I make a mental note to help him research study abroad programs, ignoring the way my heart clenches at the thought of him gone for that long. I understand better than anyone how important it is to chase your goals.

"There's time," I say.

He blinks, then smiles around the neck of his beer bottle. I nod supportively.

"You can't leave me here, bro." Jackson crosses his forearms in front of him in an X. Simone's gaze snags on the flex of his muscles. "South Bay can't lose our favorite son. You leave, and that's it."

Cooper huffs out a laugh. "Nah, man. I'd never leave you. If I studied abroad, we'd go together. Duh."

Jackson's expression shifts and clears like a new world opened up to him. "Think of the foreign chicks we could pick up."

"Now you're talking." Harris' eyes glaze over and Ty makes a noise of agreement.

Cooper doesn't chime in, but with his reputation to score, the guys take it as a given. I ignore the simmer of jealousy.

He gets up to grab the tube of sunscreen sitting on the blanket and gestures to me. I feel my shoulders and find them hot to the touch. He's paying close attention to me to realize when I need to reapply.

Or he wants an excuse to touch me without my brother flipping shit. I hide a grin while his big hands massage sunscreen into my skin.

"Um, hello," Simone drawls. "Do you think of anything other than hooking up?"

"Men are simple, baby." Jackson winks at her. "Our primary drive wants us to worship at the altar of as many goddesses as possible."

Simone squints, seeming marginally appeased. "Smooth. Nice save."

"I'll show you what else I've got that's nice."

"Dude," I say. "Sibling code. I'm right here, I don't want to hear about your dick."

Jackson holds up his hands. "Deal with it."

Simone remains suspiciously silent for a girl who loves to verbally spar with him. When I turn to her, she's got her nose in a magazine.

Cooper's thumbs dig in more than necessary to my muscles, being thorough about applying sunscreen. I smother a gasp at the divine sensation. He massages my shoulders for a minute. I'm sure the lotion is fully rubbed in, but his hands linger in the stolen touch. Making sure no one's watching, I lean back against him.

"Thank you," I murmur.

"Can't have you burning. You're a pain in the ass when you get a sunburn." I can hear the smirk in his tone.

I elbow him. "Ass. Are you guys going back out or are you done for the day?"

"We might after we eat. The waves are still good." He brushes the edge of my collar bone, lowering his voice. "Or—"

"Coop, let's go." Jackson's call breaks the spell and interrupts whatever he was about to suggest. His eyes bounce between me and his best friend. I hold my breath, worried we've been caught. "We're walking down to the Shack to grab lunch."

Cooper squeezes my shoulders before getting to his feet. "Shrimp tacos, T?"

I nod, fighting off the warmth spreading through me because he always knows what I want. "Thanks."

"We'll be back girls." Jackson grabs his wallet from my beach bag. "Anything else you want us to bring back?"

Simone flips to her stomach. "Nope. Won't even notice you're gone."

Jackson's gaze sweeps down her spine and glues to her ass. I scoff, and he follows Cooper, Harris, and Ty down the beach.

"Did he stare at my ass?" Simone asks smugly.

"Yeah. Isn't it weird? He used to date your sister."

She shrugs. "That was like a million years ago. They were fifteen." She peeks in the direction they went. "He's definitely not fifteen anymore."

"Do you like him?" I lift a brow.

She shrugs again. "Sometimes." A sly grin spreads on her face and she leers at me over her shoulder. "You're the one playing with fire with that whole sunscreen act. Smooth, very smooth. Jackson didn't even blink with Coop's hands all over you."

"That was all him." I dig out a lemonade to cool the heated flush in my body. "And he was just making sure I don't burn. It's not part of our *benefits*."

"Uh huh. Sure. That's not what that look on his face said. He couldn't take his eyes off you. If you were alone, I bet he'd want to tackle you to the sand and give you his full attention."

A laugh bubbles out of me. "No way."

Okay, maybe she had a point. We definitely haven't been able to keep our hands to ourselves for long since the night I gave him a blowjob. Even during our regular study sessions, the non-sexy ones, we end up snuggling or touching each other casually. Cooper is just a handsy guy and he's a perfect cuddle buddy.

So what if I've figured out how to incentivize his academic studies with sexual rewards?

Last night flashes in my mind, Cooper's lips brushing my skin hungrily, muttering the answers. For each correct one, I stripped another article of clothing until I was naked on his bed. I challenged him with a bonus round question that stumped him, but the moment his expression shifted into satisfaction when he knew the answer, my insides melted. He took great pleasure in reaping his reward, burying his face between my thighs until I was a whimpering, writhing mess.

"I know my truth and you know yours, girl." Simone settles back against the blanket.

Once the guys return with take out from Tiki Taco Shack, the conversation turns towards the event that marks the end of summer—Cooper's birthday. He'll be twenty in a few short weeks. The two contenders are a trip to Tijuana or a bonfire party at the cove.

After the guys demolish the majority of the food, they hit the ocean again. I read a book while Simone naps. My eyes drift to the waves to watch Cooper riding them more than once. It takes me a long time to finish a chapter.

The next time I look up, I find Cooper kneeling next to a little boy, showing him how to balance on his board. The boy's smile is ecstatic and Cooper nods in encouragement, pointing to his feet and tapping his belly. Even from a distance, it's clear to see how much pride fills him by teaching his skill to the little boy.

My breath catches when Cooper glances up and realizes I'm watching. His mouth curves in a handsome smile that makes my stomach flutter.

Cooper and the little boy's dad take him into the shallow waves, allowing him to feel like he's surfing by pushing the board. He looks so right out there, pointing out waves when they come. I picture his confident tone with ease, smiling as I imagine the way he gets this bright glint in his eyes when he talks about surfing. He could be an instructor. I think he'd like doing it.

After twenty minutes, Cooper waves goodbye and makes his way back up the beach. He sits next to me, wet suit stripped down to his waist. His knee bumps mine.

"You looked good out there," I murmur.

He glances around before brushing his lips over my shoulder. "I think I made that kid's whole month."

"I know from experience you're a great teacher." I smirk. "A total natural."

He gives me a scorching look that makes heat erupt in my core. My breath catches at the intensity of it.

"Tate—"

"Hey!" Ty calls from a distance. Harris and Jackson trail after him. "We're going to head out."

Simone rouses from her nap, sitting up with a yawn.

Jackson plants a hand on my head and tries to ruffle my braided hair. With a little growl, I grip his arm and push him off, flicking his leg.

"I'm going to head out early with them. You coming, Coop?"

"Nah, I've got plans." He looks at me while he says it.

"Aight. Tatum, get a ride home with him. We're heading the opposite way."

"Okay."

I'm barely paying attention to my brother, trying to decipher the way Cooper's looking at me. His brown eyes smolder with something that awakens an answering inferno in my core that leaves me short of breath.

"Later." Jackson messes with me once more. Then he and his other two friends pack up.

While they're leaving, Simone grabs my hand, turning her face so Cooper and my brother can't see her. She waggles her eyebrows and mouths *it's on*. I shake my head in confusion and the corners of her eyes crinkle with her amusement.

"Enjoy yourself, babe. I'm going home to lay out by the pool."

"You're done, too?" I look at Cooper. "Don't you want to surf more?"

My stomach dips at the slow shake of his head, his intent gaze locked on me. It's lucky Simone knows—not that he's aware—because he's totally failing at keeping what's between us a secret with that look. He traces his lower lip with the tip of his tongue, and an ache throbs between my legs.

I hug Simone goodbye and Cooper takes my beach bag to carry, along with his surfboard. I clutch the rolled up blanket to my chest. We don't touch on the walk to his Jeep, but once he puts the surfboard on the rack and drops my bag in the back, he turns to me, fingertips caressing my arm.

"Give me the blanket." His tone is smoky, full of confidence that makes me want to do anything he asks.

"What are your plans after dropping me off?"

He doesn't answer, just shoots me another indecipherable glance that makes my body flush warm all over.

My heart thumps in the car on the ride home from the beach.

Cooper rests his elbow out the open window, his hair curling across his forehead without his signature hat to hold it back. He reaches across and puts his big hand on my leg, tucking his fingers between my thighs. I don't think he's aware, but he does it every time we're alone in the car together.

I fight against wishing for him to move his hand up another inch, to touch me where I'm aching for him. He massages my leg the entire ride home, stoking the tension that's built between us all day.

Once we pull into the shared driveway between our houses, he kills the engine and gives me a leer that makes me swallow thickly.

"You're my plans, T," he rasps. "I need to fuck you. I'll go out of my mind if I go another minute without feeling you fall apart around my cock."

NINETEEN

TATUM

My heart nosedives into my stomach at those words. I can't tear my gaze from Cooper as he gets out of the Jeep and circles the front to my side. His eyes don't leave mine either. He opens my door and braces against it, essentially caging me in the passenger seat. His biceps bulge as he leans closer, slowly licking his lip.

"Come on." He takes my hand.

A shaky breath slips past my lips at the way he drags his eyes over me, taking in my purple bikini top and the shorts I tugged on over the bottoms when we left the beach. He mutters a curse under his breath and leads me up to his room.

"Your parents aren't home again, I'm guessing?" My voice is breathless.

He shakes his head. "Another retreat. They'll be gone all week."

We stop at his door and he pins me against it, planting his hands on either side of my head. His brown eyes are a swirl of seductive want. At last, our bodies touch and we both let out rough, desperate sounds. After not being able to touch all day while being around each other at the beach, surviving on stolen touches, this is heaven. He presses into me, the hard muscles of his body smelling of salt and sun.

"Tate," he rasps before capturing my lips in a heady kiss that has me dizzy in seconds.

I chase his tongue, deepening the kiss on my own instead of letting him take the lead. He groans, cupping my face with one hand while grinding his erection into my belly. A tiny sound escapes me when he tears his mouth from mine to trail hot kisses across my jaw and down my neck. He chuckles into my skin, making me shudder. Another gasp slips past my lips when he drags his hands down my sides and hooks them beneath my thighs, lifting me up.

My wide eyes find his and he smirks at me in a way that turns my insides to liquid heat. I wrap my legs around him and his smirk stretches into a sexy, satisfied curve.

Cooper buries his face in my throat. "Get the door, baby." He squeezes my thighs. "My hands are full."

His deep, confident tone is doing things to me, igniting fire in my veins. The ache in my core throbs with each graze of his teeth and tongue on the sensitive spots of my neck he's memorized.

Fumbling behind me, I find the handle. He keeps me pinned to the door until it swings open behind me, then carries me to his bed.

Holy shit. This is it. I'm finally going to lose my virginity to my brother's best friend.

Before I can get tangled in my thoughts, Cooper drops me to the bed and crawls over me with a sexy rumble. Taking my wrists, he stretches them over my head and traces a circle with his thumbs on the insides. I shiver and the corner of his mouth lifts.

"Do you want to stop?"

I shake my head. "Don't you dare." My thighs rub together. "I'm more than ready."

He grins. "Thank fuck." Swooping down, he kisses me until my legs fall open. He settles between them, grinding into me. I moan, arching my back when his erection rubs my clit through my shorts. "Easy, baby. We have all night. I'm going to make you feel so good."

He leans up on his forearms, dragging a knuckle down my front. Every touch sets my body on fire, and when he follows the teasing touches with his mouth, I'm so turned on I'm only able to think of the intense throbbing in my core.

"Please." I grab hold of Cooper's hair, unsure if I'm going to push him away from dipping his tongue in my belly button, pull him up for another sinful kiss, or encourage him to go lower to make me come on his tongue. "Please, I need more."

"I know, T. I know what you need, and I'm going to give it to you." He kisses my stomach above the waistband of my shorts. "I'm going to give you everything, and then you're going to fall apart on my cock. Sound good, baby?"

My chest collapses with my exhale. I nod, tightening my legs around his torso while he shifts lower. He pops the button on my shorts and drags them and my bikini bottoms down in one smooth move. Before I can process, his lips close around my clit.

"Oh god!" I cry out.

Cooper chuckles, spreading my legs wider while his tongue tortures me with sweet pleasure, lighting me up with his talented mouth. He works my pussy with his tongue and plunges a finger inside me.

"Come for me, T," he rumbles against my wet folds. "Show me."

A choked sound of pleasure shudders from me when he flicks my clit with his tongue and hooks his finger deep inside me. I swear I feel the curve of his pleased grin against my pussy when he keeps the same rhythm, earning another strangled noise from me. My hips rock as I chase my orgasm, the pleasure building until it's almost unbearable. A litany of curses and pleas spill from me while I grind on his face.

When I fall over the edge, I cry out Cooper's name.

Coop strokes my side, planting soft kisses everywhere. His face glistens with the evidence of my orgasm. It's obscene and so damn sexy.

"That was hot as fuck. Next time I eat your pussy, you're riding my face while I devour you." He gives me a sultry, lopsided smirk and grabs a handful of my ass. "Right now, I need to be inside you."

I swallow, shivering from the aftershocks of coming. "Fuck me, Coop."

His smoldering gaze travels over me and he slowly scrapes his teeth over his lip. I don't know what's going through his head, but his eyes fill with a heady desire.

"If you want me to stop, you tell me, okay?"

He sits up, reaching behind his head to strip out of his shirt. His muscles ripple and flex as he takes off his board shorts.

"I want this. I don't want to stop."

Cooper gives me a cocky grin and slips his big hand between my legs, cupping me. "Good. There's one more thing you need to know. This pussy? It's mine right now. No deals, no lessons. Today, you're all mine, T."

"Okay," I breathe, ignoring the way my heart trips over itself.

He leans over, tipping my chin up to kiss me. Kissing him is like being tossed around in a wave—an exhilarating, all-consuming rush that leaves me lightheaded. When he pulls back, his eyes are hooded. He has my bikini top dangling from his fingers. I didn't even feel him taking it off me.

A nervous jitter bolts through me. We've been naked together before, but this feels bigger because I'm on the precipice of sex for the first time.

Cooper brushes my cheek with his thumb. "There's nothing to be nervous about. I've got you, Tatum. Do you trust me?"

I smile. He's right. "I trust you."

"Good girl." He brushes another kiss across my lips, then leans over to the nightstand to get a condom.

I watch in fascination as he tears the packet and rolls the rubber over his cock. His movements are practiced, from the way he pinches the tip to the way he strokes his dick once the condom is on. It's then that I remember how experienced he is.

"Hey." Cooper cradles my face in his hands. "Whatever you're thinking about, forget it."

"It's nothing." Embarrassed, I run my fingertips over the braids Simone did for me at the beach. They're looser, with pieces of hair falling out after making out with him and writhing on his bed. "Let's do it."

A laugh huffs out of him and he moves to squeeze the back of my neck, trapping me in his sultry gaze. "Remember what I said, T. You're all mine right now. I'm the first one to taste you..." He leans in, mouthing at my jaw. "The first to be inside you..." His fingers delve between my legs and tease me until I'm panting. "This piece of you is always going to be mine, baby. Now watch."

He gets into position, hooking one of my legs around his hip. The tip of his cock glides against my folds. He makes sure I'm doing as he said, heat blazing in his gaze when he finds me watching. We both gasp when he lines up. He doesn't slam it in me, which I thought was how all guys did it from the porn I've watched.

Instead, Cooper takes his time, staring as each inch of his huge dick sinks inside me. My cheeks tingle with warmth at the reverence on his face. I focus more on the flickers of pleasure in his expression than the stretching sensation as he fills me. It's not as painful as I thought it would be, but it is new and different—more than his fingers and the toy he used on me once.

"Goddamn, that's a sight. I want to take a picture of my cock sinking into your pussy." When our hips are flush, his chest vibrates with a deep rumble. "God, you feel incredible. Are you okay?"

"Yeah." I gasp when he rocks his hips slightly. He grins, then adjusts to move again. The pressure deep in my core makes me dig my nails into his shoulders. "That's not what I thought it would feel like."

"You good?" He kisses my jaw. "I want to move so fucking bad and ruin you, T. But I don't want to hurt you."

"You're not going to hurt me." I bite my lip when he pulls that rocking move again that feels like it does when he gives me head, but deeper. "Whatever you're doing right now is the opposite. Please move more."

I feel the curve of his smile against my throat. "Keep those gorgeous eyes on me."

Cooper braces on his forearms and rocks his hips harder. I feel a slight twinge, but it quickly dissipates with his steady rhythm. He distracts me by swooping down for a filthy kiss, keeping his pace slower than I want. I bite his lip and he startles, staring down at me.

"I'm not fragile, Coop. You're not going to break me." I thread my fingers into his hair. "Come on."

He gives me a crooked smile that brings out his dimple. I yelp when he flips us over in a smooth move that puts me on top of him. Blinking, I stare down at him. His hands find my hips and he lifts me, then slams me down as he thrusts up into me. My head falls back with my cry of pleasure, fingers scrabbling against his chest for balance while he fucks me.

I can feel how wet I am each time my pelvis grinds down. He touches the place our bodies are joined and gathers some of the slickness on his fingers with a smirk, using it to rub my clit.

"You're soaking me, baby," Cooper rumbles, thrusting sharply. "You like that?"

Breath catching, I'm capable of little more than nodding. Even his chuckle makes the coil of arousal tighten in my core. He rolls again, putting me on my back. Hooking a hand beneath my knee, he snaps his hips, finding that spot again that makes me clench around him.

His head drops back on a groan, but he doesn't miss a beat, driving me closer to coming. "Fuck, T. You're so tight. I'm going to end up addicted to this hot, wet little pussy." He circles my clit with his thumb, hooded gaze roaming my face. "You going to come for me, baby? Cream my dick."

Cooper's dirty mouth, his clever fingers, and his cock filling me do the trick to tip me over the edge. I shudder with a garbled moan, clinging to him while I ride out the waves of ecstasy.

"Oh my god," I repeat deliriously, vaguely aware of him praising me.

He grabs my hips and picks up the pace, burying his face in my neck. I wrap my legs around him, still trembling from my orgasm. He tenses, his strong muscles seizing as he groans against my throat. I feel a pulse deep inside me as he comes. It stokes a strange warmth in my chest, a well of emotion pricking my throat. I tighten my arms around him, irrationally afraid that this is it. Our deal is up.

Cooper doesn't pull away, even minutes after he finishes. He pets my sides and doesn't complain about my stage five clinger development. His movements are sedate, but he tugs me closer, adjusting so we're both comfortable.

When he pulls out to discard the condom, he kisses the top of my head before scooping me into his arms. I blink against the drowsiness I always feel in his arms.

"Where are we going?" I murmur.

"To clean up."

He sets me on a cool counter in the bathroom. I peer around while he wets a cloth with warm water in the sink beside me. There's a sauna shower and a large tub.

Cooper's fingertips find my chin and guide me to look at him. His brown eyes move over my face while he slips the washcloth between my legs. I wince, and he nods with a hum.

"I read that you can be sore after the first time. Come here." He lifts me again, not letting me get to my feet. We step into the shower sauna and he puts me in his lap once the steam setting starts. "This will help, then we can take a soak in the tub."

"You read about it?" I tilt my head curiously.

"Mm." Cooper undoes my braids, carding his fingers through my hair until it's loose. "I told you before, I've never been someone's first time. I wanted to make it good for you."

My cheeks fill with heat. It's not from the steam. Ignoring the swell in my chest, I lean against him, closing my eyes.

We spend a few minutes in the sauna before Cooper runs a bath. He sits behind me and draws me back so I'm laying against his chest, cradled in his embrace. He doesn't stop touching me once, caressing my skin anywhere he can reach.

I didn't need my first time to be something special or perfect, but he made it exactly what I needed. Part of me—a worryingly large part —wishes this was real, because he and I fit so well together.

Cooper's words from earlier burn into my brain: *this piece of you is always going to be mine, baby.*

TWENTY
COOPER

Ever since Tatum gave me her virginity, I've had this phantom feeling of holding her in my arms like I did for an hour in the tub afterwards. I wanted nothing more than to sink my cock back into the divine wet heat of her body, but I also was seriously worried about hurting her. The most I allowed myself was fingering her in the tub, which led to me propping her on the edge of it while I lapped at her pussy until she couldn't form coherent sentences.

It's only been a couple of days, but I've been weirdly anxious since she left my house late that night. A girl has never stuck in my head so much, not before I fucked her, and definitely not after. But with Tatum, all I can think about is the next time I'll see her, the next time she'll be in my arms.

I'm getting in over my head with this deal shit, yet I can't bring myself to call it off.

The way I think about her, look at her—it's not how I should look at my best friend's sister. My gaze slides to Jackson. He balances on his board next to mine in the water, unaware of how little I'm beginning to care if he found out. It should scare me that I'd risk our life-long friendship when he'll kill me when he finds out I took his sister's virginity.

"Dude." He splashes me, snapping me out of my thoughts.

"You've slept on the last three good waves. That's enough saltwater for you today. You zone out any longer and the next wave will knock your ass right off that board, even if it's a little one."

"Yeah," I agree because it's easier than admitting why my head isn't in surfing today. I watch the calm horizon line. "The waves seem dead today, anyway."

It's weird to find something that occupies my mind more than the thing that I love doing the most. I scrub a hand over my face, raking wet strands of my hair back as I glance at the strip of shoreline.

"You hungry?"

Jackson shrugs. "I could eat."

I grin. "When are you not hungry?"

"I'm a growing boy." Laughing, he ducks the splash of water I send his way.

We swing the noses of our boards toward the beach and begin lazy strokes to take us in. "Who's on shift today?"

Jackson twists to look back at me and I keep my face blank, hoping my question was casual enough. There isn't any question of where we're going to fuel up after surfing. We always go to the Tiki Taco Shack when we're at the beach.

"Tatum said she had work today. I don't know who else. I didn't look at the schedule last night."

Warmth unfurls in my chest at the mention of her name. If my arms cut through the water a little harder to take me to her faster, that's between me and the ocean.

When we make it to the beachfront restaurant, it's popping with customers. Two swing seats are open at the bar and we grab them. Tatum spots us and gives us a nod in greeting from the opposite end of the bar while delivering a basket of tacos and topping off a drink. Her hair bounces in the high ponytail and the cut-off shorts she wears hug her ass, drawing my eye. I tear my attention away before her brother catches me checking her out.

I fold my arms over the rough hewn wooden bar top, watching her work while joking with Jackson. By the time she checks in with all of her customers, I've shaken off the strange anxiety that has clung to me since I last saw her.

"Don't you guys ever go anywhere else?" Tatum says as a greeting. She makes a face at her brother, then winks at me. "If the shrimp tacos weren't so good, I might think you're stalking me."

"I think it's called keeping an eye out for you." Jackson strokes his chin, mimicking deep thought. "Besides, if we went anywhere else, Marco would give us an earful about not eating here."

She shakes her head with a wry eye roll. "Two orders of al pastor and fish?"

"Stat," Jackson says.

Smirking, Tatum pushes away from the bar and heads for the back to put our orders in. I snag a free bowl of tortilla chips and put it between us before the tourists grab it. A pair of girls on the swing seats beside us are too busy taking selfies for Instagram to notice.

"Could you take a photo for us?"

I crunch down on a chip and turn toward them. A girl with trendy silver hair braided in pigtails holds out her phone to me. Her friend bats her long fake lashes at me. Who puts on that much makeup to go to the beach? The kind of girls I used to end up hooking up with, ones just like these.

"Yeah, sure."

I take the phone and they pose on the swings with their margaritas and sunglasses. I snap a few and they keep working the camera.

Jackson leans around me, his attention fixated on their tits practically spilling out of their tiny bikini tops. "Are you visiting from out of town?"

"Uh huh. It's our girls' weekend before we fly home to Dallas." The one with gray hair presses her boobs in our direction. "What about you guys?"

There's no mistaking the inviting lilt in her tone. I don't want to be a dick, but I also don't have much interest in talking to them. Usually I'd be all over flirting with these chicks. They're hot and clearly interested. They also remind me of exactly why I felt like shit with a revolving door of hookups until Tatum proposed her crazy idea.

I glance at Jackson and bite back a dismissive response. He's definitely down to score. I should help by being a good wingman at least. Tatum enters my periphery carrying two baskets.

"South Bay boys, born and raised," I say.

Jackson smirks and flexes by pretending to lean closer. "The surfing is the best in the area. You've come to the right place."

The other girl with the white bikini top and blond hair eyes him up and down. "I'll say."

I stiffen as Tatum reaches the bar to drop off our lunch, feeling as if I'm doing something wrong by talking to the flirtatious girls. Her gaze is like an arrow piercing my profile.

My hand twitches with the need to reach across and grab her wrist to stroke the soft skin until she smiles at me. I can't, though. Not with Jackson right there. I meet her eyes and swallow at the hardness in them.

"Your tacos." Before either of us can thank her, she busies herself with other customers.

Jackson digs in without picking up on the moment of tension between me and his sister, carrying on a conversation with the flirty tourists.

Poking my tacos, I hold back a sigh. My gaze flicks up to search for Tatum, finding her hovering around the end of the bar while ignoring the side we're seated on. She won't look at me.

I didn't do anything wrong and I don't want these girls. The one I do want is the only one who isn't really mine. So why am I left feeling like crap?

TWENTY-ONE
TATUM

It's after dark when my shift finally ends. I park my brother's car in front of the house and lean back against the headrest with a sigh. I can hear the muted rhythmic bounce of a basketball against concrete and Cooper's deep laughter. They're shooting hoops in the shared driveway between our houses.

I hold out as long as I can before I angle my head to peek at them.

I bite my lip. Cooper looks unfairly hot, his gym shorts riding low enough to see the cuts of his hip muscles, his unruly hair curling around his ears, escaping beneath his backwards cap. He's shirtless and grinning, sending my heart into a wobbling dive off a cliff into uncharted waters.

Nodding smugly to my brother, he dribbles the ball lazily, bouncing it down between his legs and catching it one-handed from behind. Once he has Jackson lulled into a false sense of confidence, he makes his move, running his lay up and taking a perfect shot that sinks through the net with a satisfying *swish*.

I hated the burst of jealousy that rocketed through me when I saw Cooper working his magic on the beautiful girls at the Shack. I'm not that girl, the one who goes crazy over nothing. I don't even know what they were talking about; I was too chickenshit to hang around and watch him flirt with them.

But that's who he is—the playboy with an easy smirk who sends girls into stupidsville over his charm. I thought I was getting to know him as someone else beneath all that. I need to remember what we agreed to before I get hurt.

It'll be my own fault for falling for a guy I can never have.

Groaning under my breath, I get out of the car. Logical Tatum would ask Cooper straight out, but I don't know her right now. She went into hiding right about the time I cooked up this insane plan to lose my virginity to my brother's best friend.

Why is this my life? Why do I do this to myself?

Questions for future Tatum, because I've got nothing at the moment. Nothing but a pit in my stomach and an odd burn in my chest whenever I see Coop with someone else.

"Okay, cool it crazy," I mumble to myself as I lock up the car before trudging up the driveway.

My hopes of playing it cool and walking past them without incident go up in smoke the second my eyes lock with Cooper's. He catches the ball against his chest with an *oof* when Jackson passes it to him.

"'Sup, T," he says in that charming deep tone that makes me swoony.

Stop it, I chide myself. I can't help it. All I see when I look into his handsome brown eyes is the cocky little smirk he gives me when he knows I'm about to come, the way he held me close and cared for me after we had sex, and the wicked gleam that lit up his eyes before going down on me when he said he had to taste me again or he'd go wild.

How can he be that guy and the playboy?

I tuck a loose strand of hair behind my ear. "Hey."

Oh god, awkward much? This is ridiculous. I force out a breath through my nose. He's not some unobtainable god—he's *Cooper*. My neighbor. My brother's friend who's always around. I need to chill out.

"How was work?" Cooper asks.

I shrug. "The usual."

Jackson lifts a brow, bouncing his gaze between us. Before he can point out the air of stiffness, his phone rings. When he pulls it out, he nods toward the house.

"Harris is FaceTiming me. I'll be right back."

Once he disappears to take his call, my shoulders slump. Cooper steps up behind me, massaging them. I smother a moan of pleasure before it escapes me.

"What's wrong, T?" he rasps against my ear.

"Dude." I stiffen, reluctantly stepping out of reach and away from his magic fingers working the kinks out of my tired muscles. "Jackson could come back out here any second. You shouldn't risk it. Rule three. The big one, remember?"

He sighs. "You're right. I can't help it. You've got this pouty thing going on with your mouth and I want to make you feel better."

I bite the inside of my cheek to distract myself from the way my misbehaving heart expands. "It's nothing. I'm just tired from work. I'm due for a day of self-care."

He waggles his brows. "Want my help?"

I shake my head wryly, ignoring the swirl of desire in my core. "I'm pretty sure you helped me plenty the other day after the beach. Does that make us square?"

"Huh?" A crease appears on his forehead. "Nah, not in the slightest, baby. There's so much more you have to learn and we only have a couple of weeks left before the semester starts."

Damn it. My stomach dips at his suggestive tone and the affectionate way he calls me baby. It has the effect of something I haven't managed since this afternoon—setting me at ease. Our deal might be unorthodox, but we're both on the same page.

"Well, thanks for wanting to rub me down." I grin and set my purse down.

He chuckles, retrieving the basketball. Dribbling slowly, he moves around me, glancing at the house before he leans in to speak.

"I want to do more than rub you. If we were really alone, you'd already be moaning my name."

"Oof." I bite my lip. "So confident. Ladies and gentlemen, we have a bonafide smooth operator."

"You know damn well I can back it up." He closes the small

distance between us, ducking his head to give me a smoldering look. "And that I only speak the truth. I know exactly how I'd have you making a mess for me without taking your clothes off."

Whew. I need to get away from him because I'm in danger of throwing caution to the wind and forgetting the rules of our agreement.

"Oh yeah?" I fake to the right, then steal the ball, dribbling around him.

"Ohh," he draws out. "She thinks she's slick, folks. Let's see what she's got."

Laughter bubbles out of me. He blocks my shot, using our height difference to his advantage. He offers a smirk, then steps aside with his arm out. Squinting at him, I get ready to shoot the ball. I gasp when he steps behind me, grasping my waist.

"What are you—?"

"Take your shot, T."

Cooper lifts me up so I can reach the net easily. Sliding my lips together, I dunk the ball. He whoops for me, but we both ignore the ball bouncing off to the side. Butterflies fill my stomach while he lets me down slowly, massaging my waist.

My throat tightens. I desperately want a kiss, but we shouldn't chance it, not when my brother is right inside. He could return at any minute.

Taking a steadying breath, I turn in Cooper's arms, meeting his burning gaze gradually. I see the same want reflected in his eyes when he drops them to stare at my mouth.

"Tate," he rumbles.

Screw it. This all started because I wanted to own my body and take what I wanted. I'm not letting fear stop me.

I press up on my toes at the same time his head dips, meeting in the middle with a kiss. A faint groan sounds from him and he tugs me closer, delving his tongue into my mouth. I cling to his bare shoulders. We're throwing caution to the wind and I don't care.

When we're kissing, it's the only thing in the world that's ever felt so right. I'm falling for my sex tutor and there's nothing I can do to stop it.

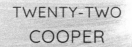

Kissing Tatum is a risky as hell move, just like she warned, but fuck it, because this is too good to stop. This is what I was missing earlier at the Tiki Taco Shack—touching her, claiming her, making her shiver for me.

The slide of her tongue against mine aligns my world. I cup the back of her head to bring her closer, deepening the kiss. It's a crazy desire, but I wish I could do this with her out in the open without having to steal every touch.

It would mean making her mine. Breaking my promise to my best friend.

My loyalty to our friendship wars with the way I've wanted Tatum Danvers for longer than I care to admit.

Tatum's content sigh winds around my heart as we kiss. Shit, for this girl, I might risk it all.

"Yo, what the fuck?" Jackson's outraged bark cuts through my consciousness.

Tatum goes still as panic surges through me. We break apart and turn to Jackson. He's silhouetted in the doorway to his kitchen, phone in hand. I push Tatum to arm's length, my dazed brain scrambling to come up with an explanation.

"I swear, man, it's not what you think." The words rush out of me and I want to take them back right away when Tatum sucks in a sharp, pained breath. Fuck. I'm messing this up already. This is why I never wanted him to find out, but I'm the one who broke our rules and got us caught. "I mean—"

"You shithead! My sister?" Jackson stalks toward me and takes a swing at me.

"Jackson!" Tatum yells in a thick voice. "Stop it!"

I duck, hands up as I back away from him. "Listen—"

"No, I don't want to fucking listen!" He throws up his hands. "What kind of asshole goes behind his best friend's back to seduce his baby sister?"

"Oh my god, Jacks," Tatum snaps. "Are you serious?"

"I didn't seduce her." My thoughts race with a way to explain this without giving away what we've actually been doing. If he finds that out, he'll be more enraged and ready to cut off my balls for touching her. "This isn't what it looks like."

Tatum crosses her arms, her expression tight. Her shoulders hunch and it twists my guts up to see her like that.

"Then tell me what the hell it is, because it looked like you were kissing my sister." Jackson glares. "The one you swore up and down you'd never touch, Coop. So what the fuck?"

"Okay, yeah, we were kissing." I run a hand over my hat and blow out a frustrated breath. *Think.* I need a good explanation for why I was sticking my tongue down her throat. I know my reputation—Jackson helped me cultivate it as my wingman. My stomach drops like a lead weight with dread. "It was just a kiss."

"Bullshit," he snarls.

Shaking his head, he charges me again. I throw up my hands to block him and we end up locked in a hold. He knocks my hat off and grips the back of my neck, gritting his teeth while he tries to wrestle me to the ground. I grunt when he catches me across the jaw with one of his fists. It's nothing more than I deserve for breaking my promise to him. If he only knew how far it's gone, so much further than a tame kiss.

"Come on, man," I bite out. "Calm down."

"Not until you fucking answer me," Jackson growls.

"It's none of your damn business," Tatum says. "God, why does it even matter who I kiss?"

The laugh that escapes him is disbelieving. "Are you serious?"

"This is ridiculous!" A look of fierce determination settles on Tatum's face. "Stop, you freaking heathens!" Like a tiny, unstoppable bull, she wedges her way between us, fearless and stubborn. My heart pangs with longing as her back plasters to my front to face her brother. "Jackson. Look at me."

Panting, he narrows his eyes and gives her attention while still locking my head in his arms. She plants her hands on his chest and shoves hard. He finally backs up, swiping the back of his hand over his mouth.

Huffing, Tatum gestures to me. "We're dating and we didn't know how to tell you. You and I had a promise, and you had the same one with him. It just happened. It's—new."

Jackson blinks. "What?"

"Coop is my boyfriend. He has every right to kiss me."

My chest heaves as I try to catch my breath, my eyes widening as the lie she spins to cover our asses filters into my brain. I want to ask her what the hell she's doing, but I also can't blow up our spot with the truth or make Jackson realize this is another lie. This is what we trying to avoid—why the fuck is she telling him we're dating?

Her move makes sense when Jackson's brows furrow and he sighs. "For real?"

There's no taking back the kiss he saw. He knows there's something. If we have to pretend to date as a cover for what we've really been doing, so be it. This is more acceptable than the truth. It's not like I have a girlfriend to worry about. The only girl who has stirred my heart lately is the same little firecracker standing beside me.

"For real," I say hoarsely.

If we're going down, we're doing it together. Clearing my throat, I put a hand on her shoulder in support, squeezing. She plows on, ignoring me.

"We didn't want to make it awkward if it didn't work out." Tatum shrugs. After a beat, she backs up until she bumps into me, standing as a united front against her brother.

I gauge his reaction, afraid he'll tackle me if I touch her the wrong way in front of him. I settle for putting my hand on her shoulder again. It's a neutral place, in no way sexual.

Jackson's nostrils flare anyway. His gaze bounces between us. He doesn't say anything, but anger still rolls off him in waves, his shoulders tense and his jaw clenched.

"I'm sorry we lied to you," Tatum says with genuine regret. "But you don't have a right to control who I do and don't have feelings for."

My chest tightens at the hitch in her breath. I'm impressed by the conviction infusing her words. Even I believe her lie.

Part of me—a selfish part—wishes it were true.

Now I have another fake thing I can't have. Permission to touch and kiss Tatum whenever I want—but it's still not fucking real.

Without responding to Tatum's apology, Jackson shakes his head, working his jaw. He spears me with a hard look that makes me want to fall back a step. We were fine ten minutes ago until I screwed everything up. Damn it. My best friend since we were kids looks at me like he hates my goddamn guts. And it's all my fault.

Jackson turns on his heel and stomps away.

"Where are you going?" Tatum calls.

"To blow off steam," he says. "Don't follow me or call me. Tell Mom and Dad I'll be home late."

"Jackson—"

He cuts me off without looking back. "Don't. We're not cool."

We both watch as he gets in his car and slams the door before driving off with a squeal of tires. Tatum sighs, rubbing her temples. The fight bleeds out of her and she leans back against me. It makes my insides feel weird, but I'm happy she still naturally turns to me for support. I wrap my arms around her in a hug and rest my chin on top of her head.

"Thank you, big mouth," she mutters.

"Mine or yours?"

"Mine. Both. I don't know."

This is a bigger, more complicated mess than we started with, but we'll figure it out.

TWENTY-THREE
TATUM

After Jackson storms off, the reality of what I've done sets in. I cover my face with my hands. It doesn't block out the worry bubbling up in my chest.

Cooper rubs my arms. "He'll get over it."

The assurance is appreciated. I expected him to freak out on me worse than he did when I first propositioned him with my plan, but he picks his faded blue baseball cap up from the ground, slaps it against his leg, and fits it back over his head with an easy smile. His arms flex and his tan bare chest reminds me I've just tied us together in an even bigger lie.

"I'm sorry," I say. "It all just spilled out."

"Don't sweat it, T. We'll figure this out."

Cooper heads for his house. I follow him, not ready to be alone while my brain processes everything that just happened. When we reach his room, I start pacing at the end of his bed while he sprawls on it with a deep sigh.

My thoughts race faster and faster through my head with the ramifications of this lie. My brother thinks we're dating—he could tell our parents, or Cooper's. His friends. This could get out of hand before we even know what we're doing.

What does this lie mean for us now? Do we go with it, keep

pretending as a cover for our real deal? I can't ask Cooper to do that with the semester starting up so soon.

I can't believe I did this. Massaging my throbbing temples, I wrangle a groan.

"You're making me dizzy," he mumbles after a few minutes. "What's up?"

"Are you serious? Hello, were you not downstairs getting punched because we got caught kissing?" I whirl to face him, planting my hands on my hips. "We need a plan of action to deal with this."

"You dealt with it already with the cover story. Good thinking on your toes." He folds his arms behind his head, closing his eyes. "It'll work out once Jackson cools off. He's always had that temper."

"I—you—work out?" I splutter. "Coop."

"Hmm?"

"Are you going to sleep?"

Sighing, he rolls to a seated position. I scold myself for watching the contraction of his core muscles. He scoots to the end of the bed, bracing his elbows on his knees.

"What do you want me to say, Tate?"

"I don't know. I figured you'd be pissed. I just trapped us in a bigger lie to hide what we've been doing. I panicked."

"So did I." Taking off his hat and dropping it on the bed, he rakes his fingers through his messy hair, distracting me again with the flex of his bicep.

"I'm sorry," I repeat.

His brows furrow. He rises to his feet and cups my shoulders. "It's gonna be fine, okay? And it's not your fault, babe. I was there, too." He ducks his head, flashing me the suave look that got us into this mess. "I wanted to kiss you and ignored your warning."

"Okay, so we both suck."

Cooper blows out a breath. "T..." He draws me into his embrace, squeezing me in a bear hug that helps the stressed out tension bleed from my body. "Quit being so hard on yourself."

I allow myself twenty seconds to enjoy this, shutting my eyes. He smells like a day at the beach, the salty air lingering on his skin, mixing with his natural musk. It's both comforting and alluring.

Down, girl.

Thirsty Tatum is not allowed out right now. This is a situation that calls for Logical Tatum to come out of hiding to deal with this.

"We'll break up."

Cooper goes rigid, pulling away to gape at me. "What?"

I lick my lips, rolling with the idea as it forms. "Yeah. That's how we'll deal. We can stage a break up to fix this."

A crease forms between his brows. "It does make it easier to play off what we've got going on."

"I think it's run its course. We should just call the whole thing off." It kills me to say it, but it's the responsible thing to do. Cooper clearly disagrees, pulling away from me completely with a hard expression. "I'll still help you study, but it makes sense to end this with a bang. Well—not that kind of bang."

Cooper huffs, but unlike his usual easy amusement, this is infused with annoyance. "Yeah, okay. Except you didn't want to stop it, so you decided to say we were dating. Why go through that if you just wanted to end the deal?"

I flap a hand, no answers coming to mind. "I told you, I panicked." I back up toward the door, setting my jaw. "Think about it —it's win-win for you. I'll keep helping you study, but you free your-self from your sex student. You could've been making out with one of the girls from the Shack right now if you didn't have to worry about teaching me."

This is for the best. It's the only way I know how to distance myself from the feelings screaming at me to shut the fuck up. I won't fall further the more I remind myself Cooper Vale isn't mine and this had a time limit from the start.

"Are you serious?" He shakes his head. "No, T, those girls were nothing—I don't want—"

"But I do," I blurt. Oh shit. Damage control, stat. "I...I want to be able to experience college to the fullest." My eyes widen and he freezes. "It's why I cooked up this plan, remember? So it works out like that. We've achieved our goals."

"Tate…" Cooper trails off, cutting his gaze from me. He blows out a breath. "If that's what you really want."

"Okay." Awkwardness sets in as we stare at each other. I can't take the stand off anymore. I gesture at the door with my thumb. "So I'll just… Yeah, I'll just get out of here."

My chest is tight as I dart for the door, regret clanging through me.

A strong hand grasps my elbow and spins me around to face him. His gaze bounces between mine like he's committing me to memory.

"Don't go yet."

"I should," I whisper.

"Just—not yet." His head dips. "Hang out for a little longer. We can put on one of those documentaries you like on Netflix."

My heart clenches. Damn it. Why does he have to know me so well?

When I shrug, he nods in relief, releasing my arm. "I saved one on the Barrier Reef restoration for you. It popped up in my recommendations when you weren't here."

It takes me a moment to swallow the lump forming in my throat while he searches the room for his laptop, ruffling his hair absently.

"Coop?" He stops what he's doing. I square my shoulders, gathering my courage. "Tell me one thing."

"Anything." He pins me with those brown eyes that see right into my soul.

"We'll still be friends, right?" I bite my lip, hoping he doesn't hear the uncertain waver in my voice. "I hope we didn't mess that up between us."

Cooper's eyes flash and he swipes his fingers over his mouth. "We can't be friends, T."

The rough, rumbled words stir heat in my core. I secretly-not-so-secretly love it when Cooper brings out the growly voice. But then his words register. My throat pricks with a sharp sting.

Smothering a gasp, I meet his intense gaze. "We can't?"

He closes the distance between us, crowding me until my back hits his bedroom door. Moving with the prowling grace of a man who knows what he wants, he plants a hand against it, towering over me.

"No. No way in hell, baby." Cooper shakes his head, his gaze roaming my face. "There's nothing friendly about the ways I think of you when I do this."

Swooping down, he captures my lips. I gasp and his tongue slips into my mouth. He cradles my face as he kisses me. It's possessive, all-consuming. He rules my senses with the irresistibly seductive kiss and his touch as he strokes the side of my throat, continuing down until he takes my hands and pins them overhead against the door.

Arousal floods my system with each glide of our tongues, our mingled breathing growing thicker and heavier. With a low rumble, he drags his hands down my arms and slips them beneath my shirt, peeling it over my head in a smooth move. He tears away from my mouth, his lips moving down my jaw, attacking my throat until the ache between my legs becomes too much to bear.

"Coop."

My breathless whisper is lost between us as his hands dig down the back of my shorts to massage my ass. I wrap my arms around his shoulders, holding him in place to torment the sensitive skin his tongue teases on my neck. A strangled cry catches in my throat as he uses his grip to lift me, grinding his erection into me when he uses his hard body to pin me to the door.

His lips find mine again in another friendship-obliterating kiss that has both of us groaning with desperate need. He peels us from the door, carting me to the desk. Setting me on it, he pops the button on my shorts and wrestles them off me in seconds, along with my panties. He shucks his tented shorts while he digs through a drawer for a condom. As he searches, my hands close around his dick. The hot, silky soft skin always fascinates me, and I love the sounds he makes when I stroke it.

He pauses, burying a groan in my neck. "Jesus, fuck, baby girl. You're killing me." Nipping my flushed skin in retaliation, he slams the drawer shut and delves his finger between my thighs, teasing my folds. "Always so wet for me."

It's true. My clit throbs and I suck in a breath as he brushes it with his thumb.

Friends don't get this wet for people they're *just friends* with.

The thought flies out of my head once Cooper rolls on a condom and squeezes the back of my neck, encouraging my attention to fall to his cock lining up.

"Watch," he rasps.

I sink my teeth into my lip, lashes fluttering as he enters me in a smooth stroke. The sight of him fucking me is filthy, but I can't take my eyes off it. Not until he guides my leg higher on his hip and finds an angle that makes me throw my head back. This time it feels different from our first time, the pleasure more intense.

The desk rattles the wall with our frenzied romp. He takes me as hard as I beg him to, my nails scraping his shoulders as I shatter over and over for him.

"T," Cooper murmurs repeatedly while he takes me apart, branding me with his touch.

The way he says it is a hot, possessive claim. I want it. His claim over me. I don't want to let go of this, even if it's fake.

Closing my eyes, I tighten my arms, memorizing every place where our bodies touch to have this for a little longer before I need to walk away to protect my heart.

TWENTY-FOUR
COOPER

Hours after Tatum leaves, I'm still awake, staring at my ceiling. It's been a while since insomnia kept my mind going, not since Tatum and I started messing around. Netflix has asked four times if I'm still watching the nature documentary we put on before she left. I kept it on once she was gone because it made it feel like she was still nestled against my side, tickling my stomach absently while she watched the restoration on the Barrier Reef.

I scrub my hands over my face and release a bone-deep sigh. "You fucked up."

Tatum's comment about what I could be doing instead of spending time with her has stayed with me. So does my reaction to the idea of her staging a breakup to fix things between me and Jackson.

When she turned her back on me to leave, something panicked rose up in me. I couldn't let her go, not without branding myself on her first. I came up with the excuse to watch Netflix just to have more time.

Then she had to go and turn those beautiful blue eyes on me and drown me in their depths to ask me to be something I know we can never be.

Friends. That was my breaking point. I don't want to be Tatum's fucking friend.

It took her saying it was over—that I couldn't touch her anymore —to realize I can't let her go yet. The thought of letting her go, of not having this thing between us anymore by cutting things off early, hit me hard in the chest.

It might have been Tatum's idea to start this deal, but I want to change it because I'm not ready for us to be over. I'm not about to lose her over this. Except she doesn't even see herself as someone on my radar, believing I've spent all summer biding my time until I could have someone else.

I need to pitch this like a mutually beneficial project, the same way she approached this, offering me her tutoring strengths (academic) in exchange for my tutoring (spicy). That adorable Tatum Logic I love inspires my middle of the night thoughts, helping me form a plan that will help me work her up to the idea of us.

This is the perfect chance to clean up my image. Everyone sees me as this playboy thirst trap, and I'm not about it anymore. It's kept me from having the kind of connection I really want in a relationship. Tatum believes it, just like everyone else.

I need to prove to her I'm not the guy she thinks. I'll need time to pull it off. If we keep pretending to date, she'll believe she's helping me retire my playboy ways by learning how to have a real relationship, all while I'm making her fall for me.

The idea begins to form in my head. I stroke my chin, squinting at my ceiling. A hint of Tatum's coconut lime shampoo hits my nose, her scent lingering on my sheets. I close my eyes as want spears through my chest.

When I think of someone to give my heart to, it's been her in my head, hands down. Tonight she as good as told me she doesn't see herself as mine the way I do.

What she said about wanting to experience college to the fullest runs through my head. If I ask her to be my girlfriend outright, maybe she'd say yes. It's the worry that she might turn me down that's got me solidifying this plan in my head.

Pretending to date gives us a better cover for the pull we both have trouble fighting. We won't have to suffer and steal touches. No more hiding from our friends. No more girls hitting on me because I'll be able to grab Tatum and kiss the shit out of her like I always want to. She'll never worry about me wanting anyone but her.

Still not fucking real yet, but the idea's grown on me the more I think about it. I'll take anything I can get when it comes to her.

Tatum saved our asses after getting caught by her brother by telling him we were dating, but too afraid to tell anyone. Rather than walk it back like she proposed, we'll lean into it hard. We'll make everyone believe we're the most sickeningly in love couple. Romeo and Juliet won't have shit on us.

It's what I'll need to patch up my oldest friendship. Jackson is pissed at me, but we're like brothers. He's probably more angry that I broke a promise I made than he actually is about what happened. Loyalty means something between best friends, and in his eyes I spat all over the trust we have in each other.

I did, but not in the way he thinks. I frown, scrubbing my face. He can't ever find that out, though.

Tatum's timeline for her original plan was up until college to prepare herself. I need this to go on longer than that. First, I need to fix things with my best friend. Then I'll convince her until she can't refuse me, just like I stood no chance refusing her.

* * *

The following night, the air in the Danvers' house crackles with tension. It took nothing to get an invite to stay for dinner. Mrs. Danvers has treated me like one of her own since I was a kid.

"Pass the salad," I ask.

Jackson ignores me, mouth set in a flat line. A worried crease forms between his mom's brows. Tatum huffs in exasperation between us and reaches across Jackson to grasp the bowl, passing it to me.

"Thanks," I say.

She nods awkwardly, shooting me her fifth curious glance from the corner of her eye. I didn't tell her my plan, and she showed up after her and Jackson's shift at the Shack while her mom and I were in the middle of cooking dinner. My lips twitch at the memory of her eyes bugged out all cute when she saw me.

Jackson forces out a breath through his nose, stabbing his chicken with agitated movements.

"Was work busy?" Mrs. Danvers asks him.

His jaw works. "No."

"Is something else bothering you, then?"

Jackson opens and closes his mouth, gaze sliding to me. His eyes narrow and he shakes his head.

Mrs. Danvers hums around a bite of vegetables, chewing thoughtfully before responding. "If you aren't willing to talk about it, then you can save the aggressiveness for after dinner. We're happy to listen if you change your mind."

Tatum chokes, smothering a laugh behind her hand as their mom sweetly tells Jackson to knock it off. She's always had a gentle approach like that with both of her kids. He grunts an agreement, no longer taking out his irritation on his dinner.

The meal continues like that, Jackson giving us all the silent treatment, only offering clipped answers when his parents speak to him directly. Tatum elbows him, but it doesn't help.

As dinner winds down, Mr. Danvers lets his family know he has some time off. They're working out their schedules for a weekend trip before the fall semester starts.

"I have work every day that week," Tatum says. "I'm trying to scrape every second I can to save up in case I don't find a job on campus during the semester."

I sense the opening I've been looking for throughout dinner.

"Not on Saturday, you don't," I say.

She turns to me. "What?"

"I already requested off for both of us with Marco." I drape my arm over the back of her chair, making a statement to her family. It feels good to be able to do it without hiding it. "I was going to wait till after dinner, but I want to take you to the pier."

"What? Like a date?" Tatum squeaks.

I give her a crooked half-smile, but I'm distracted from answering when the loud scrape of a chair interrupts. Jackson gets up, snatches his plate, and stomps away from the table without a word. The sink runs in the kitchen for a minute, then the kitchen door slams. My stomach clenches with the worry that Jackson is pissed enough to drive off again, but then I hear the muted smack of the basketball against the driveway.

"I see," Mrs. Danvers murmurs, brows lifted. She gives me and Tatum a soft smile. "I'm so happy to hear you're dating. Your father and I always said there was something between you two. We'll figure out another weekend to take a trip. Have fun, kids."

Her easy acceptance stirs warmth in my chest. She's like a second mother to me, and having her admit she always thought Tatum and I belonged together makes my heart thump.

"Uh, but I—" Tatum pauses when I drop my arm to her shoulder, playing with the end of one of her French braids. "Yup. Sorry we didn't say anything. It's still new. We weren't trying to sneak around."

Mrs. Danvers laughs. "Sweetheart, you forget that your father and I were, believe it or not, young once. You've both had every talk imaginable—probably twice over for Cooper between us and his parents. Be smart, be safe, and know you can always come to us with anything."

"Every generation feels like they're having a unique experience," Mr. Danvers says.

"Dad," Tatum complains. "Jesus."

He chuckles, pouring more wine for him and his wife. "Just wait until you get to the hereditary portion of your classes and you find out what else isn't unique to you."

Tatum groans, leaning into me. Her parents grin, toasting to each other. My lips twitch and my chest expands every time she turns to me for support.

"Do your parents like to gross you out with embarrassing stuff like this?" she mumbles.

"Worse, babe," I murmur. "They're yogis."

I relax and finish off my dinner. Tatum's parents took it as easily as mine did when I texted to tell them I was dating her. Step one done. Next step, smooth things over with Jackson.

After I help clear the table, I tell Tatum I'm going to talk to her brother. She meets my eyes with hope brimming in hers. I chuck her beneath the chin and wink.

Jackson pauses when I step out, leaning against the door to his house. His expression twists and he takes his shot. It sinks in perfectly.

"Nice," I say.

"Shut up."

Sighing, I push off the door. He passes me the ball and I dribble while I mull over how to say this to him. "I want to fix this."

"Then you shouldn't have touched my sister," Jackson bites out, crossing his arms. "We had a deal."

"I know." I catch the ball and squeeze it between my palms. "I never expected... I was never going to break it. We shouldn't have gone behind your back."

Jackson's brows flatten. "Yeah, sure. You're a patron fucking saint. Why do you think I made you swear she was off-limits in the first place?"

The comment stings. Has he always worried I'd make a move on her? That I'd hurt her? That's not me.

"Tatum snuck up on me." Turning away, I take my shot, attention trained on the basketball. "She's funny and smart. She's helped me figure out my degree. She took me by surprise, man. I like her."

Truth bleeds into my words. It backs me up for the lie, but it makes my chest feel hollow from the Tatum-sized hole carved out of it. This plan has to work.

"But she's my sister, you dick." He watches the ball roll by his feet without retrieving it. "You could have your pick of any chick in town. Hell, out of town, too. Why her?"

Jackson's sister. Friend. My mind rejects both things.

"Why not her, dude? She's perfect. I came over to talk to you so you could see that this isn't going away. But I don't want to fuck up our friendship. You're still my boy."

He scoffs. "Are you asking my permission?"

"I guess."

"You're supposed to ask a girl's dad for that."

"Well, yours took it just fine." I blow out a breath, running a hand over my hat. "Look, nothing's changed. We've all been hanging out and it hasn't been a problem."

"How long?"

"What?"

"How. Long," he snaps.

Shit. I should've waited to go over this with Tatum before talking to him. Fuck it, we'll have to roll with whatever I tell him now.

"The bonfire," I decide.

Jackson works his jaw, nodding slowly. "You're an asshole. You've been lying to me for that long?"

I strive for a calm that's growing difficult to maintain. "I told you—"

"You just want a side piece with easy access," Jackson accuses. "What happens when we go back to campus? She hasn't seen that side of you."

My jaw clenches and I ball my hands into fists to keep from decking him for talking about Tate that way. He's playing overprotective brother, but I'm not just any guy. An impulsive urge hits me and I give in to it, digging my phone out. In quick succession, I edit my TikTok and Instagram profiles, adding a heart emoji and Tatum's handle in both bios. When I'm done, I shove my phone at my best friend.

"I'm serious about her," I insist. "I get you want to protect her when you know what I'm like—"

"Exactly, man." Jackson shifts his glare from my phone to me. "I know what the fuck you're like. You don't do feelings. You barely did girlfriends until Kayla."

Frustration rakes over my patience. I can't believe I thought what I had with Kayla was a real relationship. What I have with Tate is more real than what we shared, and what we have is fake. The things I craved when Kayla was with me—having someone want me for more than a warm body, being needed, being there as someone to lean on—are all ten times better with Tatum.

"That's what I'm trying to tell you. I've changed. Being with

Tatum—" I ignore the pained grimace that crosses his face. "—helped me realize what I want."

His frown deepens. "What about all those chicks you cycle through? Kayla?"

"I'm done with them." I slash a hand through the air. "All of them."

Even before all this with Tatum, that's the direction I was headed. I've outgrown that guy.

My phone buzzes in my hand and the moment of finally believing me vanishes when he catches sight of my screen. It's Kayla calling me. My blood boils and my grip tightens on my phone.

"Okay." A caustic laugh punches out of him. "Yeah fucking right."

"Just—wait." Gritting my teeth, I answer the call. "What?"

"Baby, what the fuck?" she hisses across the line. "Why is there some other bitch's name in your Insta and TikTok bios? You never did that for me. I've been trying to c—"

"Kayla." She keeps trying to speak, so I talk over her, keeping my tone firm. "We're done, girl. We've been done after the last time you started a fight. I'm not yours. I'm not falling for your manipulative shit again. You need to lose my number. I'm seeing someone else."

Her screech is enough to make me hang up and block her number. It feels good to tell her how it is after leaving her on read a few weeks ago when she tried to say she missed me in the middle of the night while she was drunk. Jackson watches the entire call with a guarded expression. I lift my brows pointedly.

"I'm not that guy anymore," I mutter. "And I'd never do anything to hurt your sister."

Jackson scrubs a hand over his mouth. "You're for real?"

"Yes. Are we chill, or are you going to punch me again?"

The corner of his mouth lifts and the tension ebbs out of my shoulders. He holds out his arms and puckers his lips. "Fine. Kiss and make up?"

I saunter across the driveway and plant a hand over his face. "I'd rather kiss your sister."

He shoves my hand off with a groan. "You're still a dick." He grabs me by the collar of my t-shirt, his amusement vanishing. "You hurt my sister, I break your face."

"Got it."

Jackson grins. "Sweet. Go get the ball. I'm going to kick your ass on the court since I can't beat you up for this."

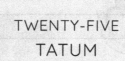

TWENTY-FIVE
TATUM

When Cooper comes back inside, he thanks my parents for dinner, then snags my hand. My stomach dips. I'm only holding hands with him, and it's just Cooper, but still.

"Come out for a walk?" Cooper asks me with the crooked grin that makes my heart clench.

Dad smirks, wrapping an arm around Mom's waist. "Don't keep her out too late."

Mom grins, pinching his side.

"Dad, come on," I beg, cheeks flushed.

Cooper ducks his head and clears his throat. The tips of his ears are pink at my parents' teasing. I'm still surprised they accepted Cooper casually asking me out on a date at dinner so readily. And I won't even touch Mom's comment about always thinking there would be something between us.

Nodding, I allow him to lead me out the door into the warm summer evening, the sky awash in pinks and purples. We pass Jackson in the driveway. He watches us closely, no longer as angry as I last saw him. I exhale in relief that I didn't come between my brother and his best friend.

Cooper squeezes my hand and we continue down to the street, strolling aimlessly. We make it to the corner before I finally speak up.

"So…" I gulp when he pins me with his sultry brown eyes. "We're off to a great start of being friends."

His grip on my hand tightens and his eyes flash. "I told you, I can't be your friend, baby." He tugs me closer, bringing his lips to my ear. "Do I need to repeat what happened after I said that? Because there isn't a second of the day I don't want to be inside you."

My breath catches and I sway into him, shivering at the memory of last night. His deep chuckle wraps around me. "Ok, but seriously. I thought we were going to figure this out together and strategize out how to end it. Now we're dating? And I'm the last to know?"

Sighing, he plants a kiss on my temple. "I knew it was stressing you that Jacks was bent out of shape over this, so I came over for dinner to talk to him." He pulls me to a stop and takes me by the shoulders. "I'm proposing we change the plan. We're going to pretend we're together."

My brows shoot up. "Why?"

"Why, she says?" An amused huff leaves him and he adjusts his signature backwards cap, shaking his head. "Babe, I need you to realize what a catch you are. Any guy would be lucky to pretend to be your man, let alone actually date you." My cheeks heat and I open my mouth. He grasps my jaw, dipping his head into my space. "But they don't get you. Not while you're mine. Only me."

"Coop," I breathe.

For a moment, I believe his rumbled words and the possessiveness threaded into them. It's insane to think a guy like him would want to claim me.

His eyes bounce between mine, then drop to my mouth. "Last night you said it was win-win if we stopped, but I call bullshit. It's win-win if we keep this going. It's the perfect cover, and…" Trailing off, he swipes his thumb across my lip. "I want people to stop thinking thirst trap and fuckboy when they see me. I want a reformed image."

"Reformed," I echo. "But why do you need me to do that? You could pick any girl. You could get a real girlfriend and just put your best foot forward."

His forehead rests against mine. "T, for someone so smart, a lot goes over your head. When I'm with you, I don't have to freak out about what to do next, because I know you're there to talk it out with me. I trust you. When I'm around you, I'm able to focus and see the future more clearly. You help me be the kind of man I want to be. That's why it's gotta be you, baby."

I'm taken aback, a warm glow expanding in my chest.

Cooper's fingers sink into my hair, massaging my scalp in the way that makes me melt. I become putty in his hands. It occurs to me we're not hiding anything right now, standing on our street corner in the golden rays of the evening. I put my hands on his chest, enjoying the slight ripple of his firm muscles.

"This way we don't have to sneak around. Do you have any problem with faking it with me?"

There's a hint of vulnerability in his question that pierces my heart, making me forget my own concerns. What he's saying makes sense, and I get the vibe like he's not going to let this go.

He's helped me this far with an even crazier deal than what he's asking of me right now. I want to help him, too.

"No, I don't have a problem."

"Good. By the way, our first date was the bonfire. Jacks made me tell him how long, and I figured it was the easiest thing to remember since it was when it all started." He pauses, offering me a lopsided smile. "Check your Instagram and my TikTok profile."

He waits while I pull my phone from the back pocket of my cut-offs. The Instagram notification is on my lock screen, so I check it first, eyes widening when it takes me to his profile and shows my username next to a heart. Switching to TikTok, I find the same, rolling my lips between my teeth.

"Um." I peek at him. "I'm mentioned in your bio."

"Exactly. Tag me in yours, too. I'm yours and you're mine, T."

A flutter moves through me and I feel like I've stepped into a dream world as I enter his handle into my bio.

I bite my lip. "What about me being prepared for college?"

Cooper smirks, and it sends warmth into my veins. "You'll be more prepared this way." He grasps my waist and tugs me against him, his words taking on a slight growl. "I'll be able to stay close to you and ease you into college life. Real world experience, T. Isn't that the kind of learning you thrive on? Parties, the social scene—all of it. Consider me your training wheels college boyfriend."

A laugh escapes me. "You've really thought of everything."

The curve of his mouth turns seductive, and he grazes his nose against mine, murmuring in a smoky tone that goes straight to my core. "Best of all, I can touch you anytime, anywhere. Like right now, because I really want to kiss you."

My lips part and he takes advantage, dipping his head to kiss me. It leaves me dizzy by the time he pulls back, hovering his mouth over mine with his eyes hooded like he can't decide if he's done kissing me or needs another. My heartbeat thrums.

"So fake dating," I murmur. He hums in agreement, still fixated on my mouth. "Okay. I propose a practice run. We know we've got no problem between the sheets, so selling our chemistry won't be a problem." He interrupts me with a gravelly chuckle that makes me bite my lip. "What we need is practice to make sure we're believable as a couple."

Cooper grins. "I expected nothing less from you, which is why I was serious about taking you to the pier."

I lift a brow. "Presumptuous."

"Prepared, baby," he rasps with a charming wink. "Prepared, confident, and anticipating your needs, like a good boyfriend."

My heart stutters. The playing field has been effectively leveled, but now we're in an all new game—one where we've gone from Cooper being my sex tutor I'm crushing on to pretending to date to cover up being friends with benefits.

If there's one thing Cooper was right about, it's that we can never be just friends. Not anymore.

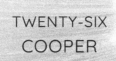

TWENTY-SIX
COOPER

An odd sensation fills my chest as Tatum and I arrive at the pier hand in hand for our practice run. Our first fake date. I picked it because it's a basic one to set her at ease.

Tatum looks cute as hell today in a denim overall dress over a cropped white t-shirt. The tantalizing peeks of her skin on the sides tempt me to map every inch of visible skin.

"We'll need to get our story straight," Tatum says when we're in line for tickets. She pulls out a travel-sized notebook from her backpack purse and twirls a pen. She peers around and lowers her voice, playing it off like she's whispering something flirty to me. "How we got together, that sort of thing."

Tatum being Tatum about this makes my chest feel tight and warm.

Satisfaction rushes through me as I wrap my arms around her. She stills for a moment, then relaxes into my embrace. I'll never get tired of being able to do this without worrying about getting caught.

"We'll keep it simple. Build it backwards from the bonfire." I keep her in my arms, shuffling us forward when the line moves. "The rest works from there if we stick with the story that we were dating on the DL because of Jackson."

She nods, bracing her notebook against my chest to jot down

notes. "We'll need a whole new plan for how we're going to do this because rule one is officially out the window."

Tatum's right. There won't be any chance of taking it slow. Not when I feel like I go crazy from how much I want her. This isn't about learning and body talk anymore—we know we're good on that front.

"I have some thoughts." Tatum flips through her notebook to a different page. "I've been thinking about them the last few days and jotting them down. Oh, I think one might be on my phone, too. I woke up in the middle of the night and wrote down *feels timeline*." Her face scrunches. "I'm not really sure what I was going for with that, but 4am Tatum thought it was groundbreaking enough to pull me out of a dead sleep."

A raspy chuckle rolls out of me and I grin. "I can picture it. You get this specific look on your face when an idea strikes."

Peering at me through her lashes, she bites her lip. "Like what?"

The line moves again, and I resist the temptation to pick her up and carry her, settling for nudging her thighs with mine. "Your eyes go all bright and you get this little line right here." I brush hair away from her forehead, tracing the space between her brows. "Every time."

"Sometimes my thoughts race too fast, so if I don't stop and give the idea attention, then write it down, I forget it. Writing something down is a proven method of strengthening memory retention." Sliding her lips together, she waves her notebook. "Anyway, my study blocks are already mapped out with my class schedule. Send me yours and I'll see where we line up to nail down a game plan that covers boyfriend and girlfriend time, study time for both of us, and—" Glancing around, she lowers her voice. "—*study* time."

Heat shoots into my veins and a rumble works its way through my chest. "Now you're talking, babe. We can multitask. Library quickies are my specialty."

Tate's lips part, a gleam of arousal flickering in her blue eyes. I want to explore that later for sure, my mind filling with all the ways I can take Tatum apart while she tries to stay quiet.

She forges on, staying on task as always. "I think we'll need to be seen together a minimum of thirty percent of our time on campus between classes. We can grab meals together when our schedules line up."

I struggle to hold back a smile at her serious expression. She taps a pen against her lip while talking out her plan. And I can't help myself. I swoop in, capturing her mouth in a kiss, swallowing the tiny sound of surprise she makes. Our lips glide together and something feels like it shifts into place.

"What was that for?" Tatum murmurs.

I smirk. "Anytime I want, remember?"

She blushes. "Right."

"I was thinking more like taking photos together. Want to post a TikTok of our date? My followers will eat it up. I saw this guy post a whole series about telling his crush he liked her and the video of their dating update had like a million views." My brows pinch. "Well, the hardcore simps will probably get emo about it, but whatever. It helps solidify the cred that I'm a taken man."

"Viral marketing." Tatum nods in consideration, tapping the pen against her lip once more. It stirs the urge to kiss her again. "That could work. Good thinking. It'll spread more quickly."

We make it to the front of the line and I take out my wallet. Tatum shuffles off to the side. Brows furrowing, I snag her waist and bring her back to my side.

"Where are you going?"

"Oh, I was going to let you go first."

I put my hand over hers to stop her from rummaging in her purse. "Nah, babe. I've got this."

"You don't have to. It's just pretend. I'll feel bad if you pay."

"Two tickets," I tell the attendant, sliding my credit card through the window before turning back to Tatum. "Too late. It was my idea to go out. That means I pay."

Tatum frowns. "But..."

"You can buy lunch. Will that make you feel better, Miss Independent?"

She lifts her chin. "Yes. It'll be more fair that way."

"Okay." With a wry smile, I collect our tickets and put my arm around her waist to guide her to the pier. As we walk, I hold up my phone and record. "What's up, everyone? This is T, my girl." I pan to include her in the frame, raking my teeth over my lip. "And today we're at the pier in South Bay. How many prizes should I win for her?"

"Hah! I'm totally kicking your butt at the water gun races," Tatum sasses.

I flash a grin at the camera, waggling my brows. "We'll see about that, baby."

She yelps when I yank her close and plant a kiss on her cheek for the camera. I stop the recording and our eyes meet. Warmth unfurls in my chest, winding around my heart at the amused look on her face.

Clearing my throat, I busy myself posting the video. "What do you want to do first?"

"Let's get cotton candy. It'll make a cute prop for photos." Tatum takes my hand and pulls me toward a stall. Darting a look over her shoulder, she squints. "I'm buying this."

I hold my free hand up in surrender. "I know not to get between you and your determination once you make your mind up."

"Damn right."

Chuckling, I release her hand to swat her ass, leaning close against her back to murmur in her ear. "It'll make you feel better because I'm serious about kicking ass at the game stands. I'm on a mission to win you the biggest prizes they have."

"Those are fighting words, Coop." Tatum mimes rolling up her sleeves. "You're on. I'm going to win *you* the biggest one."

Once we have a big cloud of pink cotton candy, she picks out a spot with the pier rides in the background. My arms slide around her waist from behind and she leans into my chest. I dip my head over her shoulder, brushing my lips against her cheek while she snaps photos. My stomach tightens with each frame when I catch sight of how we look on the screen.

We look real.

My heart thumps. She looks so much like that photo I have of us from the pool party in my room. Her eyes are bright, crinkled at the side, her grin wide enough for her crooked tooth to show when she turns her face to offer me the piece of pink fluff sticking from her mouth.

"Mm. Let me taste."

I switch the phone to record a video, making a show of taking a big bite. The sugar melts on my tongue, but it's not as sweet as licking the taste from her lips and kissing her. A shuddering breath escapes her and her eyes are darker when we part. Our gazes remain locked for a few seconds before she quickly ends the recording.

"That should be plenty to get us started. We can take some more later." Tatum's voice is higher, like it goes when she's embarrassed.

Squeezing her, I brush one more kiss against her temple before letting her go to give her the space she needs to process. I post the cotton candy kiss video.

"Our first post already has a ton of views." I grip my phone harder at comments thirsting after her. Putting it away, I bump my shoulder against hers. "Ready to have the biggest, most ridiculous prize won in your honor?"

It works to clear the odd look from Tatum's face. She perks up, smirking. "You're on."

I offer my hand, chest burning when she takes it without hesitation.

Everything feels more natural than I expected. All with the girl I never allowed myself to want. I always thought we could be great together and now I know it, feeling the connection I've been craving. Getting caught by Jackson has opened up a path I never thought was possible.

PART TWO: FALL

TWENTY-SEVEN
TATUM

A text from Cooper lights up my phone, letting me know he's waiting for me downstairs in his Jeep for tonight's bonfire. It's the annual end of summer hurrah, and the party we all consider his birthday celebration. After tonight, it's crunch time. The final countdown is on for my first semester at South Bay College starting next week. The excitement I've felt all summer crossing out days on my sea turtle-themed calendar is present, though now it carries a tinge of jitters with it.

I couldn't wait to start college to begin living my life to the fullest, and here I am about to kick off my first semester with a boyfriend —*fake* boyfriend.

Tatum: Be out in a minute.
Cooper: The longer you take, the more you cut into our parking lot make out time before we party. I'm gonna need to reacquaint myself with your perfect lips. Take too long and I'm sending in a retrieval team [wink emoji]

A breathy laugh escapes me. Before I lock my screen, the number of notifications on my TikTok app makes my heart skip a beat. I should turn them off. The numbers on the little red circle keep climbing, well into the four hundreds since I last checked this morning.

After Cooper's two posts from our first fake date went viral, my account has been bombarded with comments on the videos he tagged me in, new followers, and DM requests. I never expected anything like this.

When I agreed to the new plan, it was because I wanted to help Cooper. He presented logical reasoning for this change in our situation to work out for both of us—training wheels college boyfriend to help me acclimate to college life and a sensible girlfriend for him to reform his playboy image.

I thought I was cool with this. Turns out, I might be in over my head.

It wasn't until I realized I have no idea what comes next that my habit of over analyzing kicked in. At the pier I was going for a fake it until I make it approach, projecting a calm and collected vibe to keep myself from freaking out every time he touched me freely. The practice run was a good idea, something I definitely needed as a baseline. Tonight would be a disaster without it.

I don't know how to be in a relationship, so if I'm going to help Cooper, I need to know what to expect in every situation—how I'm supposed to act around him in public, ideal times for PDA, and how much of myself I should be. My YouTube search history is full of teeny bopper vlogs capturing dates with their partner. I scoured them for ideas on how to navigate the date at the pier. It went okay, but I'm ashamed of how many videos I watched to get inspiration from couples over four years younger than us.

How am I the right girl for the job when my experience level was still at the starting line until I went to him?

I thrive on studying the development and behavior of the human mind, yet faced with choices and opportunity, I freeze up, second-guessing every little thing. When I'm with him, it's easy. Then as soon as I'm alone, my mind works overtime to attack his logic.

It's like there's a secret manual everyone but me received, still leaving me lagging.

Coming out to thousands of strangers around the world on social media is one thing, but tonight we're officially coming out as a couple to our friends in South Bay. They're the ones we have to convince since they actually know us.

I thought this would be the easier part than faking it for social media, but a bout of anxious nerves has me shaking out my hands and pacing my room as I run through a mental list I've memorized from the notes I took to keep myself from freaking out about pretending to be Cooper's girlfriend in front of everyone we know. Music from one of my playlists—this one titled *songs to have a crisis to (we don't break down, we pivot)*—plays from my phone.

We first started dating at the bonfire. Kept things on the down low because of Jackson. Don't forget to hold hands. When sitting, choose his lap if there's room.

Halting my pacing in front of my mirror, I assess my outfit for the third time. I went for an off-shoulder cropped sweater with a pastel rainbow pattern embroidered on it that exposes my stomach and my trusty cut-offs. It's slightly out of my comfort zone, yet still me.

The girls Cooper usually dates are gorgeous and extroverted, favoring makeup, fashion, and have so much more experience. And good for them, but those things don't come easily for me because I spent so long focused on my studies rather than building up my confidence in social settings. Even after the last several weeks with Cooper, I'm a baby in terms of coming out of my shell. It's not that I want to be exactly like the girls he's usually with, just...believable as Cooper's girlfriend. I don't want it to be obvious and fail at faking this.

How was this so much easier to navigate when it was only about losing my virginity and learning the bedroom skills I lacked to fit in at college?

A knock at my door startles me, then warmth spreads through my body at the voice on the other side.

"Ready to go, babe?" Cooper cracks the door. "I hear your hype music. If you're up here making another list of conversation topics for the party, I'm confiscating all of your notebooks."

I shoot him a harassed look. "Do that and I won't be held responsible for my actions to rescue my babies."

He chuckles, sliding into the room. Leaning against the door, his head cocks and his gaze roams over me.

"You look great, and if we don't leave in the next thirty seconds, you're going to look even better because I'm going to rip every piece of clothing off you." His mouth curves slowly. "For real, if I come any closer, my hands can't be held responsible for their actions."

My insides coil, on board with that idea. That we have no problem with. I'd much rather do that, then curl up with him to binge a nature documentary on Netflix. It's not in the plan, though.

"I'm ready." Shutting off my playlist, I grab my phone and paste on a smile. "Can't have you be late to your own birthday, dude."

Cooper shrugs, watching me while he opens the door. As I go to pass him, he snags my waist, surprising me with a tender kiss to the forehead. "If you need it, I can wait all night, T."

I bite my lip, leaning into him. "I'm good. Let's head out. Traffic probably sucks already."

He hums in agreement, following me through my house to his Jeep. I press a hand over my stomach as he pulls out. No backing out now.

"What's that face for?" he prompts when we're halfway there.

I jump, sucking in a breath. The question startles me out of my run through of my memorized notes.

"What look? There's no look, this is just my face." I wave my hand in front of it to drive the point home. "Same old, same old."

The corner of his mouth lifts. "Nah." Reaching over, he settles his hand on my leg, fingers tucking between my thighs with a casual possessiveness that makes my stomach dip. One hand resting over the wheel, he exudes calm confidence while he weaves through the end of summer tourist traffic to reach Mariner's Cove for the party. "You forget how well I can read you, T. That face is the same as the night I brought you to your first party. It'll be chill. You have nothing to worry about, so quit overthinking before you blow a gasket."

Damn his perceptiveness. It would take longer than the time we have to drive to our destination to unpack everything that has my stomach in knots and my mind running in circles. It hasn't been quiet since he told me there wasn't anything friendly about how he thinks of me before he kissed me in a way that makes it clear we can never be just friends.

I still don't know where that leaves us when this charade of ours ends.

Cooper's thumb draws a circle on my skin absently. I suppress a shiver, his touch affecting me like I'm one of Pavlov's dogs attuned to what it means when his hands are on me. Now everyone else will see that effect without us having to hide it.

Once he pulls into a parking space at the cove ten minutes later, he makes no move to get out. "T, look at me."

Licking my lips, I lift my eyes to him. He's perfection in every sense of the word, his hair tousled by the salty air, full lips tilted in a fond, crooked smile, and understanding brimming in his eyes.

"What's up? You were chill about this last weekend, so talk to me. I can't help if you clam up and keep what's bugging you to yourself."

I shrug, wishing I had the words to explain why I got so in my head. "What if no one buys it and sees through our act? You're you, Coop, and I'm—"

"Fucking gorgeous," he cuts in, the weight of his eyes inescapable. "Don't even give me that sassy little comment about to come out of your mouth. You are."

"It's just so many people to fool." I swallow as the truth comes out. The nagging worry that I'm not good enough to be believable as his girlfriend eats at me. "What if we screw it up?"

"Not possible."

I wish I had an ounce of his easy confidence. "There's no way to know that one hundred percent."

"For sure."

"How?" I ask in exasperation. "There are too many variables—other people's opinions, for one."

He chuckles, a broad smile breaking free. "Easy. Because I've got you, my brainy little beauty, and you're the most determined person I know. When you want something? You make it fucking happen. And this?" He gestures between us, then snags a piece of my hair to play with. "You want to sell this, or you wouldn't be stressing about it."

My heart climbs into my throat at his certainty. He makes everything seem easier than it is.

"You know how you were nervous about the first party?" He waits for me to nod stiffly, running his fingers through my hair until I relax. "Confession? So was I."

I snort. "You don't get nervous. You don't have to say stuff just to be nice."

"I'm not, babe. Full disclosure, I was nervous the whole time because I was desperate as shit to kiss you." Taking my hand, he brushes his lips over the back of it. "I considered sneaking you away where we wouldn't be seen before Jackson got there. Let go of what anyone else thinks. We're a team, Tate. I've got your back, so you can stop panicking like you have to do this all on your own. We're in this together, remember?"

Oh.

The vital thing I forgot. A breath blows out of me, half laugh, half relieved sigh. Duh. I'm not alone. Cooper sets me at ease and helps me pack away the worries that reared since the pier.

It doesn't matter if I don't have experience because my partner in crime does. Where I don't know what to do, he'll fill in the gaps.

"Thanks for the reminder."

"Anytime." He kisses my hand again, shooting me a cocky grin. "Now, come here so I can kiss the shit out of you."

My laugh is silenced when his mouth slants over mine, stealing my breath. The nerves melt away, along with the world.

TWENTY-EIGHT
TATUM

The bonfire is packed already, twice the size of the usual party at Mariner's Cove. I didn't witness Cooper's birthday first-hand last year, but I saw how big this end of summer party gets by doing some light stalking of Cooper and Jackson's social media. Any out-of-state South Bay College students who finished moving into their dorms ahead of the semester have shown up in droves, plus everyone local to close out the summer.

It's because *everyone* knows Cooper Vale.

Man. Myth. Legend of South Bay for his skills on a board in the ocean and surfing a crowd to flirt with whoever falls for his swoon-worthy dimpled smiles.

Starting tonight, that legend is coming to a close so Cooper can begin a new chapter—hanging up his sultry playboy rep. And as his fake girlfriend, I'm helping him sell that change.

No pressure.

I wrap Cooper's promise to have my back around myself like a shield. It doesn't matter that I've never had a real relationship, or that I've only just crossed off losing my virginity from my experience list. As long as I remember that we're in this together, I won't crash and burn. It's hard to believe my life seemed less complicated when I was sneaking around with Cooper as my tutor in the bedroom.

As we make our way through the crowd, I keep a smile plastered on my face. A shiver races down my spine each time Cooper brushes his palm against the small of my back, tingles spreading across the exposed skin my cropped sweater gives him access to. The move feels possessive, just like the ride over when his hand rested on my leg. Even if it's for show, my body's as convinced as the rest of the girls flicking pouty looks Cooper's way and the guys eyeing me like something they wish they had themselves that I belong to him.

That thought is still taking some getting used to—I'm Cooper Vale's girlfriend.

Amidst the calls of *happy birthday* and people shouting his name, he threads his fingers with mine and shoots me a crooked smile. "Want a drink?"

My mouth lifts at the corner, lips still tender and swollen from how long we made out in his Jeep before joining the party. I nod, spotting Simone talking to Jenny, the bubbly girl we met at the last bonfire.

"There's Simone," I say.

"Let's grab drinks, then head that way."

He doesn't release my hand, grip tightening each time we're stopped by someone wanting to slap his back. Someone hands him a drink they poured from a keg when we reach the drinks table.

"Happy birthday, dude," the guy says. "No empties for you tonight."

Cooper chuckles. "Thanks."

They talk about surfing times during the semester. When I make to slip away to grab a water, he keeps me by his side, tucking his hand in the back pocket of my cut-offs.

"I'll catch you later, man. See you out there." Nodding with his chin, he snags a water bottle for me and steers us toward Simone and Jenny. His lips brush my temple and his voice lowers to a murmur meant only for me. "You have no idea how close I was to doing this last time."

"Last time?" My brain short circuits from the feel of his strong hand tucked against my ass.

"The other party. When I was dancing with you. When that guy was all over you." Cooper's voice grows rougher, making me swallow thickly. "Now I can show them all you're mine."

"Is that so?" He nods and I bite my lip. "By that logic, I can do the same."

Ignoring the flutter moving through my stomach, I act before I can overthink it, sliding my hand into his back pocket. He stills our slow amble for a moment and I feel the curve of his mouth stretching into a wide smile against my temple.

"Claiming me back, Tate?"

"It's only fair, right?" I hesitate, peering up at him. "I mean, it should be equal."

Cooper gazes at me with hooded eyes. "It's fucking hot. Guys love it when their girl gets all confident like that."

Heat prickles in my cheeks. "Noted."

He tugs me closer, the firm line of his body pressed against my side. "If we really want to sell this, we should slip away to the cave around the bend in the cove."

Humor dances in his tone, but I recognize the hint of seriousness. I prod him with my elbow.

"I doubt that'll rehab your playboy reputation," I joke.

"It makes me a good boyfriend," he counters, amusement shining in his eyes.

"Explain your postulation," I prompt.

Cooper grins and brings his mouth to the shell of my ear. "Because I can't stop thinking about sneaking away with my girlfriend."

I shudder at the smoky allure filling his tone. It's working. I'm half-convinced that's a great idea. While he pretends to flirt with me for the benefit of the people we pass, my determination returns. I'm going to help both of us by doing this, because past his reputation, Cooper is the best guy. He's thoughtful, genuine, and attentive to the needs of those around him. Once everyone stops seeing him as a play-boy, he'll find the perfect girlfriend.

My chest twinges, but I breathe through it until the ache eases.

"There you are," Simone says slyly when we reach the girls.

"Hey," Jenny greets with a bright smile.

179

I return it with one of my own. "Hi. All ready for the semester to start?"

She nods. "Totally. You should text me before our first class. We can meet up early and grab seats together."

A warm feeling bubbles in my stomach at how easy that was. Granted, I met Jenny weeks ago at the last bonfire Cooper took me to, but the semester hasn't started yet and I've already made a friend with one of my classmates.

"Sounds perfect," I say.

Simone flicks an assessing gaze over me, smirking in satisfaction. "Only an hour late to your own birthday, Coop. But I get it. When your girlfriend is as hot as my bestie, how can you resist?"

"Dude," I interject with a nervous laugh.

I had a whole prepared conversation written out in the notes I memorized to officially announce us as a couple to our friends, but Simone doesn't bat an eye that we're here together.

She's the only one who knows the truth about what we were before this. The truth that we weren't really secretly dating, but in more of a friends with benefits agreement. I didn't tell her about this new development after Jackson caught us kissing. Making our act believable to our closest friends is the real test.

"If it were up to me, we'd be another twenty minutes at least." Cooper kisses the top of my head. "Where are the guys?"

"Organizing the beer pong tourney," Simone answers. "They're waiting for the guest of honor to get started."

"Come on then." After Cooper finishes his drink off, he holds up a fist for me to bump, grinning when I knock my knuckles against his. "You and me, babe."

"Me? I've never played beer pong." Last time I watched while the guys played.

He shrugs as he ditches the empty cup, then steers me toward the tables being set up past the roaring bonfire people crowd around. "Don't worry, you've got me. We both know what a great teacher I am."

I roll my lips between my teeth, pulse thrumming at the double meaning hidden in those words. His hands find my hips and he moves me to walk in front of him where the crowd is thick, bouncing to the music. The girls file through behind us.

My eyes grow wide and I tip my head back against his chest to look up at him. "Can I even play if I'm sticking to water? It's a drinking game. Isn't that against the rules?"

"You can do anything you want." Cooper meets my eye, brow pinching. "I'd never force you to drink if you weren't comfortable with that."

A pang echoes in my chest. "I know."

"Good." The corner of his mouth lifts. "Now I'm going to teach you how to be a bomb ass beer pong player. It's all in the wrist."

"There he is!" Harris crows as we approach.

Cooper receives another round of raucous back slaps from his friends. They each nod to me in greeting.

Ty smirks, gesturing between us. "You turn twenty and start cradle robbing."

"Shut up, you dick," Cooper counters with an easygoing laugh, wrapping his arm around my waist. "Who's up first?"

"Your pick, bro." Jackson saunters over, gaze sliding to me for a beat. "You partnering up with me, or—?"

"I'm playing with T," he says. "We play together all the time."

Jackson nods slowly, smirking. "Cool, that just means I'll kick your ass."

"Not if we kick yours first," I shoot back.

My brother snorts. "You've never even played this, have you? Piece of cake."

I frown. "You play, so I doubt it's that hard to pick up."

"Ohh," Simone drawls, shadow boxing a one-two combo. "She got you, Jackson."

He narrows his eyes at her and lays off with a muttered, "Whatever."

I glance between my brother and Cooper to gauge if there's any lingering hostility between them after the way Jackson blew up at him for kissing me. As far as I can tell, they're back to hanging out. Jackson has kept to himself around our house, but I've heard them playing basketball in the driveway.

Cooper squeezes me in a half hug. "Ready? We're up first against Jackson and Ty."

I nod, latching on to the bubble of determination rising within me. "Bring it."

He grins. "That's my girl."

We move to one side of the table while our opponents move to the other. "How does the game start?"

Picking up the ping pong ball, Cooper positions me in front of the pyramid of cups on our side and puts it in my hand. He stands behind me. "The first shot is taken at the same time. Jackson usually does it when we play together. Stare him down and sink your ball first." His lips are warm, brushing against my ear as he lifts my arm and takes me through the motion of a practice throw so I get the feel for it. "You just stay loose and guide the ball like this."

Across from us, Jackson and Ty talk shit, but none of their words register past Cooper's rasped advice.

"You've got this, Tate."

His belief in me is palpable, boosting my confidence. It occurs to me I've come so far from the girl at the beginning of the summer so desperate to live my life, longing to fit in. All of my worries earlier were for nothing. A grin spreads across my face while the ocean air whips through my hair and I meet my brother's eye as he prepares to throw.

The crowd counts us down as a group, led by Simone. "3... 2...1...go!"

I don't blink or take my eyes off my brother as we both send our balls sailing. My heartbeat stutters when his hits between two cups and bounces off the table. Ty and Harris groan in unison. Mine rebounds off the edge of a cup, then circles the rim of another before sinking in. I forget to breathe for a second, until Cooper's rowdy whoop startles me.

Holy crap. I actually did it!

Cooper's arms circle around my waist and he lifts me off the ground. I can't stop smiling, soaring high on the feeling of success. We still have an entire game to play, but that first shot felt amazing.

"Damn, babe. You're a natural." He sets me down and cradles my face, hovering his broad grin over mine. "The more you show the world who you've been hiding, the more I can't help myself."

Before I can ask what he means, he seals his mouth over mine in a deep kiss that makes my brain go *oof*. People cheer around us. I savor the feel of him smiling into it until we part. He tucks my hair behind my ear, his piercing gaze stealing my breath.

"Are we playing or what?" Jackson calls.

"We're playing," I assure him. "That was fun and I want to do it again."

Cooper holds up his hand for the ball Ty tosses his way, catching it deftly. He drags his fingers through his messy hair and winks at me before taking his turn, sending the ball sailing smoothly into one of the other team's cups. Jackson hangs his head back.

My competitive spirit kicks in as the game continues, bolstered by discovering I have a knack for this. The first throw wasn't a fluke. Simone, Jenny, and I victory dance each successful shot while Cooper watches with a sexy smile that has me warm all over. Not long into the game, I find myself having fun.

I was afraid it would be hard to pretend in front of everyone because it would be obvious we were forcing it, but the fear evaporates. Pretending to date Cooper isn't that different from how we've always been. It's easy and natural to hold his hand, to hug him every time he sinks a shot, and to kiss him when we crush Ty and my brother. In every way, we feel like we fit together.

TWENTY-NINE
COOPER

For the first time ever, I walk into a meeting with my advisor without battling crippling dread that I'm fucking up my future. This confidence in my choices, in making a plan, must be how Tatum feels all the time. Thanks to her, I understand the appeal. It no longer scares the hell out of me to look ahead. I'm ready to put in the work to achieve everything I want.

"So, you're ready to declare a major, Mr. Vale?" Karl asks as I take my seat.

I wait for the stomach cramps and rapid pulse that used to come when I'd get overwhelmed thinking about the future, but neither happens. With a relieved smile, I nod.

"Hell yeah." A newfound courage floods my voice. Karl huffs in amusement, lifting a brow. I clear my throat. "Hell yeah, sir. I thought about it all summer and I know what I want to do now."

The idea of Vale Surf Co. shifts in my mind the more I think about it. Some days it's a surf camp intensive with a busy season aligning with South Bay's tourism, and others it's a school with workshops and classes. Once Tatum had my interests in physical things down, she made it easy to pick out a course schedule for the semester focused on balancing what I like with prerequisites that will lead to the degree I'll be studying for.

He scans my transcript paperwork spread across his desk. "I'm glad to see you prepared to apply yourself. This semester's schedule tells the story of a completely different person."

"Not totally different," I say. "Just getting serious about a lot in my life."

"Good. That's an attitude SBC likes to foster in the students here. So tell me more."

"I want to enter the business degree program." Karl nods along. I flex my hands on my thighs and continue. "With a minor focus in body science."

There's a moment's pause before Karl hums in surprise. "That's certainly the opposite of an undeclared major. You'll want to keep on top of your classes and assignments to keep your GPA in line with the credit requirements for those study focuses."

"I know. I'm prepared for all of that."

"As long as you're committed, you'll do fine."

His approval feels good. It strikes me that the first person I can't wait to tell about how this meeting went isn't my mom or dad, but Tatum. They know about my school plans after I talked with them to get their perspective on the goal of starting a business. I haven't told her yet.

On my way home after the meeting, I stop at the store to grab stuff for my classes. It's a first for me. Usually I wait until after they start to even think about getting a notebook or the required textbooks.

That kind of attitude towards my degree won't fly anymore. I'm serious about applying myself now that my future is becoming clearer. All I have to do is reach out and take it.

I pause halfway down the aisle of pens and sticky notes when a pack of pastel hearts catches my eye. The sticky notes remind me of Tatum and her huge collection of quirky notebooks and stationery armory to match every mood. I've watched her coordinate a notebook and highlighters with the focus playlist she chose for one of our study sessions—one where I wasn't undressing her and showing her every skill I have to make her come undone.

The corner of my mouth lifts and warmth expands in my chest. I grab the pack on a whim. It's like taking a small piece of Tatum with me.

* * *

"I still don't get why you wouldn't let me load up your car last night. We could've been on our way to campus by now." Tatum's Logic Tone drifts across the driveway as she and Jackson step out. "Moving day check-in starts at eight. Now we'll have to wait in line."

Jackson pulls a face and darts his confused look at me. "What are you talking about? Coop texted me yesterday to say we were taking the Jeep. It fits more of your shit. You don't even need half this stuff. We're only a forty minute drive from home."

My mouth twitches into a crooked smile when Tate whirls to face me. She takes in my loose gym shorts and fitted t-shirt, her attention lingering on my bicep perched on the hood of my ride. She looks damn good in a pair of blue tie-dye bike shorts that hug her ass and a flowy tank top that offers a peek at her sports bra.

"Morning, beautiful. All ready for move in day?"

"You're here," she blurts.

This plan was totally worth it for the pleasure of surprising her. She's not used to having a boyfriend to rely on, and I'm enjoying being there for her. It's the kind of guy I've always wanted to be. I'll work on planting the idea of us in her mind and grow the seed until she sees we're meant to be together.

"I am. Sorry, I didn't have time to grab us coffee like I promised." I adjust my backward baseball cap and shrug. "We can get something after we get you moved in."

Her brows raise at the plan she wasn't aware of, and she motions at me with a bright purple shower caddy full of toiletries. "As in, you're not already at campus."

A soft chuckle rolls out of me. "Why would I be there instead of helping my girlfriend move in?"

"Oh," she says in a small voice. She glances at her brother, realization crossing her face. "Well—"

"Move." Jackson nudges her aside. He circles around the Jeep and I follow him to help. "You two can make eyes at each other all you want on the ride, but let's get this loaded up first."

Between the three of us and Tatum's organizational skills, we have the Jeep packed in under twenty minutes. Out of habit, she goes for the back. Jackson smirks, cutting her off.

"I'll ride bitch. I'd rather zone out on my phone than watch you two sneak glances at each other or whatever in the rearview mirror."

A snort jerks my head. "We're not that lovesick."

What's nice about fake dating my best friend's sister—as far as she knows—is that things don't feel that different when we're hanging out. Other than his pissy groans when I kiss her in front of him. Worth it.

"You don't have to look at the two of you when you're around each other. For real, I don't know how I didn't see you were hooking up before." Tatum tenses, blood draining from her face. I curb the urge to react, keeping my face blank. Jackson shakes his head. "Like, you're so obvious, even when you're trying to be sneaky."

Tatum lets out a nervous laugh. "Okay, so don't keep so many tabs on us, stalker."

I rest my hand over the wheel when we climb in the front. "Did you have a smoothie for breakfast?"

She nods and flexes her cute little biceps that have nothing on mine. "Oatmeal, banana, and almond for energy."

"So a pit stop for breakfast burritos because I can see you bouncing in your seat with excitement from here. You'll burn off the energy boost before we even get there. I won't have you getting hangry on my watch."

Feeding Tate is a must. She's a hellacious terror when she's starving.

"Yeah," Jackson agrees from the backseat.

She opens and closes her mouth, conceding with a mumbled response. I grin as I back the Jeep out. I know her better than she knows herself some days.

The salty breeze shifts her hair as she makes a face at her phone camera, snapping a few photos. I catch a hint of that coconut scent I love.

"Marking the moment for your memories?"

Tate drags her fingers through her hair to hold it from the open windows and beams at me. "Yup. Me and Simone are sending them to each other. We're making a move in day scrapbook in a bullet journal we're sharing this semester to keep up with each other while we expand our horizons."

"You're acting like you're never going to see her," Jackson says from the back. "She's your best friend. You're both basically stuck to each other like barnacles all the time."

Tatum ignores her brother's grumbling tone. "Of course I'll see her. We both agreed we don't want to miss opportunities because we have our hearts closed to new friendships. That's why we're not rooming together. We still want to maintain our relationship, so that's where the shared journal comes in." She fishes it out of a small backpack purse and shows it off. "Plus, our schedules don't always align since we declared different majors. We only share one required core class together."

He meets my eye in the rearview mirror and shakes his head. "Chicks are so weird."

By the time we make it to campus, it's almost ten and a total madhouse of incoming freshmen arriving with their families. Me and Jackson moved in a few days ago, but only dropped off our things in our shared dorm before heading back home until freshmen were granted access.

Tatum smothers an excited squeal, her laser-focused gaze locked on the bright blue tent announcing itself as the check-in area. She's basically vibrating on a higher frequency.

"I really wish we'd gotten here when they opened," she says.

"Not everything goes to plan and that's okay. Ride with the flow instead of against the tide." I find an open spot along the unloading curb and snag it. "You head for check-in and we'll take care of this."

Tatum jumps out of the Jeep and hustles her way across the quad, slipping between other dazed freshmen staring at the campus buildings like a pro. I watch her with a dopey ass smile I don't bother hiding.

"We trained her well," I say. "She knows her way around better than we do."

Jackson scoffs. "You expect anything less from Tatum? She has the campus memorized. Wipe that look off your face and help me."

As we get Tatum's stuff stacked on the curb, I reach into the back seat and slip a bundle of fabric into her overnight duffel to surprise her with later. Her efficient packing makes my chest feel funny and I rub at it.

Everything is organized way better than anyone I've seen on campus. Not that I expected any different. It's Tatum, after all. I picture her researching tips for the best way to pack for college, scanning her overnight bag kept separate from the rest of her clothes, the box packed with school supplies, and the rest of her things neatly arranged. When I first moved to campus for my freshman year, it took me a week to find half of my stuff. She won't have that problem.

Darting a look her way, I find her chatting animatedly to another wide-eyed freshman. She points to us and waves. It's not long after when she joins us, blue welcome packet, South Bay College lanyard, and keys to her dorm in hand.

"All set?" I prompt.

She raises the key clutched in her fist. "Yes. Even though the line was long, they kept it moving pretty fast."

"You two go and I'll watch this," Jackson says.

Nodding, I pick up a box and walk with Tatum across the bustling quad. "I saw you making a friend."

"Yeah." Tate ducks her head. "She's an education major and seemed cool. It's not as hard to talk to people as I thought it would be."

I angle a lopsided smirk at her. "It was good we didn't get here when you wanted, or you wouldn't have met her. See? It's good to ease up on planning out every aspect of your day-to-day life."

"I guess." She sighs. "But I like knowing what to expect."

"CV! Yo, what's up, man?"

The guy calling my name from one of the dorm buildings we pass jogs to close the short distance between us. He nods to Tatum with his chin, then shoots me a knowing smirk. Yeah, I know my MO.

Adorable freshman, check. Move in day heavy lifting help, check. He thinks I'll have her in my bed tonight. I want that, but not for the reasons he thinks.

"Hi," she greets, sticking out her hand like it's a job interview. "I'm Tatum."

"'Sup, babe. I'm Matt." His attention shifts back to me. "We going to see you on the court? The guys are already picking our schedule from last year back up."

I shake my head, putting down the box in my arms. "When I can make it, I'll be there. We've got a study schedule worked out for the semester. I've got to buckle down this year instead of coasting."

Matt laughs. "Studying? You?" His gaze slides to Tate and he eyes her appreciatively. "You've got to tell me where to find the cute tutors then, because that's the only way to get my ass in the library."

I frown, fighting the surge of annoyance. He's a good guy, but too much like the player I used to be. "Tatum's not my tutor, man. She's my girlfriend."

"My bad." He turns to her. "I didn't mean anything by it. CV isn't the long term type."

A sharp burn stings my chest until her soft voice cuts through it.

"People change. For the right person, anyone can be," she says.

"Word, girl." Matt holds up his hand for a high five. She waits a beat before clapping her palm against his. "Aight, I'll catch you guys later."

"He seems like a real charmer," she says once he saunters off. "I'm sorry if my schedule messed up your usual plans. You should've said something when we were picking out classes."

"It's all good. I can catch a game at the gym with those guys any day."

"Okay. But talk to me if you want to make changes."

"Nah. See, my plan's working like a charm. He checked out your ass when we left." My easy smile remains in place, but I have the insistent urge to deck him for it. Tatum is mine.

"Why? You just introduced me as your girlfriend. Isn't that, like, against bro code to go for your friend's girl?"

Her head turns to look back and I stop her, tugging her closer so she's fitted against my side. "It's the way guys are wired. We want what we can't have. If we see a hot chick dating someone, some part of us wishes we could have her. I guarantee you at least five guys see me all over you right now, taking notice of you."

"The male psyche is so interesting in how much it differs from female logic," she murmurs breathlessly as I tease the sensitive skin of her neck with my lips.

"Let's get this dropped off at your dorm. I know you're dying to see it."

We continue down the wide walkway for two more buildings before we reach her new assigned residence in Huntington Hall.

"Third floor," she announces eagerly.

Third floor and no elevators in this dorm. Awesome. I'm definitely counting today as leg day.

Tatum glances around the room when we get there and sets her bag down on the bed closer to the window. "You didn't have to do this, you know. You could've squeezed in one more day to yourself before we go all in with our little fake relationship show."

"Nah, babe." I find a spot for her stuff and swipe a hand over my baseball hat, flexing the worn in brim. "Good boyfriends totally do all the heavy lifting on move in day. I'm not about to leave you high and dry."

The corner of her mouth lifts. "Thanks." She turns back to her overnight bag and sighs happily as she unzips it. "Um—"

I curb my grin, watching her discover the other surprise I've left for her. She pulls out the bundle of t-shirts, muscle tanks, and a light hoodie I stuffed in her duffel bag.

"Where did these come from? I don't remember packing them."

A chuckle slips past my lips as I step behind her, circling my arms around her in a bear hug. "For nights when you miss me." I kiss her cheek, then spin her to face me. Her perfect lips part and heat burns in her gaze. With a wolfish smirk, I trail my mouth to her ear. "For you to keep up with your homework assignments."

Her breath hitches. "You want me to keep up the sexy selfies here?"

"Advanced class. Think you've got what it takes to pull it off?"

"Yes."

The indignant huff she pushes out makes me laugh again. I press the curve of my mouth to her soft skin beneath her ear. "You have no idea how much I want to see you wearing my clothes."

"Coop," Tate whispers thickly.

She tilts her head for a kiss, but we're interrupted by the arrival of her new roommate. The girl pauses on the threshold and takes in the way we're wrapped around each other.

"Hey. Tatum, right?"

"Yeah." She clears her throat and untangles herself. I keep an arm slung around her waist. "This is my boyfriend, Cooper. He's a sophomore with my brother here."

It feels great every time she calls me her man. "'Sup."

"Alison." She squints at me. "Room rule: sexual partners welcome, but no surprise booty calls while we're both here."

Tatum holds up her hands. "God, no, of course we wouldn't. I'll, uh—"

"It's chill." Alison relaxes from her stern demeanor with a soft smile. "You didn't seem like the type when we chatted on messenger. I've read about some roommate horror stories on Reddit, though. Just let me know if you need the room to yourself, and I'll do the same."

I choke back a snort. I like Alison's vibe. These two will get along just fine.

"Right." Tate blows out a breath and returns the smile. "Sounds perfectly fair."

"I'll go get Jackson and the rest of the boxes." Before I go, I take her hand and squeeze, leaning in with a smirk. "Advanced class."

Tatum nods, the determined look I've grown addicted to settling on her face.

THIRTY
TATUM

Every time I've pictured how things would be when I started at South Bay College, it was completely different from how it's been in the last week since I moved in on campus. I feared I'd feel so far behind everyone, like a kid pretending to fit in with people way more mature. Except I haven't felt that way once. I trace the back of a paint pen I've been using to decorate the daily spread in my to-do list journal down the floral page of the dreams and goals planner I kept in the basket under my bed before college began.

New friends? Check.

After the first meeting with my roommate, Alison and I have fallen into a comfortable dynamic. We're both practical and a good fit for each other. And Jenny, the bubbly girl I met at one bonfire this summer, messaged me to meet her outside our first shared General Psychology 1 0 1 class today.

Not starting college with my V-card? Check.

Check, check, checkity-check check. I bite my lip around a smile, shivering at my desk. I'm still rocking the delicious ache between my legs from last night when Cooper was over to watch a new episode of my favorite nature documentary while Alison had plans. We got five minutes in before making out led to losing our clothes and tangling ourselves together.

His rough order still echoes in my head. *Hands on the table, Tate. Keep them there.*

Boyfriend? Check.

Well, a fake one. But Cooper makes sure he fulfills every expectation I could possibly have about having a boyfriend before I've even thought of it. I'm not exactly practicing my newfound experience with anyone else, but I haven't thought about my original plan while I'm focused on helping him.

The door opens and Alison comes in with a towel wrapped around her head, fresh from a shower. She hooks a thumb at the door. "Your boyfriend is headed this way."

"What?" I check the time on my phone. My first class starts in a little less than an hour. Gathering my bag and my notebooks, I rush past her while she puts away her shower caddy. "Later."

Outside my door, he's there, one hand raised to knock and mouth tugged up at the corner.

"Beat me to it," he says.

I toss a glance over my shoulder and whisper. "What are you doing here?"

"I'm walking my beautiful girlfriend to class." His smirk stretches. "And to bring you this."

"Thank you." I accept the coffee cup he hands me, pausing at the pastel purple heart-shaped paper stuck to the side. "What's this?"

Plucking it off, I recognize his handwriting. It reads *good morning, gorgeous. Coffee is just an excuse to see you.* A thud echoes in my chest and the tips of my ears feel warm. Is this legit, or is this part of our act?

He steps closer while I'm distracted, taking my bag from my shoulder. "Ready to go?"

"I can carry those. You don't have to." Peeking around, I check that we're alone in the hall. "No one's even here to see you being all boyfriend-y right now."

"Nah, I'm doing it." He presses his lips to my forehead under the ploy of being sweet if anyone pops out of their dorm and mutters, "We agreed it's better to just keep the act going so we don't slip up."

It's the thing we decided last night, but I didn't think it would start so soon. He's right though. I close my eyes and breathe in his scent to ground myself.

"Did you sleep good, or stay up too late hyping yourself up for today after I left?"

My mouth quirks. "I slept great. Didn't you get my homework photo?"

He groans, gripping the material of my dress at my hip. "Yeah. You in bed on your stomach, wearing my shirt with the hem up high to give me a peek of your ass? I had to jerk off again before bed."

"Your shirt was very comfortable as pajamas." I need to redirect us before we end up finding the nearest private space to give in to the desire clear in his unwavering gaze. "Come on, I want to get a good seat as soon as the professor opens the door. According to what I could research on student forums, she favors students who show they want to be there."

"In an intro-level course?" He hums and takes my hand. "Most of my professors last year were pretty lax."

"And that's probably how you ended up where you were before we assessed your options."

"Probably." He shrugs. "Thankfully I have a secret weapon to keep my ass in line this year. It's do or die time."

"Oh yeah, what's that?"

He gives me that broad grin that makes my heart trip over itself. "You, baby."

I shake my head with a breathy laugh. We make it downstairs and head into the early morning sunshine splashing across the quad in the middle of the five dorm buildings.

Cooper lifts his phone while we walk across campus and tilts his head in my direction when he begins recording a TikTok. "It's the first morning of classes. I just picked up my girl and brought her coffee. It's T's first year here. Say hi, baby."

He angles the camera to me, lifting his brows and squeezing my hand when I stare. I quickly wave and hide a blush behind a sip of coffee. He chuckles and swoops in to plant a kiss on my cheek.

"So cute when you're shy." He addresses the camera again. "My marketing class doesn't start until eleven, but Miss Smarty Pants over here loves learning and decided early morning classes across the board were the way to go. Part two of our first day vlog will be linked in the comments in a bit. Catch you on the flip."

He ends with a hang ten hand gesture, sticking out his tongue and scrunching one of his eyes shut. I wait until he finishes posting before propping my chin on his arm while we walk. "So we're fake vlogging to your followers, too?"

"Hell yeah. Viral marketing, right?" He shoots me a lopsided smile. "We've gotta hit this from all sides. Besides, my followers have been hounding me for an update."

I sink my teeth into my lip. "Are they so eager to get confirmation South Bay's most legendary player is single again?"

Cooper stops, his easy smile faltering. Instead of answering, he plays with my hand. "At first, I was worried as hell that was the case."

My throat tightens at the distant bitterness in his eyes. It's like they've lost their light and I don't like seeing him like this. I search for something to say to help chase away the melancholic look on his face, but everything I think of feels forced. At a loss for what to do, I step into him and hold his hand tighter. He meets my gaze and those handsome brown eyes regain a spark of light.

Exhaling heavily, his shoulders relax and his mouth quirks up at the corners once more. "But that's not the case. They're invested in us, T. They want to hear all about our relationship. Check out the comments and see for yourself."

"Okay. After class, though. I can't be late on the first day."

He huffs in amusement. "You'll be fine."

"If your followers want updates, should we meet up later to plan out what to post when?" I bite my lip as a sense memory of Cooper's teeth scraping my neck hits me. "I know we only got so far with our game plan last night."

His eyes hood as he trails his gaze over me. The tip of his tongue swipes across his lip.

"Hey guys!"

A chipper voice breaks the irresistible tension building between us. Jenny waves from the entrance to the building most of my classes are in this semester with more enthusiasm than even most morning people have. While I'm in a breezy peach cotton skater dress with a jean jacket and Birkenstocks, she's fully done up in a boho crop top with a matching high waisted skirt that has a slit up to mid thigh and strappy platform sandals. I wave back with my coffee cup, lifting my fingers.

"You're revved up for class," I say in surprise when we reach her. When we danced together at Mariner's Cove, I totally took her for a party girl at first. "I think you've even got me beat."

"I'm a night owl." She rustles her beachy blonde waves. "I haven't been to bed yet. But after this class, I can crash until three. I thrive better that way. My mind is alive at night. Aced all my standardized testing thanks to micro study sessions between one and two, then four and five in the morning."

"Find your optimal energy level, right?" A thrill runs through me. This is what I've been looking forward to for years. College life, meeting people, yet still engaging in stimulating academic conversation. "That's great. You know what works best for you."

"Totally. The brain is so cool like that."

"Yes!"

The eager outburst escapes me before I can rein myself in. Cooper squeezes my hand and a low chuckle leaves him. Clearing my throat, I peek at him through my lashes and find him smiling at me fondly.

"Have a good class, ladies. See you later, babe." He winks, sauntering backwards away from the building and melding in with the early flow of students milling around campus.

"Girl, I can't believe that guy is your boyfriend. He's so hot." Jenny hooks her arm with mine and leads us into the squat building with Spanish mission style roof tiles. "Then again, the way he looks at you is goals AF. Gah! I'm so single. Your sweet couple-ness makes me miss being in a relationship."

"Uh, yeah." I cough awkwardly. "You should've seen him when he was ten. He was all legs."

She lifts her brows dramatically. "Stop it. You've known each other that long?"

"Since I was four and he moved in next-door. He's my brother's best friend."

"Um, yes please. High key romantic to end up together."

I swallow, keeping my friendly smile in place. It still feels weird to lie about, even if it's helping him kick the playboy reputation. All I can think about is how it's all fake. How the only thing we can ever have is fake, no matter how good it feels when he kisses me. Because even if my brother has accepted that we're together, Cooper still wouldn't actually go for me if he had the chance.

Before I throw out my coffee cup, I take off the note he wrote me and stick it in my planner to save it. Fake or not, it's the first time a boy gave me a sweet note.

* * *

Cooper is waiting outside of the room when class lets out. He pops away from leaning against the wall with a charming expression once he spots me.

"Miss me?" he asks when he closes the distance between us and slips an arm around my waist to pull me against his firm body.

Glancing around with a subtle flick of my eyes, I find we're being watched. Right. Time to play up our act as boyfriend and girlfriend.

"Yes." I wind my arms around his neck, pressing on tiptoe to reach.

"This is a nice greeting." His murmur is only loud enough for me to hear.

"Too much?"

I move to pull away, but he keeps me in place, massaging my waist. Leaning in, he brushes his lips over mine in a soft kiss that makes the rest of the world melt away. He waits until my body relaxes against him before drawing away.

"Come on." Coop takes my bag, silencing my feeble protest, and slings it over his shoulder before threading his fingers with mine. "Jackson just texted before your class finished that he grabbed a table in the student union. We should get there before Simone and him try to eat each other alive."

I smirk. "You'd think after years of trading snarky barbs, they'd find some kind of middle ground."

He snorts. "I think they like the tension. One of these days it's going to snap between them. One of them definitely thought about it. Bet."

"Shut up." Laughter cuts through my words. I elbow him as he leads us from the building to meet up with the others for lunch. "Gross, I don't want to think about my brother boning my best friend."

"Who says it's not Simone boning him?" He waggles his eyebrows, then lets out an *oof* when I attack again with my elbow. "Fair, fair. No more talk of boning."

"Thank god." I aim for a stern tone, but I can't keep the smile off my face.

He leans close, lips grazing my ear. "Unless we're talking about the things I want to do to you. Because I like thinking about that all the time."

The low, rasped words send heat spilling through me. It pools between my legs and leaves me short of breath. How can he still affect me so much that I want him all the time?

"How was your marketing class?"

I swiftly change the subject to cool my head, but I'm genuinely interested to hear how he likes the classes I helped him select to achieve his goals.

"It was good." He pauses to hold open the door to the student union for me. "We only went over the syllabus, but it all sounds interesting. There's a section on social media which I think I'll like."

"That's great!" To see him looking forward to his classes after he asked for my help in the summer fills me with joy.

Simone, Jackson, and Ty wave us over to a corner table in the back of the cafeteria by the window. We join them and she pops up, grabbing my hand before I sit next to Cooper.

"I've already scoped out our new favorite place," she says. "But we have to hurry, because it's been popping since I got here and I only have another forty-five minutes before my class."

The guys bump fists and slouch in their chairs. Cooper motions to the pasta bar before heading that way while me and Simone get in line for a grille that smells amazing. Two more people quickly join the line behind us.

"So my general psych class? It's awesome," I gush. "I didn't get to text you about it, but I already love my professor. She opened today's introductory class with an open debate on what we think psychology is. I was living my best life."

"Yeah? Good, I'm glad. I have a bio lab for my first day. Blah." She sticks out her tongue. "But once I get this class out of the way for the credits, I'll breathe easier."

"You know I'll help in a heartbeat if you need a study partner."

"Yeah, if you can let me join your little study club with Coop." Her tone is sly. I snap my head around to make sure no one figures out the double meaning—what my study time with him originated as. She laughs and hugs my arm. "Come on, bestie. That was your opening. I'm living on the crumbs Cooper's posted online for his simp army. Don't I get best friend perks here? I'm being patient, but damn, girl. The desert is dry and a bitch is thirsty for details."

Guilt slams into me again for not telling her this time when I needed her perspective before with the old arrangement. Playing pretend for everyone else is difficult, but lying to my best friend's face is impossible.

Taking a breath, I search the room for Cooper. He's back at the table with a bowl of pasta, laughing with Ty and my brother.

"It was after that day on the beach." This veers from the story we told Jackson and everyone else, but she knew the truth then. "He took me back to his place and—"

My cheeks prickle. She grins, suppressing a little squeal as she pokes me in the side.

"He said he wanted to kiss me anytime he wanted," I finish.

It's vague for her sake. Enough of the truth that I don't feel like crap for hiding this from her when we tell each other everything. She would understand why if I explained, but this isn't just my plan anymore with Cooper helping, so I don't want to betray his trust either.

"Knew it," she mutters in satisfaction. "Okay, split a Mediterranean build-your-own flatbread pizza with me?"

"Yes."

Back at the table, I don't make it into my seat before I'm yanked sideways onto Cooper's lap. Simone takes a seat across from me between Ty and Jackson, nudging our pizza closer.

"Really?" Jackson asks in a flat tone, dropping his sub to the plate.

A strong arm winds around my waist. "Try this."

I have a fraction of a second to process before Cooper lifts a bite of his pasta. I part my lips for him, meeting his eyes as he feeds me. The tart red sauce bursts with flavor on my tongue and I hum in enjoyment.

"Good, right?" His thumb brushes away stray sauce from the corner of my mouth and he licks it clean. "Knew you'd like it."

Simone swivels our pizza tray back and forth. "Well, as cute as that was, we have pizza crafted by the combined genius—"

"And hunger cravings," I interject.

"And our hormonal-induced cravings," Simone adds dutifully. "So this is about to rock."

"Dude," Ty complains.

He catches mine and Simone's unimpressed looks. Cooper chuckles, unbothered.

"Girls talk about their period. Get over it," Simone says.

"Let me in on this pizza masterpiece."

Coop pats my hip and waits. I rip off a piece of my slice and offer it to him. The warm touch of his lips meeting my fingers startles me. He covers by hugging me against his chest, splaying his palm across my stomach. It dips beneath his hand and I can't help squirming.

"Dude." It's Jackson's turn to complain.

"You're right, Simone." Humor laces his voice. "That was the best damn bite of pizza I've ever had."

It feels like every eye in the room has to be watching us after that public display. I have to remind myself that's the point of all this while my stomach flutters. It's all to help Cooper, and I'll give that my all.

So far, so good. People are eating up me and Tatum being together from the palm of our hands. If everyone else believes us, my hope is that it helps back me up to gradually convince her she doesn't need anyone else because she has me.

On top of that, I'm finding I actually enjoy my classes. The material interests me, unlike the random classes I picked last year to collect credits without any idea of what I was doing. Now that ideas for my future are taking shape in my mind, I have the drive to do what it takes to get there.

There's energy in my step as I enter the library. It's still early in the semester, only a couple of weeks into classes. I never really came here before. When I chose to study—a rare occurrence—it was always in my dorm.

Normally I'd be hitting the court or the gym with the guys I play basketball with. This year is different. Tatum meets me three times a week at the library at night.

There's a party we could be at, but Tatum insisted on study time. Strangely, I find I don't miss partying as much as I used to. As long as I get some down time to shoot hoops with my friends and get to see Tatum as often as possible, I'm content.

Somehow I beat her here. A grin spreads across my face as I

saunter through the first floor of the library to claim the table I've come to think of as ours. I get my stuff set up and pick off the next paragraph of a paper due in my marketing class next week. The topic I picked on effective communication has me thinking about how I might use the strategies I'm describing to earn the trust of a potential customer if I opened up a surfing business after I earn my degree.

A girl at the table next to ours keeps peeking over at me. It's not out of the ordinary if I'm recognized from my TikTok account. This is a good opportunity to keep working the reputation we've been building as the couple everyone's heard of on campus.

I take out a pad of the heart-shaped sticky notes I've been leaving for Tatum every chance I get and scribble something I know will earn me her cute little smile when she reads it. I plaster it to the table beside me and wink at the girl watching this play out.

"Oh my god, you actually beat me?"

At Tatum's surprised tone, I lean back in my seat, a sarcastic retort on the tip of my tongue. The smug grin immediately drops off my face once I see her. Holy fuck. Is she for real?

I left her some of my clothes, but I never pictured she'd go out in them, broadcasting that she's mine to the entire campus. The thought ignites a rush of possessiveness. My t-shirt is too big for her. She knotted it at her hip, giving me a peek of skin above her white tennis skirt.

Dirty thoughts flood my mind, picturing all the things I want to do to her while wearing this outfit. Focusing on studying while she's so close to me without being able to touch her is going to be a torturous challenge.

Pulling out the seat next to mine, she allows her bag to slump off her shoulder to the floor with a tiny pout. "I was on the phone with my mom and lost track of time. I can't believe you seriously beat me here. I'm losing my edge."

All I've got in response is a helpless shrug, too distracted by the blood flow rushing to my dick at how hot she looks in my shirt with that little flared workout skirt. My hands flex to keep from grabbing her hips and dragging her onto my lap to grind against her ass like a caveman. It's a good thing I wore jeans today, because hiding a boner in gym shorts is impossible.

Unaware of her effect on me, she says something about her parents before pausing to read the note. It says *I've been looking forward to seeing you all day* even though I saw her for lunch, and picked her up this morning for her early class as usual. The note does the trick. She uses it to cover her pretty blush, which gives the handful of students in the study area an eyeful of what a great boyfriend I am.

"Thank you," she murmurs as she tucks the note into one of her notebooks.

I lick my lips slowly, raking my gaze over her. "You look good in my shirt."

So fucking good.

"Oh." Tate ducks her head, fluttering her hand over her stomach. "Well, it's laundry day. Um, so yeah."

"Yeah..." My smoky response trails off and I skate my palm up her leg to the hem of her skirt. "I can work on my paper later. Want to run through your practice test questions first?"

An idea forms in my head when she doesn't immediately freak out with my hand resting on her thigh, hidden from the table next to ours by the way I turn my body to face her. No one occupies the other table on her side.

"Sure."

She bites her lip, dropping a hand into her lap to loosely wrap her fingers around my wrist. To anyone paying attention to us, we could just be holding hands. Her eyes lift to peek at me through her lashes. She's thinking about the same thing as me when we turned our studying into a dirty game where correct answers meant more pleasure.

"Quiz me?" Tatum prompts quietly.

The corner of my mouth lifts. When she first came to me, spontaneously fooling around like this would've made her nervous in private, let alone in public. She's come so far from the girl bargaining with me to dick her down so she could analyze and learn from the experience.

I hold out my hand for the practice test her professor passed out in class this week. She's been studying it so often that I have half the questions memorized. I scan the sheet and pick one at random.

"What is visual sensory memory referred to as?"

"Iconic memory."

"Good girl." My fingertips trace a circle on her inner thigh. I know it's a sensitive spot for her. When she suppresses a soft sigh, I cock my head with a satisfied tilt to my lips. "Next one. It's theorized that repression is an example of what?"

"Motivated forgetting."

I hum, dragging my fingers higher, stopping short of her panties. Reaching across us to her bag, I get a pen from her organized supplies case with a bright citrus fruit pattern. She tries to read what I'm writing on her test. I distract her by stroking her clit through her panties until I finish.

Eyes gleaming, I tap the question and angle the paper so she can see.

Are you wet yet, baby?

Her lips part and her eyes widen, darting around. She doesn't answer, but I don't need one.

"Ready for the next question?" It's my way of checking if she's still in or if she wants to stop.

Her chest rises and falls as a student walks by on their way out. She tracks him with her gaze and whispers, "Give it to me."

Shit, that's exactly what I want to do. I'm getting worked up the more I tease her. I have to keep reminding myself I can't rip her panties aside and push my fingers inside her the way I'm dying to.

We keep going like that. I throw a test question at her and she responds, her breathing growing strained. For each correct answer, I tease my fingers where she has to be aching and hot for my touch by now, going off the way she keeps doing these abortive little rocks of her hips to seek pressure against her clit without being obvious.

After another question, my gaze locks on her mouth. Her lips are swollen from nibbling on them to keep quiet.

Instead of answering, her quaking thighs clamp together, trapping my hand. "Coop."

The whispered plea is frayed and needy. I know that tone well. My girl needs to come. Badly.

"We can't," she breathes. "I can't stay quiet, please."

She's so goddamn gorgeous like this. I squeeze her thigh and lean into her. The corner of my mouth kicks up at the hitch in her breath when I brush against her panties again. "Come with me."

"What? Where?"

"We've earned a break from studying," I rasp against her ear. "Come on, baby. Live a little with me." My tongue darts out to trace the shell of her ear. "Promise to make it worth it."

At her uneven exhale and small nod, a low chuckle rolls out of me. Glancing around, I check that no one is paying attention and take her hand.

"Come find a book with me." I swipe my tongue across my bottom lip, trying to stay serious. "I need to reference it for my assignment."

Tatum tries to hold back a smile, attempting to give me a mock-stern look as I lead her to the stairs to go up to the next floor while desire brims in her eyes. The library might be quiet tonight, but if I'm going to get her to let go the way she needs to right now, we have to find the section least likely to get a visit from any student or staff. Just the idea that we could get caught for doing this, that's the thrill I want to give her.

We climb two floors, then cut through the science journals section. If I don't get a taste of those perfect lips, I'll go out of my mind. I can't wait until I find the right spot after teasing both of us for the last twenty minutes.

Halfway down one of the stacks, I stop to push her back against the shelf, slamming my mouth over hers. She arches into me with an urgent noise. My fingers twist in the material of her shirt—the one I gave her—and tug her closer as my dick throbs. My girl in *my* shirt, driving me fucking crazy with that peek of skin at her hip.

"Fuck," I bite out when I break the kiss. "Not yet. Let's go, T."

I thread my fingers with hers and we keep moving across the floor, both of us short of breath. She breaks on the next flight of stairs, reaching for me with a needy little cry that sends a spike of heat straight to my cock while she kisses me on the shadowy landing between floors. A smoky laugh escapes me and she swallows it hungrily.

We've never been so insanely desperate to fuck before, and I'm riding the high of wanting her so damn badly.

After another flight, we're on the fourth floor. According to Tatum, this is the least used part of the library. It's one of the random factoids and observations she told me about the first week of classes. I'm glad I filled it away as a potential make out spot. Past Cooper did present me a solid.

The floor is deserted. Even the lights are dimmed compared to the other floors, only one set of lights on. It adds to the illicitness of sneaking up here to get off. We move through the bookshelves until I'm satisfied we're hidden away in the back row.

"We don't have a lot of time." Tatum keeps her voice low even though we're the only ones up here.

Grinning wolfishly, I herd her back against the shelf for another searing kiss that leaves her panting by the time I trail my lips along her jaw to suck on her neck. "Don't worry about that. I just want you to focus on how good I'm about to make you feel."

"Oh god," she pushes out as I sink to my knees. "Why is it so fucking hot when you do that?"

Skimming my hands up her thighs, I meet her eyes and peel her panties down. She grasps the shelf and my shoulder for balance, stepping out of them. I shove them in my back pocket and fist the material of her skirt, holding it up out of my way.

Leaning in, I swipe my tongue through her folds, enjoying her bitten off gasp as much as I savor the first taste of how wet she is. Smiling widely, I cover her pussy with my mouth. I can't help myself. I love doing this to her more than I've ever loved doing it to any other girl.

When I look up and see her features twisted in ecstasy, all I want to do is make her fall apart. I hover over her and spit on her clit before pushing my face between her thighs for more, giving it to her sloppy.

"Shit, oh shit, please," she begs.

Holding her hip, I swirl my tongue on her clit, willing to suffocate if it means an earth-shattering orgasm for her.

"Yes, ah!"

With a garbled cry she attempts to keep quiet, Tatum leans against the shelves, panting as her body quivers from the soft kisses I brush over her wet pussy. God, I could eat her all fucking night. Part of me wants to, but I want to feel my cock inside the tight heat of her body as I make her come again even more.

I get a condom from my wallet and rise to my feet, kissing her again as I blindly undo my jeans and pull out my cock. Her fingers cover mine as I pump myself. Once I have the condom rolled on, I grab the back of her thigh.

"Hop up."

I lift her into my arms and her legs wind around my waist. Reaching between us, I line up and sink inside with a wrecked exhale. It's pure heaven every time my cock is buried in her pussy. My hand slips beneath the shirt I gave her to massage one of her tits as I fall into a rhythm that gets her wetter with each thrust.

Our eyes meet. Hers are heavy-lidded in the dim light, her lips parted on a silent cry. I claim her sweet mouth with mine.

It doesn't matter how many times we've been together since she first came to me. Every time feels like a perfect drop into a cresting wave, a rush that I want to ride forever.

Keeping her supported with one arm, I cup her face as we kiss. Her arms loop around my neck and she moans softly.

We're completely wrapped up in each other until the squeak of a shoe on the steps makes us both freeze. My heartbeat pounds in my ears. I block her with my body, straining my ears to listen. If we're quiet, we should be good. Unless it's a security guard.

Craning my neck, I peek through the small gaps in the book-shelves and spot a student with headphones on. He's two aisles away with his back turned to us. As long as he doesn't come this way, we're golden.

Tatum tugs on my shirt, her pussy fluttering. Is this getting her hotter? Turning back to her, I smile and cover her mouth with my hand.

"We're good," I whisper. "He's going to get a book and leave. He can't hear us, but I need you to stay quiet, baby."

As I murmur, I rock into her slowly. Her gasp of pleasure is muffled against my palm. I move at a steady pace that has her clinging to me.

I keep my head angled, darting my gaze between her and the student oblivious to what we're doing. Each time my cock sinks into her, she shivers, her eyelashes sweeping her cheeks. I'm captivated by the wild and erotic look on her face, wishing I could fuck her hard and fast to make her scream for me.

Once the student's footsteps finally echo in the stairwell after a few minutes, I move the hand covering her mouth and sink my fingers in her hair. Putting my lips to her ear, I speak in a filthy tone as I drive into her. "I could feel how close you were because we almost got caught. How badly you wanted to. Don't hold back. Come. Come for me."

Her body shudders against me, her inner walls tightening. She gasps and curses, burying her face against my shoulder as another shiver wracks her body.

"So good for me, pretty girl. I love it when you come on my cock."

Tatum's tongue swipes a stripe up my neck as she wraps her legs tighter around my hips to push me deeper inside her. "Fill me up."

Her hot little whisper rips a groan from me. She always surprises me when we're like this, revealing this sexy as fuck, confident girl I'm so goddamn gone for. I forget about staying quiet and not getting caught, snapping my hips to chase my orgasm. I only last another handful of thrusts before it hits.

Muscles tensing as my cock throbs inside her, I drop my head to her shoulder for a moment to catch my breath. After pulling out, I carefully let her down and smooth her white skirt down to cover her before I take care of the condom and tuck myself away.

If there wasn't a chance of getting caught, I'd give in to the desire to get on my knees again to keep eating her until she's a beautiful mess. That's what we're doing the next time I get her alone.

Pulling away, I give her a lopsided grin. She tips her head back against the shelves, gorgeously flushed and fucked out. My favorite look on her.

"What?"

"Worth it."

I smother her giggle with another kiss, winding my arms tight around her waist.

Once she's satisfied it's not obvious what we did, we head downstairs, pausing at the top of the stairwell to ditch the tied off condom in the trash. A smirk tugs at my lips as I watch the swish of her skirt on the way down, knowing she's still bare beneath it.

My hand pats my pocket and I chuckle in satisfaction. The look Tatum shoots me is shy with a hint of mischief at the secret freedom she's rocking beneath her skirt. I'm keeping her panties so I'll always remember tonight.

THIRTY-TWO
TATUM

The thing about pretending to date South Bay College's most notorious player is that everyone knows him. In turn, that means everyone now knows me. By the end of the first month of the fall semester, it seems like everyone has dubbed us SBC's it couple.

"Hey girl!" A student I've seen around my dorm's lounge on the first floor waves to me when Simone and I pass her on the quad.

"Oh, hi." I wave back.

"There's a mixer next weekend. Are you and Cooper coming?"

"Where at?" Simone asks.

"Hollis House." The girl plays with her hair. "It's pool party themed. You *have* to be there. It's like the party of the semester. But it totally won't be if you guys aren't there."

This is what I wanted, isn't it? Going to parties. Fitting in at college and feeling normal. I fit in, but only because I'm Cooper's girlfriend. Will I still get these invites when our agreement ends and we're no longer the campus' it couple everyone is so invested in?

I smile politely. "I'll text Coop and ask if he wants to go."

"Of course he wants to." The girl laughs like it's obvious. "Everyone will be in bathing suits. Couples have to match, so make sure you pick something good for you and Cooper."

My smile becomes strained. "Sure."

"Okay, we've got a date with our favorite build-your-own pizza masterpiece for dinner, so peace out." Simone hooks her arm with mine and leads me away.

"Bye!"

"Is it weird that everyone thinks they know me now because of Coop's viral TikTok game?" I ask.

"You don't have to go if you don't want to, dude. You know that, right?" Simone nudges me. "If it doesn't spark joy, then it's an immediate no."

I laugh. "Thank you, happiness guru."

"I do my best." She nods sagely. "But for real. And you know Cooper would support your happiness over anyone else's one hundred percent. The dude is totally gone for you."

"Yeah, I know." I bite my lip, unsure how much to say so I don't give away that we're faking this relationship. "I think I'm just not used to making plans on someone else's behalf. Like now, it's always *us* and *we*."

"Gross, that makes you sound married AF." She laughs, waving her hands in front of her while shaking her head. "I'm going to keep enjoying the single train and make pit stops to sample the local con*cock*tions on offer."

"You enjoy that."

For the first time, I don't feel the urge to do the same. I thought I wanted the experience I gained over the summer so I'd be ready, but I can't picture anyone making me feel the same rush of arousal I get when I'm with Cooper. I'm so deep in our cover story that I even have myself fooled.

"Oh, I will, babe. I will," she promises.

I crack up at her sly shimmy and eyebrow waggle, her off the shoulder top showing off her dark tan skin. We part ways when we reach our dorm building's lounge.

"Meet you back here in forty-five minutes?" she asks.

"Yup. It won't take me long to shower and change."

"Cool." She throws up two fingers in a peace sign.

When I reach my door, I find another heart-shaped note. A smile breaks free at the sight of the blue pastel paper. Cooper's so sneaky about coming by to leave them. Sometimes they're silly, sometimes sweet. Each one makes my heart flutter.

Plucking it off the message board hanging on the door, I read it.

You look pretty today. I like when you wear blue. Your smile made my day.

I roll my lips between my teeth, my cheeks flushing with a sweet warmth stirred by imagining him murmuring his message to me. I know he does this just for show, but every time he does it, my days seem brighter and more full of life.

Cooper's voice sounds behind me. I turn, expecting to find him in the hall, but he's not there. The door across from mine is open and I realize it's coming from there. Trying to be chill, I move closer, hanging outside in the hall. They must be watching one of his thirst traps.

"So I'm back today with my must-do list to keep ya girl happy. My dudes, if you're not worshiping her, you're doing it wrong."

The cocky, crooked smile in his voice is easy for me to picture. I haven't watched this video and it's not one of our planned out posts we've done to feed his followers couple content.

"One, always be ready to feed her. She says she's not hungry, but she probably is. Let the girl eat," Cooper explains. *"Two, give her kisses. Kiss her forehead. It makes her feel special. Kiss her hand. And I know you're not missing on kissing her everywhere else. Don't stop kissing her until she's getting all shivery and melting against you. That's how you kiss your partner. And let me tell you, if you can breathe, you're not doing it right."*

"God, he's hot and perfect," one girl in the dorm room says. "I would ten out of ten suck his dick. I bet it's as perfect as he is."

I freeze, guilty for listening in on them. A strange knot forms in my stomach. Am I jealous?

That would be irrational. I purse my lips, disappointed in myself.

Her roommate laughs. "Have you seen him come around? His girlfriend is on this floor. I think she's across from us. Look at his other videos. She's all over his account. Has been since late summer."

Before Cooper finishes his advice, I slip back across the hall.

I hold his note against my chest and go into my room to get ready for a shower. The line between fake and real is blurring beyond recognition. I thought I had this under control by focusing on helping him instead of getting caught up in my own feelings, but playing pretend is warping my sense of reality. What will the lasting psychological effects be?

Will I eventually believe our lie is true? And if that happens, if I forget the parameters of our agreement...will my heart survive it when the time comes to go back to being friends?

* * *

Cooper has me trained to react to the sound of my phone vibrating late at night, past open visiting hours in the freshman dorms. Heat spills through my core as his name lights up my screen while I'm sprawled across my bed writing the list of things I'm grateful for in my intentions spread of my bullet journal Friday night. Right now, I'm most grateful my roommate went home for the weekend, leaving me by myself in the dorm.

Cooper: Still up?

Tatum: Is that your booty call opener? Needs work.

Cooper: How? It's perfect. Neutral and low stakes. Better than going straight for the dick pic.

I giggle, abandoning my notebook.

Tatum: Okay, yeah. But obviously you're not going to do that unless you're alone. Hopefully.

Cooper: I'm not totally alone.

He sends a video. I open it, eyes widening at his crooked grin. A very familiar fabric dangles from his fingers. He swings his prize back and forth. They're my panties he took after we fooled around in the library last week.

Tatum: Thief.

Cooper: Fair game. You have my shirts, I get to keep a pair of your panties.

Tatum: My underwear wasn't part of our deal! And you gave me the shirts.

Cooper: They are now. You're not getting them back.

Tatum: What are you going to do with them? I sleep in your shirts. Are you saying you sleep with my panties?

Cooper: I'd rather have you in my bed. I can't stop thinking about those little sounds you tried to keep quiet in the library while I had my cock buried inside you.

Biting my lip, I close my eyes and relive one of the hottest experiences of my life before sending him a shy admission.

Tatum: I liked that a lot. It was seriously hot.

Cooper: So fucking hot, baby. Every time I think about your sweet little moans as I gave it to you, my cock gets hard.

A strangled cry catches in my throat at the photo he sends right after—shirtless, tan ripped body on display for me, gym shorts hanging low on his hips with his aroused bulge outlined by the fabric. The edge of his backwards cap is visible in the corner of the frame along with the smug, flirtatious tilt of his lips. *For me.* He's taking these seductive photos of himself for me, not any other girl. The thought leaves me breathless until my phone vibrates again.

Cooper: Are you a good girl for me?

I rub my thighs together as I type back a response. This time, he sends a voice message. Sometimes when we do this, he switches to voice messages when one of his hands is otherwise occupied. An illicit thrill arrows through me and I roll onto my back, my body warming. Heart thudding in anticipation of hearing his voice, I press play and bring the speaker to my ear.

"You're so good for me, T," he praises in a deep, sexy rasp. With a low curse and the rustle of fabric muffled in the background, he continues. "I want to see you. I want you to send me a picture of you in one of my shirts. And only that. Do that for me. Show me you're mine."

My stomach dips and my clit pulses with need at his request and filthy tone. I play the voice clip one more time, cheeks pricking with heat as my hand skates down my stomach to tease between my legs. I never voice chat him back, but I'm feeling bold tonight.

"You want to see proof I'm yours, Coop? Want to know I sleep in one of your shirts every night, bare underneath?"

Once I send my sultry message, his answer comes through in record time. I press play on the recording and let out a shallow breath at his reaction.

"Fuck. Yes." His voice is jagged and wild.

I slip off my underwear and get up on my knees, checking myself in the mirror my roommate hung on our shared closet. Out of all the sexy selfies I've sent Cooper, I feel the most like a vixen in this pose. Angling the phone slightly above me with the facing camera, I bunch the fabric of Cooper's shirt at my hip, giving just enough of a tease to tell I don't have anything on beneath it.

Cooper takes a few minutes to respond once I send the photo I like best. I expect a text back like when we've sexted before, but my phone rings with a FaceTime call instead. My heart pulses in panic, thinking it's my parents, but it's not.

FaceTime call with Cooper Vale fills my screen.

Oh my god. He's calling? We've never had phone sex before. Fire sings in my veins at the thought of watching without being able to touch each other in person.

Fumbling with the phone, I answer, only allowing the top half of my face to be seen. "Hi."

"Hey babe."

He scrubs his face, giving me a peek at the bulge of his bicep and his forearms. He's shirtless, laying back on his bed. The hand drops away from his face, running down his chest. His shoulder muscle flexes and his lips part. Is he—?

"You're so fucking sexy, T." Cooper grins. He's totally touching himself. "Let me see you."

"I, um."

My face grows hotter and I push out a nervous laugh. I like the idea of this, but doing it for the first time spontaneously when we didn't plan it out as a lesson is throwing me off.

"Tate, hey." His voice softens and he folds an arm behind his head. "I didn't mean to psych you out. We don't have to. It's cool if we go back to pictures and texting."

I shake my head. "No, I—I want to. You've got me all warm. Sorry."

"Don't be sorry. It's okay. This is new, but it's not any different." He brings his phone closer to his face, letting me see his dimples. "Go with it. Same rules apply. If it doesn't feel right, we can stop."

"What do I do?"

"I want to see you. Go stand in front of your mirror." As I get up, his voice lowers. "I'm going to tell you everything I would do to you if I were there. Your hand is my hand, got it?"

Swallowing, I nod. My nipples are already tight nubs from the want coursing through me, visible through his shirt. He groans when I flip the camera angle to show myself in the mirror.

"Shit, the sight of you in my shirt is the best damn thing in the world." His hand drops out of frame again and he releases another rough noise of pleasure as he strokes his cock. "We're starting off easy. Like when I made you touch yourself before, remember?"

"Yes, when you teased me until I wanted to come so badly." I bite my lip, peering into the mirror. "Tell me where to touch."

"I'm running my fingers up your thigh and teasing the bottom of the shirt. I don't dip under yet."

Following his directions, I skim my fingertips along the same path he dictates. My thighs press together as I imagine how his touch feels.

"Next I pull your hair out of the way and kiss the side of your neck," he rasps.

I lick my lips slowly, then bring my fingers to my lips and wet them so they feel like his kisses. Closing my eyes, I press my fingers to my neck, shivering.

"Coop," I whisper.

"That's it. Now I'm touching your tits."

We continue like that, my initial hangups abandoned as my body heats up. I'm enjoying this, my arousal heightened by the intensity of fantasy mixed with knowing he's watching.

"My turn," I murmur when my confidence grows.

His eyes hood. "Yeah? What are you doing back to me?"

He props his phone on the desk beside his bed so I can see more of him. He's shirtless, his shorts pushed down, his erection out, the tip making my mouth water with the desire to kneel between his knees and go down on him. I start with that.

"I'm on my knees and I suck you."

The corner of Cooper's mouth hitches up. He spits in his hand and closes it around his cock. He drops his head back, matching his pace to the way I usually blow him.

"Fuck, I wish your perfect mouth was really on me right now," he says roughly. "But I want more before I come, so I only let you have a taste for a minute before I get you up and out of that shirt."

He's playing dirty now. I'm not complaining. Setting the phone aside, I peel the shirt off and stand nude in front of my mirror. He curses, gaze raking up and down his screen when I pick the phone back up to show him.

"Look at you, pretty girl," he rasps. "The way I want to taste every inch of you. Play with your nipples."

I sink my teeth into my lip and suck in a hissing breath at the first brush. My breasts feel swollen and heavy, my thighs coated with slick wetness from his teasing. I arch my back as I pinch a nipple, my head falling back.

"So good," I moan.

"Yeah, baby. You look so pretty like this when I tease your nipples. Are you ready for me to fuck you?"

"Please," I beg. "Please, I need you to."

"I know, T. I've always got you. Move back to the bed and prop your phone on your desk. I want to see all of you while I fuck you."

My chest heaves with the uneven breath that gusts out of me as I scramble to follow his directions. I lean my phone against my pencil case wedged with my laptop. Once it's situated, I sit on the edge of my bed.

"Now spread your legs. Show me how much your pussy wants to get fucked." His dirty talk is killing me. He knows it, too. His eyes gleam as he stares at me through the screen when I open my legs wide. "Fucking beautiful. I love the sight of you wet for me. Lean back on one hand and run your fingers through your folds."

A flush spreads down my neck and across my chest. I can see it in the small version of myself in the corner of the screen. An ache builds in my core. I do as he says, swallowing a strained sound when the first glide of my fingers feels so damn good. My pussy feels more sensitive than ever, my clit throbbing with need.

His attention is intent, not taking his eyes off me. "Taste yourself. Tell me how sweet you taste." I lick two of my fingers and hum. "Yeah, like that. God, you look hot like that. Next I rub your clit and sink the first finger inside you."

Bliss spreads through me as I touch my clit at last. "Oh shit, that feels so good." My lips part and my hips rock in time with the circular movements of my fingers. "I won't last long. I'm so turned on by what you're doing."

"Me too."

I hiss as I press a finger inside, a thready moan escaping me.

"Now another finger," he says thickly. "I love watching you take me in."

My eyes fall shut as I lose myself to the fantasy, imagining it's Cooper's hand between my legs, his deft fingers working into me, making me feel so good. He goes faster, murmuring words of encouragement that send a burst of heat through me.

My inner walls clench on my fingers. A cry tears from me. I just need a little more.

Oh shit, I'm really close. "I want to come."

"Tatum, stop." Cooper's filthy tone makes my eyes pop open. He smirks at my trembling. "I know, baby. I know you're so close to falling apart. I want to see it more than anything. But there's something you have to promise first."

"What?" I'm breathless and ready to plead.

He rakes his teeth over his lip and his burning gaze pierces me through the screen. "Next time you touch yourself, promise to think of me. No one's touching what belongs to me right now. Got that? You only touch my pussy when you're thinking about me taking care of what's mine."

My stomach tightens at his thrilling words. How do I tell him he's always the one in my fantasies when I touch myself? That it's only been him for a long time.

"Yes. Only you, I promise."

"Good girl. Now you can make yourself come for me. Let me see you, baby." He rumbles in approval as I comply, his hand moving over his cock. "Those are my fingers fucking your pussy."

I gasp. "Yes."

"Wish it was my goddamn cock. I want to drive into you so bad." With a ragged breath, he speeds up, the sound of his jerking off obscene. "On Monday I have to fuck you on your break between classes. Wear a dress with easy access so I can eat your pussy before I make you ride me. Deal?"

"Oh god," I cry as my orgasm hits.

"Fuck, Tate." His words slur as he releases a wrecked sound.

My eyes fly open and I watch him come, muscles tensed, his handsome features contorted in pleasure. He's so damn hot. I keep circling my clit with my fingers as I watch, biting my lip as I slide into another eruption of ecstasy.

Once my body stops tingling with little aftershocks, I reach for the shirt and pull it over my head. Cooper hasn't hung up yet. He smiles lazily at the screen, always languid after he has an orgasm from my experience.

"This is the part of a FaceTime hookup that makes me wish I really was there." He huffs out a laugh. "I'm addicted to falling asleep with you after you come."

I tug on the neckline of his shirt and hide a smile. "I wish you were, too. I sleep better when you're holding me."

"How do you feel? You good?" he checks.

"Yeah. That was different, but really good." I grab my notebook as I climb into bed, not bothering to find my underwear. "Now I can check phone sex off my list in my sex journal. I also checked off public place since you smashed that one in the library. Not many things left on the list now. I'm almost a certified sexpert like you."

He gives me a heated look and smirks. "See you tomorrow. I'll bring you coffee. Goodnight, T."

THIRTY-THREE
COOPER

Hollis House is popping with tiki torches, metallic green streamer curtains, and a live DJ the following weekend. The Kappa Sig frat boys went all out for the party. Their place is packed, everyone wearing bathing suits and carrying pool floats. Unlike the bonfire parties over the summer, Tatum seems more relaxed now that she's had some practice. We got here an hour ago, and she's been deep in conversation with Jenny, the girl from her early morning psychology class.

"Jenny and I are hitting the dance floor. This song is her jam." Tatum hikes her clear pink flamingo float higher around her hips and presses on tiptoe to kiss my cheek.

"I said it was a bop," Jenny cuts in.

"Right, that." Tatum nudges her inflated flamingo head against the unicorn inner tube she picked out for me. "You coming? We can bump and grind the flamingo and unicorn."

"Is that a dirty euphemism?" I catch her around the waist and pull her back in for a kiss, toying with the loose tropical print fabric of her off the shoulder bikini top. It's a close match for the board shorts I have on. Before we arrived, we took photos and posted them to our social media accounts. "You go on ahead. I'm going to chill over here. Have fun. I will, because I'll be watching."

She's so pretty when she blushes. I wink before Jenny pulls her to the sandy dance floor the Kappa Sig guys set up in their living room inside an oversized kiddie pool. I lean against a fake tiki bar, enjoying the sound of Tatum's laugh as she dances with her friend.

I've been thinking about my plan. So far I've been fine with letting things progress naturally.

Kayla is here. I saw her with the other Theta Pi sorority girls when we got here. She keeps walking by with a couple of them, pointedly glancing my way. I'm not playing her games tonight.

I'm well aware of what she's doing. Her skimpy bikini shows more of her body than not, putting her on display for everyone here to see. That won't work. My dick is no longer interested when she flounces past me for the third time with her tits pressed out.

I feel nothing for her, no stir of arousal, no tug on my heart. It's hard to believe I ever saw anything in her or believed what we had was real. I used to look at this girl and think this was it, this was the relationship I was craving, who I wanted to rely on me to take care of her.

What I have with Tatum is more real, and it's a completely fake lie. In her eyes, anyway. For now, until faking it becomes real. Part of me worries if she's just going along for the act sometimes, but I think it's my own nerves about screwing this up.

Frowning, I swig the last of my beer and put the empty in the bucket by the bar. When I look up to continue watching Tatum, Kayla is making a beeline for me.

"Great," I mutter.

"Hey baby," she says once she reaches me.

I nod with my chin, giving the signal I'm not really down to talk. She ignores it.

"I've missed you." She pouts exaggeratedly. "I've hit up all the parties so far this semester, but this is the first time I've seen you out."

My shoulder hitches as my focus drifts to Tatum. "I'm studying hard this year."

"Studying?" Kayla laughs. "That's not like you. I didn't think you knew how."

It stings, but I let it go. Her opinion doesn't matter. Once Tatum showed me my strengths and the way my brain was wired, she figured out the best study strategies to help me retain the information.

"Anyway, I'm not partying as much."

She tilts her head, frowning at me. "You're so different now."

I narrow my eyes. "I'm really not."

I'm more focused, becoming who I want to be.

She moves closer, brushing her rack against my arm. It's not accidental. I know how she likes to tease a guy into her pants. Or her tiny bikini bottoms in this case.

When I shift over so she's not touching me, she huffs and closes the distance again.

"Kayla," I bite out. "I'm done playing around. Can you not right now?"

"What do you mean?" She acts innocent, but the determined glint in her eye is clear to see. "You're all alone over here. I'm just keeping you company."

"No, you know I'm here with my girlfriend." I point Tatum out. "See her over there dancing with her friend? So knock your shit off. I'm not interested in you. We're done."

"Cooper—"

She hates being ignored. Her bitchy tone is lost on me as I spot one of the frat guys flirting with Tatum. My teeth clench as the guy plays it off like he's dancing with Jenny and Tatum, but when he switches from Jenny back to Tate, he grabs her hips and slides his hands all over her stomach, creeping higher. Tatum frowns, trying to get his hands off. Jealousy and fierce protectiveness rocket through me as I stride across the room.

Kayla follows, making an annoyed sound.

"Dude. Anyone can see she's not into the way you're grabbing her." I shoulder him away, pulling Tatum behind me. "Do you not know how consent works?"

"Chill, bro, we're just partying over here. Don't kill the vibe. What's your deal?"

I grit my teeth. Tatum closes her fingers around my wrist. "My deal is that's my girlfriend you were about to feel up."

He sobers, holding his hands up. "My bad, man."

It's ridiculous that throwing down my claim on her is what gets him to back off more than the fact she clearly didn't want to dance with him while he grabbed her tits or ass. I don't waste another second on him. Turning to Tatum, I clasp her chin to tilt her face up.

"You okay?"

"Yeah. Thanks babe." She darts her gaze around at the small crowd watching the drama unfold, pausing on Kayla. Recognition crosses her face. "I could've handled him, but I'm glad you noticed and came over. Hi, you're Kayla, ri—"

"You rescued your little girlfriend. Are we good to talk now?" Kayla interrupts.

I pull Tatum into my arms, glaring over her head at my ex. "No, we're not good. I've made it more than clear we're done, so you can just stop."

"What?" Kayla scoffs, crossing her arms. "I just want to talk. Can't we still be friends?"

"You broke up with me, remember?" I shake my head. "You're toxic. Not the kind of friend I want in my life."

She flings her arms to her side, snapping her gaze around at the people watching her get shut down. "Coop, I just miss you, and—"

"That's enough. We have nothing to talk about. Ever." I take Tatum's hand, stomach buzzing with anger. "Do you mind if we head out for some fresh air?"

"Of course." Tatum squeezes my hand, peering up at me with a worried expression. "Let me tell Jenny where we are so she can find her friends."

She peels away. Kayla takes a step toward me until someone laughs and calls out desperate. Her lips purse and with a pissy huff she storms away, following the guy I told off for touching Tatum.

Some frustration bleeds away when Tatum comes back without her flamingo. I ditch my unicorn and take her hand, leading her outside. She traces the inside of my wrist with her other hand, hugging my arm as we stroll down the tiki torch-lined front walkway.

"Are you okay?" she asks when we sit on the grass further away from the party.

"Yeah."

Sighing, I sprawl back. It's dewy and cool against my bare back. She lays against my side without hesitation, resting her head on my shoulder. The pumping beat of my heart slows down to a calmer state. I blow out a breath, gazing up at the sky.

"Can I ask you something?"

"Shoot," I say.

"What made you want to change your reputation? I mean, other than getting serious about applying yourself."

I squeeze her hand, heart rate kicking up once more. I can't confess how I feel to her yet. But I can tell her some of the truth. She deserves to know.

"When I was dating Kayla, I thought she was my first real serious girlfriend."

Tatum hums, listening. She twines her fingers with mine as I open up and tell her something I haven't told to anyone.

"I've realized now that I don't want Kayla, or any girl like her anymore. They're the type who just saw me like a piece of meat. A dick to ride, that was it. Anyone who hooked up with me saw me as a good time and a status symbol." I swipe a hand over my mouth. "Kayla never really cared about my feelings or our relationship. She enjoyed toying with me and knew I liked it when she needed me, so she strung me along."

"Cooper," Tatum says sadly.

She leans up to meet my eyes. I tuck her hair behind her ear and caress her face. My chest aches because the girl who believes she's my fake girlfriend looks at me with more compassion than my real one ever did. I know she cares about me.

"Haven't I done the same to you?" Her throat convulses with a swallow. "God, I'm an idiot. I never knew you felt like this and all I was worried about was getting you to be my first so I could get some experience points. I used you."

"Hey, no." I tug her down into my arms. "You didn't use me, babe. They wanted bragging rights. I never once thought of it that way with you."

"Promise you'll tell me if you feel like I am? I don't want you to hide your feelings."

"Of course. Thank you." I chuckle. "It feels pretty good to talk about."

"Guys have feelings too, Coop. Gender doesn't matter when it comes to mental health and talking things out. It doesn't emasculate you to talk about them."

"Yeah. Thanks for listening."

"Always."

My arms tighten around her. It's getting harder to think about letting her go when all I want to do is hold on like this forever.

THIRTY-FOUR

TATUM

Ever since Cooper's confession at the party two weeks ago, I'm hyper aware of asking too much of him, limiting our lessons with excuses that I need to study for midterms this month. He swore he didn't think of what we're doing that way, and I'm determined to keep it that way. I never want to hurt him by treating him like an object. The look on his face after we left the party haunts my thoughts. I never want to see that wounded expression on his handsome face again. It makes my heart ache just thinking of using him the way others have.

We've been so good at faking it that I forgot we aren't real. Well, on my end things have become hard to separate. I don't know what this is for him other than me helping tame his image. I ignore the twinge that thought causes in my chest. He deserves a girlfriend who will see everything I do about him, not his best friend's sister helping him out as a cover.

Another heart-shaped sticky note from him shows up on the message board of my dorm when I get back from my afternoon class. The sight chases away the cloud hanging over my head. If my feet move a little faster down the hall to get it, that's my business, not anyone else's. I'm already smiling before I finish reading the note.

Miss you, overachiever. Wear this and be ready by 6pm. Can't wait to see you in it.

The arrow points down to the bag hanging on the doorknob.

Oh my god. My smile falls, overtaken by shock. Did he get me lingerie and leave it out in the hallway for everyone in my dorm to see? I picture the message in his seductive croon and heat floods my face.

Peeking inside, I find the unmistakable SBC school colors, light blue, navy, and red. The wad of fabric is shiny and definitely not lace or silk. My lips roll between my teeth. That rules out lingerie.

I can feel the attention from other girls on the floor waiting for me to open it, especially from the girls across the hall who follow Cooper's TikTok. They all know he's the one who leaves me notes. Is this another surprise he's sprung on me? I want to check his account to scope out new posts for a clue, but I can't do it with anyone watching.

Whipping out my phone, I shoot him a text while I take the bag inside my dorm room.

Tatum: Dude. Everyone thinks you left a naughty gift with this suggestive note.

Cooper: Good idea. I'll keep that in mind for next time [smirk emoji] Did you open it yet?

A pleasant, aching heat lances through my stomach at the thought of wearing something sexy he picked out for me, and my mouth curves as I type out a reply.

Tatum: Not yet. What are you up to?

Cooper: You'll see, babe. See you soon.

Tatum: I was going to study tonight.

Cooper: Nah. Boyfriends take their girls out on dates. You'll like this. Go with the flow. Besides, you've been cramming hard and deserve a break.

Holding back a smile is impossible because I hear the response in his lazy, confident tone, complete with one of his heart-obliterating winks. The studying excuse was a weak one. He knows I've been on top of my midterm prep regimen and one night off isn't going to make or break my exam scores. Opening what he left for me, I find a South Bay basketball fan jersey just like the one I know he has.

An idea pops in my head to get him back for making everyone on my floor jump to conclusions about the bag's contents. Stripping out of my jeans and shirt, I pull on just the jersey and hold my phone up for a selfie. I've done this hundreds of times since the summer, practicing it so often it feels natural to give the camera a flirtatious smirk as I kneel on my dorm bed. I tug the material suggestively between my legs to show off a hint of side boob, then attach the picture to our message thread and shoot it to him with a sly grin.

Tatum: Is this what you had in mind?

His reply comes back seconds later.

Cooper: Damn it, T. Now I have to leave the gym with a boner. Fuck, you look good like that.

I fall back against the bed with a laugh. Another message comes through.

Cooper: Wear a shirt under that. I don't want anyone else seeing what's mine at the game tonight.

I bite my lip, fingers hovering over my keyboard to type out a reminder I'm only pretending to be his. I don't say it, secretly enjoying it when he gets like this.

* * *

The basketball arena is huge and packed with fans when we arrive shortly before the game begins. Cooper laces his fingers with mine so we don't get separated as we weave through the crowd to reach the section he got us tickets for. His hand engulfs mine and he holds on tight, using his body as my buffer from getting jostled.

"This many people go to college games?" I ask over the din of chatter.

Cooper shoots me a lopsided grin over his shoulder, his dimple visible through the face paint decorating his cheeks. "Hell yeah. People go nuts for college basketball. Tonight's the first game of the season."

Simone and Jenny jump up when they spot us and Jackson nods

to Cooper. Ty and Harris have seats in the row ahead of ours. All of them are decked out in school colors, though we're the only pair matching with our coordinating face paint Coop did before we left my dorm.

"Success! You dragged her away from the library," Jenny cheers.

Cooper gives her a fist bump. "All it took was a little bribery and sweet talk."

I tuck my lips between my teeth, thinking of the note and the jersey I'm wearing. "Since when are you and Simone secret sports fans? The only basketball I've watched is when the guys play in the driveway." I steal some of Jackson's popcorn while we filter down the row to the two open seats. "I don't even think I know the official rules."

"My dad and I watch basketball," Jenny says. "I'm kind of a nut for it."

Simone shrugs. "It's a home game and my roommate had tickets she couldn't use. Sounded fun." She offers me some of her nachos. "Plus, snacks."

"Point," I concede. "The snacks are bomb."

"It's all about being at the live games. It's a totally different atmosphere." Cooper leans in to kiss my cheek when we sit, draping an arm over the back of my chair. "Way different from watching any sport on TV. You'll see."

I peek past him at the girls elbowing each other on the stairs between sections. They recognize Cooper, snapping a photo they'll likely text to a group chat. They might recognize me, too. We can't avoid it when we're together now. Everyone's invested in both of us as the school's favorite perfect couple.

Their label for us is starting to sting, chipping away at our lie. I remind myself Cooper needs my help. That's why I have to keep going, for him. This is all so that he'll find the right person for him when his reputation is successfully reformed. I never want anyone to feel like they can use him for his body or as a status symbol again.

Fierce protectiveness bursts in my chest as I snuggle close enough to him I could probably climb on his lap, peering up through my lashes. "Good thing I have my boyfriend here to explain it all to me."

Butterflies tickle my stomach. It doesn't feel as strange to call him my boyfriend now as when this first started.

He smirks, playing with one of my French braids. "Seems fair, considering you explained the cornerstones for my economics class in a way I could grasp it to pass my last quiz. I'm sure someone as smart as you will pick up on things easily without needing me at all."

Forgetting about keeping up our act, I beam in genuine pleasure. "You did?"

"Yeah. We just got the scores back today." His eyes soften and his smirk stretches into a wide smile. "Not only did I ace it, I still retained an understanding of everything you explained. It's finally sticking."

"That's amazing." I squeeze his knee when it bumps against mine. "But take some credit for yourself. You earned that grade. I only helped you study."

"Love birds, separate for five seconds and take some pics with us," Simone announces. "There's a hashtag contest tonight that Student Life is doing. Most school spirit wins a free dinner at Bluewater."

"Fancy."

I waggle my brows, biting my lip at the mental image of Coop in a crisp, fitted button down with the collar open and the ocean breeze in his hair. His sleeves are rolled up too in my imaginary date night, because obviously. I'm as weak for his toned forearms as all of his followers are.

"We've got this on lock. Here, make an S with your fingers." Cooper takes my hands and molds them how he wants them, then loops his arms around me and holds up a B he makes with his own hands next to mine.

His firm chest is warm against my back and his jaw grazes my temple as he hugs me close. It feels good, making me forget about everything that's been on my mind.

"That's cute as fuck. God, I hate how good you guys look together. Kidding, no I don't. I love it. But for real." Simone snaps a shot of us, then angles it for a selfie. "Okay, everyone in. Go sharks! Give us free crab cakes!"

Jenny perches on her lap and Jackson presses in on her other side. The rest of us echo her enthusiastic cheer and we take some photos, then a Boomerang for the hashtag contest.

My brother is still leaning into Simone's personal space, looking at the photos while she swipes through them. "Looks good."

Her eyes flick to him. "Yeah."

She jumps when a loud air horn sounds, followed by a lively DJ mix to hype the crowd. Jackson sighs and leans back in his seat, slouching low with his popcorn.

The music gets Jenny and Simone dancing. I join in with a laugh when they turn their attention on me. Cooper grins at me, his warm brown eyes gleaming as I shimmy. He lifts his phone and records a video of me, gaze shifting between the phone and me.

Players jog out to the court followed by the announcement of their name after the song ends. The energy in this place is wild and thrilling.

Cooper was right. Something comes over me once the game is underway, driven by the deafening cheering filling the arena. When the South Bay players push the ball down the court, passing it back and forth with impressive speed and skill, my heart drums in time with the smack of the ball against the waxed floor. Every time they score points, I'm jumping to my feet along with everyone else, holding Cooper's hand as we victory dance. I even participate in a wave, much to Simone's amusement. She shows me the Boomerang of me on her Instagram story during a break between quarters.

While we wait for the game to start again, the jumbotron hanging at the center of the arena switches from player stats and game high-lights to a kiss cam, searching the crowd for couples to match up. My heart skips a beat when it stops on us while we're standing up and swaying to the music with his arm wrapped around me. Simone and Jenny whoop, nudging me.

Eyes wide, I whirl to Cooper. I was having such a good time, I wasn't thinking about pretending to be together. Are we doing this?

His attention is on me, his gaze full of something I can't decipher that makes my stomach dip. The arm around my shoulders tightens.

"Come here, gorgeous." His words ghost over me. "Let me show them all that you're mine."

Cooper doesn't hesitate. His hand cradles my face and draws me near until his mouth slants over mine. The kiss makes my heart swell and I forget we're being broadcast to an entire stadium of people. It doesn't matter that our friends are right there, that my brother is watching.

All that matters is my favorite feeling in the world—Cooper's lips on mine.

THIRTY-FIVE
TATUM

After midterms are over, I feel like I can breathe easier. I'm confident in how my grades are going. What's even better is the spark of pride in Cooper's expression after his exams finish up. Midterms week hasn't been easy on him, even with my help to study.

I decide it's my turn to surprise him by doing something special for him to destress and celebrate making it through midterms. He's been working hard to apply himself and I can see him looking toward the future without any of the dread haunting his features over the summer.

At first I'm not sure what to do. He likes it when I let go of my planning-obsessed nature and embrace spontaneity. It turns out to be the right call when I'm randomly browsing the campus' ticket site for students on a study break while listening to one of my new hype up playlists in the background. I find a music festival happening this weekend in L.A. One of the bands he likes is playing in it.

"This is it," I whisper excitedly.

My phone has another new tag notification when I grab it. Someone tagged me in the kiss cam from the basketball game again. It's been all over social media. Scraping my lip with my teeth, I watch the short clip again, heart glowing when Cooper murmurs to me—*Let me show them all that you're mine*—before kissing me in front of thousands of people like there's no question that I'm his girlfriend. For a second, I imagine it's true, closing my eyes against the wave of longing that passes over me.

But we're not real. Those are the rules of fake dating. It's right there in the name. Sighing, I push it all down. If I'm not careful, I'll fall for our cover, too. Then when it ends... I don't want to think about that, either.

Swiping to my messages, I text Jackson for his help to pull off the surprise I want to give Cooper. He doesn't take long to answer me.

Tatum: Are you guys playing a game today?

Jackson: Yeah. I'm on my way to meet Coop and Ty at the gym's court.

Tatum: Cool, perfect.

Jackson: I don't think we're playing a full match today. We're short on players so we'll probably just shoot hoops for a while. Why? Miss your boyfriend? [Eye roll emoji]

Tatum: It's a surprise. [confetti emoji]

Jackson: You don't do surprises.

Tatum: I do now. Keep him busy while I work my magic.

A smile tugs at my mouth. It turns out surprises aren't so bad. All I needed was the right person to show me how to appreciate them.

Once I snag tickets for the festival and book us a hotel room, I dig through my notebook stash for the one with floral-patterned paper before hurrying to Cooper's dorm. After the guys play basketball, he usually heads back to his room to shower before seeing if I want to get dinner with him. That leaves me enough time to leave him a message and pack while Jackson keeps him occupied. We can grab dinner on the road if we leave tonight.

Old Tatum would want to prepare more, say we should at least leave in the morning, but I'm not her anymore. I'm embracing the adventure of an impromptu weekend away.

Elated jitters build in my chest. This is exhilarating. Is this what Cooper means by going with the flow? If so, I think I like it. My entire body is alive with an electric spark from the thought of dropping everything and going right now.

The note I leave on his door is much like the one he left me last weekend before the basketball game. I give him directions to pack an overnight bag and be ready for pick up. Can it be a pick up if we're taking his car? I shake my head to dispel the habit to think about logistics, then fold the floral patterned paper into the shape of a heart to match the pastel sticky notes he leaves me.

When I finish packing, my phone vibrates in my back pocket. I tug it free from my jeans and grin at the photo of the note I left on Cooper's door.

Cooper: I'm rubbing off on you.

Tatum: Don't say it.

Cooper: [angel emoji]

Tatum: I mean it [laughing emoji]

Cooper: Can't help it. I could be rubbing off *on* you [smirk emoji]

Tatum: Dude!

It's impossible to tame my grin. I zip up my bag, texting Alison and Simone to let both of them know I'm going off campus for the weekend. My roommate messages back to ask if I mind if her friend spends the weekend while I'm away, and my best friend sends a bunch of emojis only I can decode as her excitement for my impromptu plans.

Cooper: All packed. What am I packed for?

Before I respond, I take a photo of myself wearing one of the shirts he gave me. It's a concert shirt for the band we'll see live this weekend. I remember when he and Jackson went to one of their shows while they toured the country last year.

Tatum: You'll see. I promise to show you a good time.

Cooper sends back a voice message. His smoky tone stirs heat between my legs when I play it.

"I love it when you say that."

THIRTY-SIX
COOPER

When I got behind the wheel yesterday, Tatum told me to drive. I never expected we'd end up in L.A. for a music festival. I saw the announcement on Phantom Knockout's Instagram that they'd be playing at the beginning of the semester, but I forgot all about it. My girl went big with this surprise, and I've enjoyed it so much, keeping a dopey ass grin off my face has been impossible all day.

Phantom Knockout's set is the last one of the night on the main open air stage. I rest my chin on top of her head, my arms tightening around her. She leans back against me, whooping with the rest of the crowd hanging in front of the band's stage when they come out to greet the fans.

"Thank you for this." She twists to give me a smile and I kiss her temple. "This weekend's been one for the books."

"I'm glad you liked the surprise. You've done so much for me, so I wanted to do something for you." The opening notes of one of the band's most popular hits starts up and she sways. "I really like this song."

Something expands inside my chest. "Yeah? Me too."

"I totally need this one on my playlists. It'll make me think of you."

The expanding sensation grows. I forget to pay attention to my favorite band, too focused on her singing along.

"This is it, take a chance. Your first ride, flying high. Don't forget —you promised all your lasts to me," she belts out.

Fuck. I love her. Sometimes it slams into me by surprise, reminding me how deeply she's imprinted on my heart. Being with her makes me feel like I'm constantly riding a wave, an endless, exhilarating rush.

I've had so many of her firsts. I want to be all her lasts, too.

Releasing her, I shift to the side to record her singing one of my favorite band's songs so I'll always remember today. I've taken dozens of photos of her. Every time she smiled today, I've needed to capture every one.

"Want me to take a photo of both of you?"

I glance at the couple who's been hanging out beside us for the last two sets at the main stage. Both of us arrived around the same time to get a good spot to see Phantom Knockout.

"Yeah, thanks. I can get one of you both, too." I hand off my phone and pull Tatum into my arms. "Smile, baby."

Tatum throws her hands up with a cheer and I catch her wrists, sliding her arms around my neck.

"Oh shit, that's so cute." The girl with my phone snaps a few and motions to her girlfriend. "You don't mind taking some of us?"

"Not at all," Tatum says. "Come over here so I can get the stage in the background."

She hypes the couple up while she takes their photos. My attention fixates on her. Even in the middle of a live concert, the world falls away when she's smiling.

"Thanks so much," the girls say when they finish.

Tate returns the phone. I snag her hand, dipping my chin to bring my face close to hers.

"This is so cool. I can't believe we're here right now," she gushes.

"You're the one that put it together on the fly." My nose grazes hers. "Surprised the hell out of me."

I mean more than the weekend trip she sprung on me.

Hope builds in my chest that this could be what I've been

waiting for. I keep putting off the vital step I need to reach—the part where I take this from fake to real. At first I wanted to ease her into the idea as she got into the swing of the semester, then midterms crept up on me. She might be ready now that she's used to being with me.

My thumb brushes Tatum's knuckles and she shoots me a thrilled grin. I return it, letting myself enjoy the moment.

The band gets the crowd going with song after song until we're all consumed by the infectious energy of watching the show. It's an indescribable magic that ties us all together in this bubble, this moment where we feel on top of the world. Getting to experience it with Tatum by my side, squeezing my hand and dancing excitedly makes my heart drum harder. It has nothing to do with the loud music or singing song lyrics until our voices fail us.

A soft chuckle leaves me when I feel a raindrop near the middle of the set. I tuck her beneath my arm to shield her, though neither of us are dressed for rainy weather.

Another one falls, splattering with a heavy splash on my nose. Tate moves to stand in front of me with a gorgeous, untamed smile. She holds her arms out, tipping her face to the sky as the clouds open up on us.

I hold her waist. "What are you doing?"

"Living in the moment. It feels awesome."

Her carefree laughter is my favorite sound in the world.

THIRTY-SEVEN
TATUM

Our laughter echoes through the hotel room when we stumble into it completely soaked from the downpour of an early season storm. The open air concert venue got completely washed out in the middle of the last set and by the time we made it to the Jeep, we were drenched. Neither of us have stopped smiling or laughing since the first raindrops fell.

"Is your underwear soggy?" Cooper snorts at the way I wriggle and helps me strip out of my wet clothes after grabbing towels from the bathroom.

"I don't think there's any part of me that isn't soggy right now." My nose scrunches through my giggles. He drapes a towel over my head and I pat him down with another. "But that was so much fun!"

I've never had such a good time doing something that was completely unplanned. The music festival was amazing. When I showed him the tickets on our drive up last night, I loved the look on his face at my surprise. But nothing will top getting rained out near the end of the festival with him holding my hand. I'll never forget the experience.

"It was." Cooper kisses me lazily while we peel each other's clothes off until we're naked. He parts only far enough to speak against my lips. "Are you cold? I don't want you to get sick."

I press against him, my pebbled nipples grazing his chilled skin. His arms snake around me. "You either. I guess we'll have to share body heat to warm back up."

He gives me a languid chuckle and tilts his head toward the bathroom. "Want to shower?"

I shake my head. "Too tired."

He hums and lifts me, carrying me to bed. "I guess I'll just have to take care of you here."

We only have one big bed. I was booking the room so fast, I didn't even think about getting separate beds. It definitely wasn't a problem last night as Cooper made me keep my hands on the headboard while I rode him. After that, there wasn't a question of sleeping arrangements. He pulled me into his arms just like our epic post-orgasm naps over the summer and joked that I could check hotel sex off my list, his voice rough and deep against my glistening skin.

A shiver moves through me at the memory, my thighs rubbing together as we climb under the fresh covers.

"Spontaneity is a good fucking look on you, baby," he murmurs against my lips.

"I learned from the best."

I gasp when he captures my mouth with his again, his fingers sinking into my damp hair. We kiss for a long time. Our bodies move together with familiarity. It starts off sensual until it becomes an act of simply remaining connected.

There's no pressing urge to go any further. He's hard and my body is warm, but he smiles at me when he breaks away and continues tracing patterns on my jaw affectionately. We don't need words. Our bodies do the talking, angled close together, lips meeting without any purpose other than the pleasure of kissing.

I'm not cold from the rain anymore. Neither is he. We're warming each other up as we remain entangled beneath the sheets, his mouth slanted over mine. The euphoric kiss drifts from one into the next for so long I lose track of time.

When we eventually stop kissing, I roll over. My lips are puffy and tender. His arms slide around my waist and tug me back against his body where I fit. Where I belong. His heartbeat echoes against my skin and mine matches his. Our two hearts beat as one.

"Goodnight, beautiful." His rasp is followed by the brush of his lips against my bare shoulder.

"Night," I murmur.

Cooper's fingers thread with mine and he moves our joined hands to rest over my heart. It feels like he's mouthing something else against me, but I can't be sure.

I've made plans and goals for everything in my life. It's a strategy I've clung to for so long, not only for my academic dreams, but anything I've ever wanted to do. The structure helped me deal with crippling anxiety of what to do next. By having the steps to visualize how to get from ideas and goals to reality, I didn't feel like that anymore.

I've always been afraid to let go of my planning crutch. If I don't have a guided path to reach my goals, they seem unattainable. My brother's best friend is the one who helped me see it doesn't have to be like that all the time. Not planning doesn't mean failure.

Cooper taught me to be confident in myself. To let the waves of life take me where I'm going instead of planning out every second. It feels amazing to let go and just be, to not know what's coming next or after that.

This summer might have started with one of my craziest plans ever, but somehow it's brought me so much more than my original goal that's been met countless times over. And the thing is, this was all to ditch my V-card before college and catch up with everyone else's experience level, but I haven't thought about seeing anyone else. Not once.

I no longer fear I'm not fitting in because I spent so long focused on my studies. New people come up to me all the time on campus and I don't freeze up while wondering how I'm supposed to act. I go to parties and have time to study for everything I'm working toward to achieve my five year plan.

I'm living the college life I wanted thanks to Cooper. He didn't only become my tutor in the bedroom. We're far beyond that. He's become so much more; taught me so much about myself.

A drowsy, content sigh from him ghosts across my skin, piercing my thoughts. He holds me closer, his arms locking tight around me. It always feels like he doesn't want to let me go when I'm in his arms. The way his lips automatically graze my shoulder and he inhales as if he's trying to commit me to memory makes me smile. I squeeze the hand he has tucked against my fluttering heart.

This feels so right.

We haven't had an audience to play this up for all night, yet we've still been like this. I don't want to lose this. I like who I am when I'm with him.

Could we make this work? Instead of posing as a couple...could we become a real one? I bite my lip. A few months ago, I would've shot down that thought immediately. I never believed I was the kind of girl he wanted.

Except people's types don't matter. With billions of people in the world, we connect with who we fit with. Our hearts don't care about whether we make sense on paper or based on our social media followings.

Love isn't something that can be planned, it's a rogue wave that defies logic to crash with all its might over us.

Tomorrow. I grin to myself in the darkness, surrounded by Cooper's comforting masculine scent. I'm going to tell him the truth tomorrow.

There's a thrill in what kind of possibilities awaits me in the next moments and I'm embracing it. I have no plan. No fallback if the wave I'm riding overtakes me.

All I have is this feeling in my heart when I'm around him. I don't want to lose it. I don't want any of this to be fake anymore.

I'm done pretending that I'm not in love with Cooper Vale.

THIRTY-EIGHT
COOPER

Tatum is still asleep. I gently brush her hair away from her face, then trace the plump curve of her lips. The dream I had lingers, my chest expanding with a warm glow as I picture the white dress she wore on her way down an aisle marked by flower petals in the sand until she reached me.

Last night I mouthed *I love you* against her skin while we warmed each other up from the rain storm we were caught in. I meant every word.

She makes a soft sound, her lips pulling into a sleepy smile. "I can feel you staring."

The corner of my mouth kicks up. "Yeah. And? The view is spectacular."

A husky laugh leaves her and she rolls into me, tucking her face against my chest. My arm slides around her, hugging her closer. We both fell asleep naked. As much as I always want to have her, this is nice, just laying together like this. It makes me feel closer to her without anything between us.

She peeks up at me and my heart climbs into my throat. I want to make her my girlfriend for real.

"Do you want to head back right away or hang out here for a bit?"

A rumble vibrates in my chest as I roll her beneath me. "You know my answer to that." My hips settle between her thighs and I grind against her. "I always want to be right here."

Tatum winds her arms around my neck, arching her back. "Mm. I meant do you want to get breakfast?" She hesitates in the same way she does when she's working out a problem. Her mouth opens and closes, then she seems to reconsider. "I was thinking if you want, we could use the clips we filmed from the concert and record a morning after vlog for some new couple content on your TikTok."

My shoulders tense. Couple content—what she calls the couple-focused thirst trap content I've mainly switched to since we started pretending we were together. Instead of filming clips of myself stripping out of my wet suit after a surf or playing basketball with the guys, I only posted things with her in them. I haven't thought about our viral tactics since I uploaded the clip of the kiss cam one of the guys on the basketball team forwarded to me.

When I don't respond, she gets up to pull on a loose tank top and one of her stretchy tennis skirts that drive me crazy. I watch for a few moments before getting dressed.

I want her more than anything. But I need her to see me as more than her fake boyfriend and her stand in to get experience points with. My fists ball. I know she's nothing like the girls who only want me for a ride on my dick. When I opened up to her about it after running into Kayla at the party, she was worried about doing the same thing to me as the girls I thought I had something real with.

Tatum's the only real experience I've ever had. It's time I stop coasting on the plan I put together and tell her the truth. No more fears. No more stalling.

We can't keep this up. She still thinks of this as fake. I have to end this game and tell her how I feel. Licking my lips, I catch her by the shoulders. She smiles, dropping her hair from the ponytail she was scraping it into.

"Hi."

My lips twitch and nerves twist my gut. "Hey. Sit down a minute? There's something I need to talk to you about."

Her smile freezes. "Oh. Yeah." She slips out of my grasp and drops to the end of the bed. "What's up?"

It hits me hard how much I love her. Everything about her steals my breath. Her luminous blue eyes. The freckles across her nose. That slightly crooked tooth from falling off Jackson's bike. Her big heart and her clever mind. She's dedicated and kind. Perfect in every way. Perfect for me.

Tatum's guidance from our study sessions filters through my head. The way she breaks things down into steps for me. I can't skip ahead. This has to go in order to make sense, to know what comes next.

"I'm tired of pretending with you, Tate."

THIRTY-NINE

TATUM

No more pretending.

Oh. Oh. It's logical that at some point faking a relationship with Cooper would have to end. We're halfway through the semester. Of course he'd want to stop.

This was always fake for him. He doesn't see a girl like me.

Everything I've tucked away in my heart rises to the surface. All those times I forgot the rules. I was never supposed to fall for this, too.

I knew it wasn't forever, so why does it feel like an undertow has me trapped, unable to breathe?

No more training wheels boyfriend, even if the thought of losing Cooper makes my heart fracture. My fingers twitch with the need to move thanks to my anxiety bubbling up, filling my chest until it's tight and uncomfortable. I shove my hands beneath my thighs, scrunching the sheets in my grip.

The resolution I made last night sits in the back of my throat. This isn't how I pictured this morning going. Waking up in his arms, smiling before I opened my eyes, I was ready to tell him how I feel about him until I lost my nerve. I only brought up breakfast to give myself time to work back up to telling him. The words won't come now, my newfound confidence taking a critical hit.

This is where having no plan gets me—blindsided with no idea what to do next.

I always thought it didn't feel like we were faking. I guess it hasn't been the same for him. I'd ask him to double check, but the thought of hearing him spell it out for me forms a leaden weight of dread in the pit of my stomach.

He's tired of pretending with me. My stomach clenches as his rasped words echo in my head. What more do I need to know than that? I won't make this more awkward by adding feelings into the mix. We both knew the rules we agreed to when we started this. I wasn't supposed to fall for him.

Swallowing past the emotions welling in my throat to form a lump, I think of what he told me at the party. The last thing I want is to be another girl using him. He doesn't deserve the way girls treat him like a perfectly sculpted trophy instead of a giving man with the biggest heart. Someone as caring and genuine as him deserves to find someone that supports and loves him, because he's more amazing than any guy I've ever met.

Cooper's eyes bounce between mine. There's something wary in his expression. Is he worried about me? This was his idea in the first place. It's his call when we stop this.

"Do you understand?" He rakes his fingers through his messy brown hair. It curls around his fingers and sticks up at the back from sleeping on it. "No more pretending—"

"Yup," I push out in a rush with wide eyes. My heart hammers as I shoot to my feet. I need to move or the anxious energy buzzing through me will suffocate me until I explode. "Of course. That makes total sense to stop pretending. I think everyone's used to seeing the guy you want to be now. The perfect boyfriend—for real this time, not as someone's beefy meat man."

His brows furrow. "Meat ma—never mind. What are you saying?"

I whip around to face him from the other end of the hotel room. He leans against the dresser, gaze locked on me. "I'm saying I get it. We're done with being SBC's it couple. It frees you up to meet the right person. It's about time I graduate with honors from the Sexy Social School of Vale, isn't it?"

He huffs out a laugh that doesn't seem that amused, swiping his fingers over his mouth. "That's what you want?"

"Well, I think we can say we've soundly achieved my goals we set out to crush at the beginning of the summer." My teeth scrape my lip too hard. "I definitely didn't enter my freshman year at South Bay College as a virgin. You helped me relax enough to feel comfortable at parties. Honestly, you've helped me feel comfortable in my own skin. I can't thank you enough for that."

His stiff expression softens and he closes the distance between us. I swallow when he grazes my cheek with his knuckles. "You were always capable of finding this girl on your own, T. It's who you've always been. You didn't need me."

His attention dips to my mouth and an ache of want burns in my chest. If we could kiss one last time. One for the road.

"No more lying to our friends," I whisper. "That'll be a huge relief."

"Yeah." His voice is edged with roughness and he tears his gaze away. "No more lying. Sorry, I didn't realize that was weighing on you."

"A little bit. I know they all believed us." I shrug. "Still, I don't like lying to people. It doesn't feel good to be lied to, so I don't want to do that to others."

"Right." He frowns. "So, just to be clear, you want to stop this?"

I nod. "This is the right call for both of us."

"Okay." He doesn't sound too relieved, even though he brought this up.

"We'll still be friends, right?" The hope in my voice is difficult to hide. "Just because we're fake breaking up doesn't mean you stop being my neighbor or Jackson's best friend."

His shoulders sag. After a beat, he nods. "Yeah. Friends. Of course, Tate. I'm always going to be here for you."

I exhale in relief. "Good. Same. If you need help studying, hit me up. We work well together."

"Yeah." He ducks his head and clears his throat, falling back a step to put some distance between us again. "We should head out. Ready? We can grab breakfast on the way."

"Yes." I move past him to pack up my stuff. "You're right. It's a long drive. It's better if we get going now."

Cooper doesn't move for a few minutes while I duck into the bathroom to get my toothbrush. When I come back out his expression is far away. He sighs again before he finally grabs his things.

* * *

The four hour drive back to South Bay is agonizingly awkward. Things have never been like that between us. It's going to take me a minute to find a new normal where I'm not touching him all the time. My heart pangs. I already miss the way he always tucked a hand between my thighs. He hasn't touched me once between L.A. and South Bay.

On the way back, I text Simone and Jenny to meet me at my dorm. Simone lets me know they're there as Cooper pulls into the student lot on campus.

"Want me to walk you back to your dorm?" He stares ahead, drumming his fingers on the wheel. "I can carry your bag."

I'm tired of pretending with you.

His words won't leave my mind. I can't endure the ten minute walk across campus while he's like this.

"No, I'm good."

"Thanks for—" He grips the wheel, knuckles turning white. "For the concert tickets. I had a good time."

"Me too." My attention darts between the clench of his jaw and his hand. He's usually so relaxed, but something is bothering him. "You good? You can tell me. We're pretty skilled at keeping each other's secrets."

My laugh sounds clumsy and forced.

He heaves a sigh and adjusts his hat, squeezing the bill. "I'm okay, T. Just thinking." His jaw works. "Just, uh, thinking about everything I have going on this week. My marketing class has a research paper assignment I need to work on."

"Oh. Right. Well, text me if you need anyone to bounce ideas off of, or if you need a library buddy." Could I sound any more desperate for an excuse to keep spending time with him? "Bye."

Tucking my chin against my chest, I rush out of the Jeep, get my bag from the back, and hustle across campus to get to my dorm. It's a miracle I make it without succumbing to the crushing weight sitting on my chest.

The girls are waiting inside on my bed when I get in. Alison glances between the three of us and gets up.

"I'm grabbing an early dinner," she says. "Everything cool?"

I nod, throat too tight to speak as I dump my bag on my bed. Simone is on her feet as soon as the door closes and practically tackles me with a fierce hug.

"Do I need to send Jenny out for an emergency milkshake?" Her words are muffled against my shoulder. She knows me too well.

"No. I don't think I could stomach anything right now. It's too..." I gulp in air and wave my hand in front of my stomach when Simone releases me to sweep an assessing look over me. "Buzzy."

"What happened?" Simone's brows pinch. "Did that idiot screw up? I thought he'd changed, but once a player always a player. He's just like your brother. All those guys are. I will stick my foot all the way up Coop's ass if he did anything to—"

"Simone." I hold up a hand and blow out a breath. My voice is tight. "No. He's not like that anymore. We broke up. Except—except we were never really dating."

She lifts a brow. "Still friends with benefits?"

"I mean, yeah. But not now. That's done. All of it's done." I rub my temple, pacing the short length of my dorm. My eyes sting.

"You broke up with Cooper?" Jenny peers between us in confusion.

My attention snags on my desk full of notebooks and my stomach twists itself in knots. They're what got me into this mess. They've got to go. I can't look at them without thinking of him.

With a huff, I stride across the room and fall into a flurry of grabbing handfuls of the organized stacks of planners and journals, packing every one of them away in a purple crate. The girls watch silently. When I've cleared my desk of every one of them, my chest is heaving. I shove them under my bed, hiding them behind my suitcase and another box of books I store under there.

Straightening, I prop my hands on my hips and blow a stray lock of hair out of my face. The need for action bubbles up again and I resume pacing while my mind runs through everything that's happened. None of my usual tactics to find my inner peace work.

"I know you like to move around when you're overwhelmed, but you've got to talk to us, dude," Simone says gently. "Don't keep it in. Let it out."

Rubbing my thumbs against my fingertips, I force out, "I need to swear off any planning that doesn't have to do with my study schedule."

The only journal I left untouched is the one I keep in my back-pack with the schedule of my assignments due and exams. What's the point of planning and journaling when it leads to this? My plan failed and bit me in the ass hard enough to leave a permanent mark.

Simone's eyes widen. "What happened?" She gestures to Jenny. "Start at the beginning."

Jenny catches my hand on my next pass and tugs me next to her on the bed. I pick a spot on the wall to stare at, honing my focus on Alison's coral reef poster as a calming anchor point to keep my emotions at bay while I explain everything from my plan to lose my virginity with Cooper's help to his idea to use fake dating as a cover for both of us when the fall semester started. All of it pours out of me in a breathless rush, my voice shaking.

"I really messed up," I mumble when I finish. Simone strokes my loose hairs back after she braided it for me while I let the complete truth I've hidden from her flood out in the open. "I wasn't supposed to catch feels."

"Oh babe. How do you know he doesn't feel the same? Because I swear Coop looks at you like you're his world. There's no way he's that good at faking that." Simone lifts her brows encouragingly. "Did you ask him?"

"I couldn't. He was pretty clear about ending this." Fear of rejection choked me.

"You should talk to him," Jenny says. "Tell him how you feel. Even if it's hard, communication is best."

"Logically, I know that. Emotionally?"

I lean on her and she puts an arm around my shoulders. We sit like that for a moment and my body relaxes. Simone squeezes in on my other side to hug me. My racing heart finally slows as I start to calm down with their support. I wipe away the tears threatening to fall.

Without panic, heartbreak, and fear scrambling my brain, I'm able to think clearly to analyze what I'm feeling. "It's sound in theory, harder in execution. I'm...scared of how many different ways it could go."

What if I misinterpreted everything between us because I was never able to tell where the line between fake and real was drawn? If he had feelings for me, he would've said something. He wouldn't let me go, like the last time I suggested we be friends. I don't think my heart could handle Coop letting me down easy.

It's not fair to him if I dump my feelings on him right now after we just agreed to end it. We both need time.

We've been in each other's pockets since the summer. Simone even said we sounded married once. Maybe I got swept up in what we were doing. I was so worried about orchestrating the perfect first semester of college that it's about to pass me by.

As much as it hurts to carry these feelings for Cooper without any hope of him feeling the same, it's not like he's gone from my life. We're still friends. In time, I'll get over this. After all the work he put in to help me put myself out there, he wouldn't like it if I just shut myself away.

The thought of his exasperated smile makes a thick laugh escape me. No, what I need to do is live my life. To embrace whatever happens one day at a time instead of worrying about my next five steps. I swallow. To go with the flow.

"Thanks for letting me tell you guys. That really helped." I sit up. "I think I could go for that milkshake now."

Simone smiles. "You can have all the milkshakes you want, babe. Want to see a movie after?"

"Yeah, that sounds good." Time hanging out with my friends is exactly what I need at the moment.

"We'll support whatever you need to do," Jenny says.

"We're here for you," Simone says. "Whether you want to go full dramatic and coordinate a flash mob in one of his classes to confess or keep it more low key. Or if you don't want to have anything to do with him right now, that's cool."

I snort because that's probably the last way I'd do it. "I love you. I think what I want to do is give us both some time to cool off after pretending for so long." My heart pangs, but I know it's what has to happen. I glance at my desk, no longer piled high with my notebook collection that got me into this mess. "Spend some time focusing on myself first before I do anything else."

Simone nods. "Respect. We don't need no man—"

"Or woman. Or non-binary partner," Jenny says with a bright smile.

"Yes," Simone and I say in unison. She hugs me as we get up. "There's no right or wrong way to handle a breakup, fake or otherwise."

I hug her back. "I don't know what I'd do without you."

"Suffer, obviously," she intones dramatically.

All three of us laugh. It helps soothe some of the pain radiating in my chest.

I cast one more look at the empty desk on our way out. It's time I let go of my need to regiment everything and just live.

FORTY
COOPER

I've played the morning after the concert in my head over and over every minute of the day for the last week in an effort to work out where the hell I went wrong. Telling Tatum the truth that this hasn't been fake for me from the start crashed and burned. Then she launched into an agreement complete with sound Tatum Logic. She caught me off guard. Even though I wanted to tell her everything, I backed off and listened to her, taking her hasty acceptance of ending things as a sign she's still not ready for the truth.

I won't push her into anything she doesn't want. Even if I can't be with her the way I want to be, I'll still put her needs first.

After half a semester of pretending to date her—with no actual pretending on my part—she still doesn't see me as the guy she should be with. If she did, she wouldn't have said she was done being my girl when I asked flat out if this is what she wanted. I failed my goal. Wiped out before I had a chance to tell her I'm in love with her.

There's no one else for me. She let me go with encouragement to find another girl. I could date every girl on the SBC campus and none of them would compare to her.

Tatum Danvers is the only one I want. The only girl I've ever truly wanted, even when she was off-limits.

The thought of her doing the same with other guys is killing me.

I'm distracted in every class, picturing another guy getting to know her laugh, the cute way she scrunches her nose, the fact she likes to have music on to hype herself when she's working out her problems, the fucking sounds she makes when she's about to fall apart.

It takes everything to keep a tight leash on myself, to stop from barging into her classes to keep every guy away from her. I could make it happen without her knowing, get every guy on campus to keep it strictly friendly with her. It's only the look I easily imagine if she ever found out I pulled something like that making me kill the idea before it fully forms. She'd be disappointed in me for lying to her in the hotel room when we were talking this out, and I can't stomach the thought of her disappointment.

That was my chance to say something and I didn't take it because I didn't want to pressure her.

My professors notice how distracted I am. When one of them mentions it to me at the end of today's lecture, I tense. Tatum worked hard to help me figure out what I wanted. I can't throw away what she's helped me achieve by slacking off again. I decided I wouldn't coast through my life anymore.

It's why I'm venturing across the quad to her dorm building at the end of the day. My chest constricts the closer I get.

She usually gets ready to meet me for dinner around this time. I left my notes there last week, not realizing then we'd be over before the weekend was out. I need them for my economics class, and the notebook also has the business plan I've started working on for the surf school I want to open after finishing my degree.

The girls in her dorm side eye me hopefully as I make my way up to the third floor. Word's spread across campus that we broke up. Some give me the look I've come to recognize as an open invitation to fuck around. I ignore them like I've been doing to anyone giving me that look. They have no chance of getting with me.

I stop in front of her door, staring at the message board I've left countless heart-shaped pastel sticky notes on for months. They're in my bag out of habit. I don't have the heart to take them out.

All week I've written little things I love about her on them to curb the urge to go to her and tell her in person.

The door opens while my hands are braced against the frame. Tatum halts with a startled squeak, staring up at me with gorgeous wide blue eyes. My fingers clench on the frame to quell the need to pull her into my arms.

"Oh. Hi."

"Hey." It comes out gruff.

She licks her lips, gaze flitting over me. "I haven't seen you around this week. Not since..."

"I know. Sorry, I was—" An idiot. I'm still an idiot. She wants to be friends, but I have no fucking clue how to be around her when all I want is to kiss her, to hold her, to never let her go. "Is my notebook for econ here? I need it."

"Oh. Right." Her expression falters, shuttering in a way I don't like. "Come in."

I dip my head and take a step, needing to be closer to her coconut and lime scent. She jolts into action, turning her back on me to dig through her drawers. I sigh, stopping in the middle of her room. She's the only one here.

The notebooks are missing from her desk. My brows furrow. It's on the tip of my tongue to ask where they are when she makes an adorable noise of triumph that sends warmth flooding through me.

She brings my missing notes. "Can't study without these."

"Yeah." I hate the distance I put between us when it's been so natural to be around her.

This is how it has to be. In order for her to really see me, I couldn't keep hanging on to her like a safety net, standing in the way of what she wants. I have to let her go to finally show her the man I am—the one who loves her. She needs time to feel like she's experiencing her life. Once she's had her fill, I'll be ready.

I'll wait a lifetime for her if that's what it takes. The only lie I didn't tell in the hotel was that I'll always be here for her, however she needs me.

Right now Tatum needs me to be her friend, and as much as I hate that word when it comes to her, I'll give it my goddamn all.

"Are you heading out for dinner?" My shoulder hitches and I curl my fingers around my notebook to keep the impulse to run them through her hair in check. This is why I stayed away all week. I didn't anticipate it would be this hard not to touch her. "I don't know if you have plans with anyone, but we could grab something to eat together?"

"I had a late lunch." She snags her keys and motions for me to leave, locking up behind us. She glances at me shyly. "I'll walk you out, though. I do actually have plans."

The spiral binding of the notebook digs into my palm. Shit. If she has a date and I see the guy, I might deck him. A possessive irritation that I have no right to simmers in my veins all the way to the sidewalk outside of her building.

We're almost to the junction that splits between the rest of the dorms and the path to the student union when I stop her by grabbing her wrist. "Are you okay? Do you regret it?"

Her brows furrow and she glances around. There aren't many people out this time of day. "Regret dating you? Of course not."

I huff, shaking my head. "The real deal. I know you said over the summer you only needed me as your sex tutor because you wanted someone you could trust with your first time."

She gives me a thin smile. "Honestly, not one of my best ideas."

I drop her wrist, tucking the notebook in my back pocket before crossing my arms. She reaches out to rub my tense bicep.

"I don't regret any of it. I'm fine. I meant it wasn't my best idea because it put you in a tough position with all the sneaking around we had to do." She stares at me and bites her lip, lowering her voice to a scratchy whisper. "I probably would've been better off just learning the spicy ropes myself instead of approaching sex as a subject to study."

I grunt, rubbing at the burn in my chest. I hate the thought of all her firsts with some random dude. "Look, guys can be idiots when it comes to getting their dick wet, babe." Her mouth pops open. Fuck, that slipped out by accident. I blow out a harsh sigh. "I just want you to be careful. If you ever feel like you're not in a safe situation, you call me, understand? It doesn't matter where you are or what time it is. I'll always come get you. Cool?"

Tatum closes her mouth, rolling her lips between her teeth. She nods with a little hum of agreement. "Thanks. You're...you're really the best, Coop."

I take a step closer. I can't help it. Shit, I want to kiss her.

Her breath catches. "I'd better go. I'll see you later."

My hands flex around emptiness rather than reaching out for her again. I watch her walk away from me for the second time in the last week.

"What the fuck?"

I whip around, pulse stuttering at Jackson's angry tone. Tatum's out of ear shot and doesn't hear her brother. He steps out from behind a tree in workout shorts, ripping ear pods from his ears. Jesus christ. Déjà vu hits me square in the chest at his furious expression. Except he's way more pissed off than the night he caught me kissing his sister.

Neither of us saw him out on a run. I was too focused on Tatum and her back was turned away from the tree Jackson hid behind.

"Jackson," I say cautiously. "Listen, whatever you think you heard, it wasn't—"

"Wasn't what it sounded like? Fuck off," he spits. "You're not tricking me with that bullshit again."

I tear my hat off my head to scrub at my scalp. "I'm not lying, man. It wasn't as bad as you're thinking."

Jackson pushes me and I fall back a step. "Not lying? You've been lying to my face this whole time. What did you do to my sister? What the hell was that shit about sneaking around?"

I grimace. He's going to kill me. "I wasn't lying. We were pretending to date because we were fooling around, but I wasn't faking it."

"Who the fuck does that?" He shakes his head and shoves me again. "I'm serious about her, Jackson. I've changed, Jackson—you're a fucking liar."

I grapple with him, not about to take a hit because he wants to play protective older brother. "No I'm not," I grit out. "Throw those words in my face all you want, but they're still true."

"Sounds like some cocked up idea for an excuse to touch my sister." He glares at me, jaw clenched.

I scoff. "I didn't need any excuse. She's grown up and made the choice all on her own. You heard it yourself. It's over now. She was the one too good at pretending. She doesn't want me anymore. I'm just looking out for her as a friend."

He grabs two fistfuls of my shirt and hauls me close to growl in my face. "Stay away from her. I don't want you around her."

My head jerks. "We're friends. That's it."

"I don't trust anything you say. If I see you hanging around her, you're dead to me. She doesn't need you to fuck up her head. She's smart, man." He shakes me. "Leave her the hell alone."

"Whatever." I tear out of his grip and stalk off with harsh breaths. My veins burn.

My best friend's words cut deep because they've never felt more true. I'm only making something of myself because of her help. Only looking to the future because she taught me how. Without her, I'm nothing.

FORTY-ONE
TATUM

There's another note on my door when I get back from class. Like always, my heart flutters at the sight of the pastel heart. I don't have to wonder who it's from. *Cooper*. Air rushes out of my lungs and my throat stings as I pluck it from the message board.

Saw you smiling in the student union. I'm glad you had a good day.
— Coop

This one is a pastel purple. I have a collection of them on my desk. If I didn't hide my notebooks under my bed, I would tuck them between the pages. Instead I have a small mountain of colorful notes from him taking over my desk.

Every day for the last two weeks they've appeared on my door. He's making it so hard to move on from him. He's been avoiding me—not that I've made that much effort to see him, too cowardly to face him—yet the notes still come.

He's given me song recommendations for my playlists, some with a simple smiley face, one telling me about going for an early morning surf, and wished me luck on a quiz.

Plopping in the chair at my desk, I trace the letters of his name. Thank god Alison has her afternoon lab today so I can wallow in how much I miss him alone. Sighing, I bring the sticky note to my nose and inhale, searching for any hint of the clean, salty ocean breeze scent that reminds me of him.

Swallowing past the lump in my throat, I add the latest addition to my pile of hearts. Part of me is grateful for the reprieve of not seeing him around campus. I asked if we could be friends, yet I don't think these feelings will be so easy to let go of. I'm a mess just from every note he leaves. How would I handle hanging out?

My days have been filled with taking a chance on every path that opens to me. I've joined a corn hole game on the quad the physics club put together. I went to a poetry reading at the library with Jenny. Used my gym access with Simone and Ty for the first time. I had dinner with an exchange student I met in line at the coffee cart yesterday. Any invite that comes my way, I accept it.

I'm fully embracing going with the flow and have a blossoming social life because I'm putting myself out there. He'd be proud of me. The only things I allow myself to plan out are my study blocks. It's making me appreciate college, but something's missing now. I place a hand over my heart and hang my head.

There's a giant Cooper-shaped hole missing from my life. And I don't know how to fix it. I don't know if I want to fix it, because letting go of the love I feel for him is as terrifying as facing him is.

But, god, I miss him so much. My days seem so dull and lifeless without him. It doesn't matter that I've made new friends. I could befriend every student on campus and it still wouldn't make up for his charming smiles, his raspy laugh, or his warm hugs.

A text from Jackson distracts me from my thoughts. I roll my eyes when I scan it on my lock screen.

Jackson: Heading to the gym. Ty and Harris reserved a court. Want to come chill?

Tatum: For the hundredth time, I see through what you're doing. I told you already. I'm fine. Stop being the overbearing big brother, it's not your vibe at all.

He sends back a middle finger emoji and I huff. He's checked in with me a few times a day. I don't know how, but somehow he knows the full truth of what went down between me and Coop. Simone swears she'd never tell him and I believe her.

That only leaves...

Licking my lips, I open Instagram. The last photo Cooper posted was from the concert with our faces pressed close together, the stage Phantom Knockout played in the background. Five minutes after we took the photo, the rain started. The heart emoji with my name isn't listed in his profile anymore. My throat tightens and I switch to TikTok. It's not there, either.

With a sigh, I rest my forehead against the edge of my phone. What am I doing?

Is it healthy to stalk his social media like I used to? Definitely not. Can I help myself? Definitely not.

There aren't any new posts. I trap my lip between my teeth as I stare at his smiling cover image on the most recent upload after the repost of the basketball game's kiss cam. It's titled *Ways To Treat Your Girl Right Part 10*. I'm too afraid to ask Jackson if he's seeing anyone. Thankfully, he hasn't brought his best friend up when we've spent time together.

Clicking on the video, my heart climbs into my throat. We took a break from one of our study dates in the library to come up with the ideas he put in this post for our couple content. I pause it when he's done introducing the video's hook before his chuckle is my undoing. The comments are close to a hundred thousand, way more than I remember being the last time I looked at his account. Curiosity gets the best of me and I open them.

The top liked one asks where we are, begging for Tate and Coop content. There are a dozen more with similar sentiments flooding the comment section. He hasn't responded to any of them.

I pick another video, then another. All the comments are the same, asking where we are. Some seem to be South Bay students that have taken on answering comments with the news of our break up. People question how there's any hope for them if a perfect couple like us can't stay together.

I shake my head. We lied to so many people and made them

believe we were perfect all so people would see past Cooper's thirst trap reputation.

Scrolling back, I pick one of my favorites from his posts before I became a feature on his account. He's at the beach, his surfboard stuck upright in the sand. He smirks at the camera in that playful way I love, water droplets dotting his handsome face. When the beat drops, he covers the camera with his hand, then reveals his wetsuit peeled down to his hips, muscular tan chest on display while he does the trending dance of that week.

I lose myself to watching his videos, both my old favorites and going back through the ones we made together.

He's hot, that's always been undeniable. But as I let the video loop, I stare into his eyes and remember the way he says my name. The warmth of his hand resting on my knee or holding mine. His smile when one of the concepts from his classes clicks for him once I break down the explanation.

"This is tragic. Why are you sitting there with your backpack on? You're not even ready to go."

I turn at Simone's voice, eyes unfocused and limbs stiff from staring at my phone screen for so long. Oh. I got sucked into watching TikTok and lost track of time. I didn't hear Alison get back from her lab or leave for her study group while I was absorbed in looking back on my fake relationship. We're late for the party we're going to tonight.

She sits on my bed and takes my phone, lifting her brows when she sees what I was looking at. "Girl."

"I know." I rub my eyes. The sting doesn't go away. It only gets worse until I feel tears leak free. The dam I've held back splinters, the painful flood of heartbreak surfacing from where I buried it until I was ready to process it. "Sorry, I just. I don't know."

Simone makes a sympathetic noise and tugs me from my seat at the desk to sit beside her. She helps me take off my backpack and wraps me in her arms. She rubs my back while I break down. "Cry it out, babe. You can't compartmentalize your emotions and just go on like everything's fine."

"I was trying to focus on me," I mumble. "It's like I don't really know how to be myself without him anymore. I'm meeting people and going out. Doing all the things he helped me find the courage to do. All I want to do is tell him about my day. How did I fall for our lie?"

"I'm sorry you're hurting. It would seriously help if he was an ass, but he's still doing that." She squeezes me and her attention slides to the pile of notes on my desk. "My mom says time is the only medicine for these things. I'm doing my best to avoid getting close enough to a guy before he can touch my heart."

My laugh is watery. "I'm getting your dress all soggy."

"Don't worry about it." She wipes my tears and smiles at me. "Do you still want to go to the party? It'll get your mind off this. We need a girls' night. Just you, me, and the dance floor."

After a moment of mulling it over, I nod. I need the distraction, or I'll end up crawling in bed wearing one of Coop's shirts.

"Want to stop for milkshakes and fries first?"

"Always, bestie." Simone kisses my cheek. "Let me do your hair."

Some of the tightness in my chest eases as we laugh and get ready to go out. This won't break me. I just have to be strong.

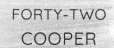

FORTY-TWO
COOPER

In the last two weeks I've thrown myself into taking control of my future. I'm not letting Tatum's help to get my life on track go to waste. Day and night I study for finals, meet with my advisor, and work on my business plan for the surf school. In my downtime, I call my parents on FaceTime while they're away at another retreat and tell them about my plans for the future. Their proud expressions and praise for doing the work feels good, but something's missing. *Someone.*

More than anything, I want to tell Tatum about these plans I have for my life because I wouldn't be here without her. It kills me that I've barely seen her in almost a month other than our trip to L.A. and getting my notebook from her dorm. It's a scary taste of what my life would be like if I'd never known her and it fucking blows.

My eyes burn from how shitty my sleep's been. Dropping my pen on the desk in my room, I sigh and press my fingers against them. I groan as the pressure relieves some of the ache. I know I look like hell with bags beneath my eyes. My back's stiff from hunching over the desk all afternoon once my morning class ended. I've been alone in here, not feeling like interacting with anyone on campus.

Staying away from Tatum is torture. Jackson isn't talking to me, either. I get the silent treatment and dirty looks when we're in our dorm together. He wears his ear pods, giving off the universal *don't talk to me* vibe. I've resorted to texting him, but he ignores my messages to hang out even though I'm doing what he fucking made me agree to.

He's never been this angry at me for so long. We rarely fight. It's always been easy to get along. I don't know how I'm going to fix our friendship when he won't even acknowledge me, let alone listen to anything I have to say.

Jackson made me stay away from Tatum, and I have. Maybe he said something to her, because she hasn't texted or messaged me online despite friend zoning me. I keep hoping when a notification lights up my phone screen it'll be her, then my stomach sinks when it isn't. When I check her Instagram—and her stories from a new account I made so she wouldn't know it was me watching them—I see her trying new things, meeting new people, and immersing herself in everything college life has to offer.

A sharp pain lances through my chest because I'm not the one giving her new firsts anymore.

The phone sits at my elbow beside my sheet of statistics problems. Temptation to check for the seventh time today tugs at me.

Except for the notes I still leave her, I've changed when I go to the student union, the library, and which ways I take to get to my classes. The notes are my way of keeping our connection alive. She's been in my life since my family moved to South Bay and I can't lose her completely over this.

Everything reminds me of her. My haven at the beach where I surf with Jackson and the guys makes me think of the times she joined us there, of our shared shifts at the Tiki Taco Shack. Songs that come on at the gym make me think of how she has a playlist for every situation. When I study, it's her voice in my head while I review notes.

All of it makes me want to talk to her. To tell her about my day and hear how hers went. I miss those moments we've shared. I miss just being with her. Fuck, I miss *her*.

Instead of doing that so I don't break another promise to Jackson, I write it all down on the sticky notes. Some I leave at her dorm, enduring the curious whispers from the girls on her floor that watch when I show up at times I know she won't be there to leave them. The others that are too personal, too full of my love for her go in the collection I'm building of heart-shaped mini confessions. I have so many I have to hide them from Jackson when he's in our dorm. I've taken a page from Tate and keep them between the pages of a blank notebook I hide under my bed.

Pushing away from the desk, I work out the kinks in my body. The room is oppressively quiet, the silence crushing in on me.

I can't keep this up. Something's got to give. The last two weeks made me realize I'll go insane isolating myself.

This isn't the guy I want to be. This isn't the guy worthy of Tatum.

First, I have to get my best friend to look me in the eye again. I know where he'll be tonight. No more ignoring me. We're getting past this.

* * *

This is my first time out since the music festival. One of the Kappa Sig guys is in my statistics class and wouldn't take no for an answer to his invite to the party at Hollis House tonight. I'm glad I caved, feeling like I need a night to chill out after I got a great grade back on my last test.

I spot Jackson at the air hockey table behind the couch in the living room when I get there. He meets my eyes and mouths *shit*. My eyes narrow in determination and I push through the crowd to the kitchen to get a beer first. I make my way through the party, nodding to people that say hi. Jackson doesn't budge when I lean against the wall beside him.

"What's up?"

He glances at me, a muscle in his cheek jumping before he shrugs. He's not stalking off. It's a start. Some Kappa Sig guys start up a game of air hockey and we end up watching until I decide to go for it.

"I've been trying to talk to you, but you've been blowing me off."

Jackson waves a hand, brows pinched. He gestures with his beer to the sliding glass door. "Damn it. If we're doing this, let's go out there. I can't hear shit over the music in here."

Popping off the wall, I follow him outside. The small deck is empty. Most people circle around the hot tub in the corner of the yard. He braces against the railing, pinning me with an unhappy look.

I sigh. "Are you going to try to hit me again? I just need to know if I should be prepared."

His lips twitch and humor bleeds into his expression for a moment. "Depends on whatever dumb shit comes out of your mouth."

"Fair." I squeeze my nape. The music from inside is muffled by the glass, the heavy bass thumping through the house. "So, for starters, I'm sorry this all went down. I never meant to lie to you or break the promise I made. The thing is, I've always really liked her. I didn't want to risk our friendship. But I did it all because love can't be controlled."

"Love?" Jackson scoffs and shakes his head, leaning his weight on the deck railing. He works his jaw. "You—the biggest player out there—"

I square off with him, lifting my chin. "I said what I said, man. I love Tatum. I never lied to you about that. All I've ever wanted is to make her happy, whether that means I'm with her or not. I'd never hurt her."

He squints, mulling over my words. "You swore you'd never go for her."

"I know. I can't help it. I'm sorry."

"Harris' lay up sucks." Jackson glances at me from the corner of his eye.

My shoulders relax and relief rushes through me. We'll be okay. He's not going to keep up this grudge.

He shifts to face me, propping against the railing. "The game's not the same without you."

"I never wanted to lose my best friend, either. A girl's never come between us. But I'd do it all again, even if it always ended the same."

My mouth pulls into a strained smile. "The chance to fall in love with her over and over would be worth it."

He snorts. "Sounds like a terrible groundhog's day if you're just going to lose every time."

A rough laugh leaves me and I swig my drink. It doesn't wash away the permanent ache of want that's taken up residence in my chest. "I'm serious. Loving her is like—like taking on the biggest wave you've ever seen and sticking it. When she laughs, when she needs me—fuck, man. All of it. She's my dream wave."

Jackson gapes at me. "That's some simp shit, bro."

I nod, blowing out a breath. "It's how I feel about her. I can't keep it to myself anymore."

He ruffles his hair. "Sorry. For what I said, and for being a dick the last couple of weeks."

I hold out a hand. "So we're cool?"

He smirks and claps his hand against mine, pulling me in for a bro hug. "Yeah. You're still a goddamn idiot. You should've told her this, not me."

The corner of my mouth kicks up and I look out at the yard when we separate. "I know. I was going to ask her out when I told her we need to stop pretending we're together. I only pitched the whole fake relationship thing so I could make her fall for me. She agreed to end it so quickly and made sure we'd still be friends. I don't think she feels the same." I nod to the house party with my chin. "This is what she wants."

"That blows." His brows furrow. "She really gave me hell for getting pissed off with you when I tried to talk to her. Told me it wasn't any of my business."

I laugh, my chest twinging sharply because I can picture it. She's always been fierce and likes to stand up for herself, even when she has both of us to protect her.

"I've been keeping a closer eye on her, and something's been off. Outwardly she seems fine, but I dunno." He drinks the last of his beer. "I need another. Let's go back in."

His words stick in my head. Is she fine? I just want her to be happy.

Jackson pauses inside the door and I bump into him. I'm about to ask what his deal is when I spot Tatum and Simone dancing. Before they see us, he grabs a fistful of my t-shirt and drags me to the kitchen.

It stings that we've gone from talking everyday, getting closer in the process, to not knowing where either of us will be at.

"Here." Jackson hands me a fresh beer.

I finish off the last of mine and stack the cups. While he gets a drink, I edge to the doorway, sneaking glances through the throng of people partying to watch her dance with Simone. Her eyes look puffy. Or maybe I'm only seeing what my mind wants me to see because I'm so attuned to taking care of her.

"CV!" A slap on my back pulls my attention from her.

"Matt. Hey, how's it going? Feels like I haven't seen you since move in day." My neck strains to catch another glimpse of Tatum, but he hooks an arm around my shoulders and pulls me away from the door.

"Good, bro. The parties this semester have been sick, but they're not the same without you." He waggles his brows. "You out on the hunt for a fine little something tonight?"

I laugh him off and nod to Jackson. "Nah, but I bet he is."

"You know it." Jackson sticks his tongue in his cheek. "The Theta Pi girls are probably out back in the hot tub by now. Let's go."

I shoot him a grateful look and edge toward where I saw the girls dancing. My blood runs cold, then hot. Simone isn't around and Tatum's standing with some frat boy by the air hockey table watching a game in progress. He leans down to say something in her ear and she laughs. My gut clenches and beer sloshes over the side of my cup from my punishing grip.

It's not her genuine laugh. Even from a distance I can tell the difference.

I've spent all summer learning her body. I know the sounds she makes when she's about to fall apart with an orgasm. Memorized the little sighs she makes when I kiss her. I'm the one who knows her better than anyone. It should be me by her side, note this Chad from the frat house making her laugh.

FORTY-THREE
COOPER

My feet are moving and I'm halfway across the room before I realize I can't stay away any longer. Tatum's back is turned to me when I reach them. The Kappa Sig guy—Ben, I think his name is, but who fucking cares—looks at me and steps closer to her. I think the fuck not.

"Tate," I say.

She jumps, whirling around. Her eyes light up at the sight of me, and, shit, they are kind of puffy underneath. It takes all my willpower not to tug her into my arms where she belongs.

"Coop! Oh my god, hi. It's great to see you."

The breathlessness in her voice makes me swallow. My gaze roves over her, hungry to take in every inch of her that I've missed. Damn, keeping tabs on her social media doesn't come close to the real deal.

She holds her drink in front of her with both hands. I remember from going over her class notes with her that it's a subconscious body language sign. She's putting a barrier between us and keeping her hands to herself.

"I didn't know you'd be here tonight." Tatum opens and closes her mouth. She starts to say something, then cuts herself off, tucking her lips between her teeth. Her eyes flit across my features, landing on my mouth. "How was your bio test? That was this week, wasn't it?"

My heart thumps when she angles her body closer, turning away from Ben. She put that barrier up, but she's babbling and all but leaning into me. Ever since she was a kid, she's had this habit of blurting everything she wants to say when she hasn't seen someone in a while. Hope flickers to life, floating through my chest.

"Good." I give Ben a dismissive glance, pushing down my jealousy. "I haven't been out in a while and one of the Kappa guys is in my statistics class. He said I had to come out tonight. Didn't know you'd be here, either. Are you having fun?"

"It's a girls' night. Simone's stuck in the bathroom line." She smiles. "Bill challenged me to a game of table hockey, so we're waiting for our turn until she gets back."

"Ben," he corrects with a plastered on smile while he checks out her ass.

I hold back a growl, jealous anger burning through me.

"Oh. Right, sorry," she says.

I smirk and focus on her. "You going with the flow?"

Her smile turns shy and she nods, her voice light. "The lesson finally stuck."

"Good," I rasp. "That's good."

Our gazes lock and my fingers twitch at my side. Her lips part when my attention falls to her mouth. Her tongue darts out to wet them. How can I ever be her friend when I know what it's like to kiss her?

"Oh, girl, this is my song!" Simone interrupts. She snags Tatum's hand. "Hey, Coop. Bye, Coop. I'm stealing my bestie for a dance."

Before I have the chance to say a word, Tatum shoots me an apologetic shrug and follows her best friend to the throng of dancers. I watch her grin and let go, as if the two of them are in their own world instead of the middle of a college party. There's a sense of relaxed freedom about her that wasn't quite there at the first bonfire party I took her to when she worried about fitting in.

"Damn, she's hot." My gaze cuts to Ben and he holds up his hands. "Dude. Don't glare at me. I'm just stating facts."

I've had enough of this. I won't stand by while guys like Ben who stink of Axe spray look at her with want in their eyes.

"Here's a fact, Ben. She's miles out of your league. Quit while you're ahead." Screw it. If Tatum ever finds out about this, I'll tell her I was drunk and forgot I wasn't supposed to play the part of jealous boyfriend anymore. "She's not an option tonight or any other night. Got that?"

He grumbles under his breath and I block his view of her, lifting my brows. He nods with a stiff jerk of his head.

"Make sure that fact gets around."

"Whatever, bro," he says as he moves off.

I track him until he edges around the room and swaggers up to a group of sorority girls. Casting one last longing glance at Tatum while she dances, I head for the door to leave.

"Coop. Cooper!" Jackson calls after me.

I wave him off. I'll text him later. Right now I need some air.

* * *

The buzzing in my head doesn't clear until I'm back in my dorm. Jackson texts me to check if I'm good. Once I respond that I'm fine, I put my phone on Do Not Disturb mode to silence all my notifications.

Sitting on the edge of my bed, I rake my fingers through my hair. Logging into my secret Instagram account, I go to her profile on autopilot. She hasn't made any new posts and there aren't any new stories today.

Needing to hear her laugh, I switch to my TikTok and watch one of the last posts she was in, leaving it on loop to hear the moment she bursts out laughing when we tried one of the couple challenges where I was supposed to flip her around. She ended up stuck, dangling upside down against me with only my grip on her tangled hands keeping her from falling. We have one where we did it right, but she insisted people wanted to see us fail it first. My thumb traces the side of the screen when she shrieks through laughter and tells me to put her down.

The comments on this post have exploded. I haven't been checking any of my accounts since I tossed up the kiss cam repost. After everything that went down, I wasn't in the mood to make new content. My brows pinch and I tap on the comment icon. My comment section is flooded with followers begging me to get back with her because they were invested.

Yeah, me too. Me fucking too.

Leaving the app, I go through my camera roll. During one of the nights I couldn't sleep, I sat up in the middle of the night and scoured my phone for every photo I had of her and saved them to an album. The most recent ones are from the music festival. Some are the tamer sexy ones she sent me in the summer.

My favorites are the ones I took while she wasn't paying attention during studying and at the beach. I stop for a while on one of her looking out the window of my Jeep with her hair blowing and a hint of her soft smile. She's beautiful and perfect.

Shooting to my feet, I rummage on my desk for a pen and get the stash of sticky notes from my bag to write down that I miss riding around in the Jeep with one hand on her leg while she surfed the waves with her hand outside the window. By the time I finish, I'm cramming my words to fit on the heart because the small notes are never enough space for all my love.

I can't give her up.

Fucking hell. I should go back to that party right now and tell her. But I messed up our chance at a real relationship by not being honest from the start. All I wanted was to do this right, because I'm in love with her. She deserves more than me tearing across campus to tell her how I feel in the middle of some frat party.

But I'm telling her. I need her to know everything.

We're not friends. We've never been friends, not even when we had benefits.

Fuck the friend zone.

* * *

Instinct drives me out of my dorm and takes me to the notebook aisle of the store where I bought the heart notes. I need to get more after writing down everything about her that makes my heart thump, plus keeping up with the ones I've been leaving her before I run out.

"Make your selections quick. We're closing in ten minutes," the teenage clerk says on her way by with a basket to re-shelve things.

"Sure," I say.

Grabbing two packs of sticky notes, I move to the notebooks. I need a way to apologize for screwing this up, but none of the colorful patterned journals jump out. I can't make it right just by getting her a new notebook.

One on a bottom shelf catches my eye. It immediately makes me think of her. The cover is stamped with the message *burn after writing* on a photo of a pack of matches with a flame design surrounding it.

A plan forms in my head once I grab it and head for the register. I know what I'll do to win her back. It's what I should've done from the start, instead of asking her to pretend to be my girlfriend.

I've given Tatum enough space to get her college experiences in on her own. It's time my girl hears the truth. I have to fight for what I want—*her.*

Once I get back to the dorm, I start recording and don't stop until I've put everything out there.

FORTY-FOUR
TATUM

Cooper remains on my mind through the weekend and my classes on Monday. I looked for him after dancing with Simone, but he was gone. Jackson said he left the party and my heart sank.

By Monday I wake up full of determination and newfound clarity. This isn't how things are supposed to be between us, and it's down to my choice not to say something when he asked what I wanted that put this impenetrable wall between us. It's up to me to tear the wall back down.

I feel ready to talk to him and see wherever it takes us. I can't hold this in. I've known for weeks that I should talk to him, but fear held me back, churning my stomach anytime I thought about admitting my feelings to his face.

After my classes end for the day, I halt outside the dorm. There's no note. My heart clenches.

I shouldn't expect them, even if I was looking forward to it after a long day of lectures gearing up to finals. Combing my fingers through my hair, I keep my thoughts positive and unlock the door. I don't need any negative energy clouding my head when I'm about to drop my school stuff off before tracking Cooper down. I need to remain in the right mindset.

"This was left for you." Alison hands me a small, book-shaped package.

There's a blue pastel heart stuck to it that says *forget rule one* in Cooper's familiar handwriting. My heartbeat stutters.

Forget taking it slow?

"When?" I breathe.

My roommate shrugs. "Not sure. It was here when I got back." She grabs her wristlet. "I'm heading down to the student union. Want to come?"

I hug Cooper's mystery gift to my chest. "Not right now. I'll eat later. Thanks, though."

It's the first time I've said no to something in two weeks. I don't feel like I'm missing out.

Alison shrugs, unbothered. "See you later."

Shucking off my backpack, I scramble onto my bed cross-legged and flip the package over. When I tear off the wrapping, I find a notebook that says *burn after writing* on the cover. Out of all the notebooks I've collected, I've never had a self-destructing notebook where I could metaphorically erase anything I put in it. An intrigued thrill sparks to life inside me.

It's the old, familiar natural high of opening a new, unmarked notebook. *Possibilities*, my mind whispers. My lips twitch. Inside the cover, there's another message in his handwriting.

Screw the rules. Life doesn't always go to plan. It's okay not to know what comes next, T. Make mistakes. That's real life.

A smile breaks free. I hear the encouraging words in his smooth, charming voice echoing in my head and touching my heart.

The first page is challenges: Be Honest (*There's No One Watching*). Cooper filled it in already with a letter to me.

Tatum,
When I saw this, I thought of you. Sorry for stealing the first page, but it's important. The back says it's about being honest and I haven't

been honest with you when it mattered, so I think I needed to fill in this page more than you do.

The thing is, being honest scares the shit out of me. It's why I couldn't declare a major without your help showing me what my interests could lead to. Why I didn't think I deserved the deeper connection I crave instead of empty hook ups. I haven't been real with myself about so many of the things I want from my life.

But you're honest, Tate. You're aware of what you want and you go for those things without holding back. I've always admired that about you.

A trembling breath escapes me while I read and I shake my head. "I'm not. I'm afraid, too."

If only he knew the biggest thing I've been keeping from him. Fear is human nature. It's how we deal with our fears that defines our bravery.

I pull the notebook closer as if it'll bring him closer as I continue reading.

I'm sorry I disappeared after we got back from L.A. You asked me to be a friend, and I crashed and burned hard. I don't think I'm good at being your friend. The last time you asked if we could stay friends, I knew I could never think of you as a friend when I need to kiss your perfect lips like I need to breathe. (Do me a favor and burn this page so Jackson never finds it. He doesn't need to know what happened after that kiss.)

I thought I was giving you the space you needed to do what you wanted because I wasn't going to stand in the way of your goals, big or small. They're important to you and I know you work hard to achieve everything you want to do. You give your goals your all. I didn't want to hold you back, not when you worked so hard to help me foster mine. Except that meant I wasn't being honest and I'm done with that.

Here's my new goal: choose honesty. Even when it's scary.

I promise to do better. See you soon. I have a lot to tell you.
— Cooper

My vision blurs and my heart swells with emotion by the time I reach the end. I blink away the moisture brimming in my eyes.

I need to see him right away. I'm not waiting another minute. The ache of missing him is unbearable.

Scrambling off the bed, I fall to my knees and dig out the hidden stash of notebooks from underneath. My smile is soft as I add the new journal to the collection. Instead of hiding the crate of notebooks under the bed once again, I set it next to my desk.

It's time for communication. I'm done putting off the conversation I should've had with him at the hotel. If he's striving for honesty, then I have to do the same.

I'm about to leave my dorm room to head to Cooper's when Simone texts me.

Simone: Drop whatever you're doing and watch this immediately! P.S. I told you!!!!

After a bunch of heart and confetti emojis, she sends a link to a TikTok video. I sigh, not in the mood to watch another video about rescue farms she's been sending me every day to cheer me up. I'm too impatient to go see Coop. Then it registers it's one of his posts and my heart beats hard, sending a pulse through my body.

Once I click on the link, he fills my screen. A noise catches in my throat. He's wearing the same thing he wore to the party. I remember thinking how unfairly good he looks with the fitted t-shirt stretched across his broad shoulders and chest. Did he film this that night after he left?

The post is already viral with thousands of comments in the hour and a half since it's been uploaded. I sink to my bed.

"Welcome back to part three of my truth series," he starts. "If you're confused, start with part one."

I scramble to his account to find the first video to watch from the beginning. When I checked on Friday, he hadn't uploaded anything new, but now I find several new posts all labeled as truth series in multiple parts. The first one was posted after lunch while I was in class.

Cooper is seated in his desk chair, arms braced on his knees. He shoots the camera a sheepish yet resolute glance at the start of the recording from Friday night. My heart swells and a breathless laugh leaves me at the way he adjusts his backwards hat, the ends of his messy brown hair curling out from underneath the faded blue edges.

"So, you've probably been wondering where I am. A lot of you have been demanding Tatum content, and I hear you. I've got to come clean, though." Cooper licks his lips slowly, chest expanding with a deep breath. "It was fake. We weren't really dating. The truth is, I convinced the girl I've always liked to pretend to be my girlfriend so I could prove to her I'm the guy for her."

My stomach bottoms out and my eyes widen. Always liked? I miss what he says next and start the video over. I restart it twice more just to be sure.

He definitely said always liked. Swallowing, I allow the video to play through.

"See, we'd been getting closer over the summer." His mouth twists into a playful smirk and he swipes a hand over his mouth, dipping his chin to peer up at the viewer through hooded eyes. I'm aware of how much looks like that make his followers swoon, and it's getting me, too. "I thought if I posed as her boyfriend, she'd realize how great we are together."

A pang echoes in my chest when his expression falls and he shows more of his real self.

"Things didn't work out like I wanted," he admits quietly. "I thought we got to a point where she was ready, but when I told her I was tired of pretending, she thought I wanted to see other people. I didn't mean I was tired of her, just that I wanted it to stop being a fake act. I lost the nerve to ask her out."

I inhale so sharply, I choke on nothing.

"What?" I hiss once my coughing fit passes.

The video starts over and I watch it through again, catching the ending I missed where he says this series is all about getting the truth out there. Shaking my spinning head, I start the next video, covering my mouth with my fingers. This time there's a pile of familiar colored hearts next to him on his desk.

"So part two of the truth series." Cooper rubs his jaw. "Here's a truth: I saw her tonight at a frat party on campus. We're supposed to be friends, but you know what was running through my head the whole time? How much I was dying to pull her in my arms and kiss the shit out of her. Some guy was talking to her, making her laugh, and I hated it. Fuck the friend zone."

He waves a hand over the massive pile of sticky notes and my attention flicks to a smaller, matching collection from every note he's written me on my own desk.

"I like to write her these. They always make her smile, and let me tell you, her smile is one of my favorite things about her. Making her smile is the best part of my day. These notes all have the things I love about her. I've been writing it all down since we broke up. Whenever I had the urge to go see her and tell her the truth, I'd write these." He gives the camera a wry smile and scoops up some of the pile, allowing the pastel hearts to flutter back to the desk. "It's an urge I have often."

"Oh, Coop." A thick, emotional laugh leaves me. I cover my eyes while his voice washes over me. "We're idiots."

This whole time we've been assuming we want other people while suffering the burden of loving each other. In his words, fuck the friend zone.

"All of these notes are ones I couldn't leave her." He picks one out at random and reads it. "When you smile, anything feels possible." Then he picks another. "Nothing compares to your eyes lit up when you're happy." Another. "I watch old videos just to hear your laugh. If I don't hear it, my day isn't right."

Each confession steals my breath.

A tear spills down my cheek and a lump lodges in my throat. I didn't think it was possible to fall any harder for Cooper than I already have, but he's proving me wrong as he reads out countless things he loves about me.

He reads every note on his desk for two more videos. By the time I reach the end of his truth series posts, there's a new video just posted a few minutes ago while I was watching the others. This one's labeled get the girl and when I open it, he's no longer in his room.

Cooper stands beneath a tree somewhere on campus in a sea of colorful heart notes. They're hanging from the branches, swaying in the breeze.

"Hey, so this is the last video in the truth series. This is the part where I get the girl." His handsome smile is more confident than the previous videos he created after the party. He winks. "Hopefully. I need to shoot my shot. I'll be here waiting for you, because I love you Tatum Danvers. Come find me."

FORTY-FIVE
TATUM

Cooper's last video plays on repeat while I run across campus from my dorm to find him. Students that recognize me shout when I pass them.

"That's her!"

"Go get him, girl!"

I wave as I rush to where he's waiting for me. My heart pounds hard with a mix of adrenaline and excitement.

When I finally reach the tree near his dorm building, there's a small crowd watching. I stuff my phone in my back pocket and take in what he put together for me. The colorful notes are even more vibrant in the afternoon sunshine. I spot Jackson and Simone filming my reaction.

Everyone falls away once my attention locks on Cooper. South Bay's hometown heartthrob has eyes only for me. He's everything I've ever needed. He stares at me, holding out a hand.

My feet move, taking one faltering step, followed by another until I break into a run. I crash against him and he lets out a gust of air, strong arms locking around me. Distantly, I'm aware of people clapping and cheering. I bury my face in his chest and tears spring to my eyes at his comforting scent.

"Hi baby," he whispers against my hair in a gravelly tone. "I missed you."

Clinging to the back of his shirt, I lift my head to meet his eyes. They gleam with happiness and relief.

"You told three million people you love me before telling me, Cooper Vale?"

Out of all the things I want to say to him, those are the first words to fall from my lips.

He gives me that swoonworthy dimpled grin I love so much and cups my cheek. "Go big or go home, right? You're my everything, so I had to go big to make sure you finally saw me as I wanted you to." My eyes flutter when his thumb brushes my skin affectionately. "I'm sorry."

"Me too." My grip tugs on his shirt. "I wanted to talk to you at the party, but you were gone. I was going to come tell you today, but then Simone sent me one of your posts."

His warm brown eyes bounce between mine. "I want to keep you, Tate. If that wasn't obvious after all this, that's what I was going to tell you at the hotel. I want you to be mine for real this time."

I huff and slide my hands up his back to his shoulders. His arm tightens around my waist. "I can't believe we were both ready to go all in a few weeks ago and both of us put ourselves through this misery of missing each other like crazy, and for what?"

His sharp jaw goes slack. "Wait, seriously?"

"Yeah. I'm in love with you, too. I wanted to tell you when we went to L.A." My brows furrow in resignation. "I thought there was no way you felt the same.

He pushes his face into the crook of my neck, grumbling unintelligible words. He mouths at my skin and I gasp, shuddering against him.

"Coop. People are watching this."

"Just showing them all you're my girl." He lifts his head and smirks. His fingers thread into my hair and tug lightly. "So you gonna answer my question or not?"

"Be crystal clear with me this time so I don't assume you mean something else," I tease.

He rumbles, hovering his mouth over mine. "Be my girlfriend, T?"

I grin. "Yes."

The hushed agreement barely leaves me before he kisses me. I melt against him, swept up in my favorite feeling in the world.

"There you are," he says when we part. "I have about a month's worth of kisses to make up for, so I hope you're ready."

I can't stop smiling. "With our average number of kisses to hours we see each other through the day ratio, my lips might fall off. How will we fit time to study for finals in?"

"Nah, I'll always take care of you." He steals another quick kiss, then one more. "Your lips are in good hands."

A fake gagging sound draws my attention from Cooper to my brother standing nearby. Simone elbows Jackson and gives me a thumbs up. My gaze moves around the heart notes surrounding us.

"All those notes you left me made my day. I've kept them all." I reach out to touch the closest one while he splays a hand on my lower back to keep me in his embrace. "When I didn't see one today, it almost threw my groove off. Thanks for the new notebook, by the way. It's really cool."

Cooper regards his creation with pride gleaming in his eyes. "You're incredible and I wanted everyone to know it."

Warmth expands in my chest. "I really love you."

His grin grows slowly. "Say it again."

I bite my lip around my beaming smile. "I love you."

"I won't ever get tired of hearing you say that." He rests his forehead against mine.

"Jesus," Jackson mutters. "I'm not filming anymore, bro. This is enough."

"Jacks, come on," Cooper says. "I thought you said you'd help?"

Jackson throws his hands in the air. "I helped you hang these all day and recorded the last five minutes of—" He waves a hand at us tangled together in exasperation. "That. Which I'm now going to go bleach from my brain."

"I think it's sweet," Simone says. "Let them have this. You

wouldn't understand since the longest, most serious relationship you've ever had is with your hand."

Jackson scoffs. "You have no idea. You wish, though."

Cooper guides my face back to him and gives me another heartfelt kiss. My brother and best friend's bickering fades away.

Once they realize the public display is over, our small audience disperses. I pull out of Cooper's grasp to read the notes dangling from the branches.

Simone tugs on Jackson's shirt and starts to move off with the rest of the students. "Text me later."

"I will." My gaze slides to my brother. He helped his best friend put this all together. "Thank you."

"Whatever." He smirks and points at us. "Now you owe me. And the same rules still apply."

Cooper brings his lips to my ear from behind once we're alone. "Want to go find somewhere quiet for a study session after we get these down? I have a lot to catch up on."

Heat rockets through me at those words. "Yes. I've never needed to study so badly in my life."

He takes my hand, twining our fingers together and everything that's felt out of sorts clicks into place. The corner of his mouth lifts and he tucks me against his side where I belong.

EPILOGUE

TATUM

Three Weeks Later

I've never been so relieved to finish a test in my life. My first semester of college is coming to a close and I'm finishing it strong with top scores (duh), new friends (plus an actual thriving social life), and a boyfriend (real this time, no more training wheels). My dreams are clearer than ever and my five year plan got an adjustment to take pressure off myself so I can fully enjoy this time of my life.

With my last exam of finals week over, I rush to meet Jackson before he leaves campus to go surfing.

He leans against his car with a bored expression when I reach the student lot. "Finally. I almost left."

"You would've had an ass kicking waiting for you when you got back to campus." I punch his arm playfully, then hold out a hand. "Keys."

He dangles them out of my reach overhead, snatching them back when I jump for them. Pointing at me, he peers over the rim of his sunglasses. "Do anything on my side of the room and you're both dead."

"Ew. Never. We don't even go past kissing when we're in your room." I shudder. "It's too weird."

"Keep it that way. It's bad enough my sister and best friend are dating."

He tosses his dorm keys in the air and I catch them, then flick his arm. "Deal with it. Besides, it's not any different than before. We were basically dating this whole time. Thanks for these."

"What are you planning?"

I shrug with a wide grin. "Don't know. I'm going with the flow."

I haven't fully reclaimed planning. Only for my dreams and goals academically. The obsession with it was a crutch to deal with my anxiety in every situation I faced, my way of controlling the outcome by being prepared for every step.

But life doesn't always go to plan, and that's okay.

I've let go of the rest, living my life as it comes at me rather than planning every little thing. No more checkboxes for things like *lose virginity*. Life experiences will happen when the time is right.

Cooper's last test should be done soon. I go to his dorm and steal one of his shirts to change into. Slipping off my leggings, I kneel on his bed and tease him with a little underboob by holding his shirt up while I take a few photos. I pick out my favorite and text it to him.

Tatum: For boyfriends who finish finals [heart emoji] [fire emoji] Meet me at the gym.

Grinning, I get dressed. I leave his shirt on instead of switching back to mine, knotting it at my hip.

On my way to the gym, people call my name and wave. Between the viral videos and the time I spent throwing myself into every opportunity I could, a lot of people on campus recognize me. Once again, Coop and I have become SBC's favorite couple. This time it's for real.

I thought it would be different, but it turns out he wasn't faking anything. It's just like things were before. He walks me to and from class and leaves me notes every day. Today's good luck message he stuck to the coffee he brought me this morning telling me to crush my last test is still tucked in my purse.

Cooper comes up behind me while I'm dribbling the ball, lost in my thoughts. He lifts me in his strong arms and buries his face in my neck.

"Damn it, T. I had to walk out of my biology class hiding a boner. You know what it does to me when you wear my stuff." His teeth scrape my skin, making me shudder. "My girl's too fine."

I laugh, twisting to kiss him. We have a bet to see who can hold out the longest until finals are over. Making out is fair game, but whoever initiates anything past first base forfeits. Neither of us have cracked yet and we've both found ways to up the ante of our psychological sexy warfare between studying for our exams. He lets me down and goes to get the ball.

"How was your last final?"

It comes out slightly breathless as he dribbles the ball casually while he saunters in my direction, hitting me with the full force of his smoldering gaze. It's his easy confidence that makes him look so hot doing that. Paired with the signature backwards hat and his thick brown hair curling from underneath and his smirk, I'm in full on thirst mode. Damn. I repeat, *damn*.

"The flashcards you made really helped. I definitely did better than midterms. I felt like I understood everything on the test." His smirk stretches into a grin. "If you're done checking me out, let's shoot some hoops. Unless you're ready to admit defeat."

"Never," I crow.

I'm determined to win bragging rights that I seduced him before my sexpert boyfriend could make me break first. The competition is fierce. I've been putting everything he's taught me to the test, enjoying it more and more every time he groans before tearing himself away.

We start a game of one on one, chasing each other around the basketball court. Instead of blocking me, he holds my waist and lifts me to throw the ball at the net.

"That's cheating." My head falls back as I laugh.

"It's a handicap for your height. Take it, Danvers, because you won't beat me," he croons against my ear.

I bite my lip. "I dunno, I feel like I'm winning."

The game continues when he gets possession of the ball. I jump to block Cooper's shot, but he's got me beat with his height. His body moves languidly and I'm struck for a moment by how good he looks as he releases the ball. His focus shifts to me and he grasps my waist, pulling me against his firm body.

"This is the real winner," he rasps.

Then his lips slant over mine before the ball finishes dropping through the net. I smile into the kiss, winding my arms around his neck. Both of us ignore the basketball bouncing off to the side of the court.

EPILOGUE
COOPER

Five Years Later

It's early. My favorite time of day when I'm surrounded by the slosh of waves heading for the shoreline, saltwater speckling my lips. The sunrise hangs just over the beach, backlighting Tatum in a beautiful golden halo.

Damn, she looks good like this. Straddling a surfboard in bikini bottoms and a snug rash guard shirt, gaze trained on the ocean's horizon to search for the next good wave.

"You're ready." I run a hand over her thigh from my seat beside her on my own board.

We bob on the steady rise and fall of the water's surface, two of the few surfers out this morning. I've been teaching her before peak season hits so she's not overwhelmed by how crowded it gets when tourists come to town. I've wanted to get her out here for years, but at the start of her break from her doctorate program, she finally accepted surfing lessons from South Bay's top surf instructor.

I swipe water over my board. "This is the last step of beginner lessons for all my students—getting out there. You've got this, babe. You know what to do."

We've been practicing in shallow water after graduating from learning the techniques to move her arms and spring from a horizontal position to getting upright once she catches a wave on the sand.

She gives me one of her cute, determined little nods. "You're a good teacher. I'm just visualizing the kind of wave I want."

I chuckle, splashing her with water to break her concentration. Leaning over, I steal a kiss, letting another good wave pass by because there's nothing that keeps my attention more than her.

"Don't overthink anything, just go for it," I murmur against her mouth.

She hums, eyes hooded and focused on my mouth when I pull back. Smirking, I tug the nose of her board toward me so she doesn't have to swing all the way around when she picks her wave. I know the moment she spots one, a spark lighting up her eyes. Her lips part and she checks with me. I nod in encouragement.

"Show me what you've got, T."

Her bright smile is my own personal bottled sunshine, the warmth piercing my chest. "This is exciting."

An amused breath puffs out of me while she stretches out on her board, her ass looking good enough to take a bite out of. I follow suit, planning to catch the wave with her in case she needs to bail. I'll be with her every step of the way, always ready to support her and care for her. She peeks back at the approaching wave once she has her board pointed to shore and starts paddling with her arms before I prompt her.

My lips twitch and my heart thumps. Good instincts. She's a natural, great at assessing the potential for an excellent ride. The wave begins to crest and years of muscle memory takes over. I look over just in time to watch Tatum pop up on her board once we've got enough momentum and grin.

She holds her arms out for balance, concentrating on the shore. I whoop at her, totally fucking captivated by my girl. If I'm honest, she never fails to captivate me.

I'm so attuned to watching her that I nearly wipe out, whipping the nose of my board to the top of the wave and back down for a twist to correct my balance. Our momentum slows in the shallows near shore as the wave loses some of its power and I fall back into the water once she jumps off hers with an excited yell. A deep laugh rolls out of me once I surface, shaking water from my face and scrubbing the damp tendrils of my hair back. I'm tall enough to stand here, but she bounces off the bottom on her toes.

"I did it!" Tatum squeals and jumps on me, towing her board behind her by the ankle strap.

My arm wraps around her waist instinctively and I haul her against me while my mouth crashes against hers in a salty, hot kiss that sends fire into my veins. Each glide of our tongues and lips says the same thing: *I love you.*

"Great job," I rasp. "You looked incredible out there. How did it feel?"

"Amazing!"

She looks out at the ocean with a gleam in her eye I recognize. She's got the surfing bug now. As much as I want to spend all day surfing with her, today's important.

The future no longer makes me anxious. I'm a man who knows what I want. With Tatum encouraging my dreams, I feel like I'm capable of anything I put my mind to. I finished my double major in three years and was able to open Vale Surf Co. where I teach different levels of surf instruction and host seasonal camps for locals and visiting tourists. Business is booming. In a short time, it became one of the top schools in the area.

I'm proud of what I've achieved and I'm proud of what she's working hard for. After she graduated from South Bay College last year with her degree in Psychology, she started studying for her doctorate while helping me run Vale Surf Co.

There's one more dream I'm chasing. The most important one I've ever wanted.

I guide Tatum's legs around my hips under the water and squeeze her ass. "We'll go out again tonight. I'm starving. Let's head back to the house for breakfast."

"I'm holding you to that." She kisses the corner of my mouth while I slowly move us closer to the beach. "I love that we can do this together. It's an upgrade. As much as I love watching you from shore, it's totally different being out here."

A pleased hum vibrates in my throat and I massage her ass. "Me too. And you look fucking good doing it."

She buries a smile against my shoulder. "What's for breakfast? And before you say me," she interrupts in an amused tone, rolling her lower body against my torso in a way that has my dick fighting the cold water as blood rushes south, "I want to remind you I am, in fact, hungry for food."

I nip at her neck. "You know I'll keep you fed in every way you need."

Forever. That's the plan.

* * *

Tatum remains in the shower after I fucked her lazily as I washed her hair until she shivered from my languid strokes sinking into her and made the most gorgeous sound when she came for me, sending me over the edge.

While she finishes up, I cook our breakfast. Nerves rattle around my stomach while I set the breakfast bar of our bungalow attached to Vale Surf Co. The view of the beach through the banana palms reminds me to create the life I want with the girl I want to spend it with.

I left a note for her on the sundress she spread on the bed that says how much I love her in blue. It's our ritual. I always leave her notes.

Another one sits next to her plate that makes my heart thump harder. I've been saving the heart-shaped sticky note from the packs I used to buy in college for this occasion.

Releasing a shaky breath when I hear her coming downstairs, I rake my fingers through my damp hair.

"Mm, smells good." She winds her arms around my torso from behind and presses on tiptoes to kiss my cheek. "Thanks for breakfast. And the food."

I smack her ass playfully when she moves around me. "I take care of my girl."

My gaze roves over her wet hair braided into pigtails, the freckles on the bridge of her nose, the way her sundress makes her blue eyes stand out. Five and a half years together and it still takes me by surprise that I got the girl of my dreams who fits with me in every way. I love her more than anything and I'm ready for more. I'm ready to make her mine for good.

Tatum sits at the breakfast bar, scanning the spread I made for us. She freezes when her attention lands on the purple sticky note waiting by her glass of lemonade—her mother's famous recipe.

"You already gave me today's note." Her curiosity is shot through with warm affection as she picks it up. "You haven't used these ones in years."

"I was saving the last one," I murmur.

It's the most important note I've ever given her. A long time ago I had a dream of her in a white dress walking a flower-lined aisle in the sand toward me. I want to make that a reality. My fingers twitch, ready to get the ring box I hid behind the fruit bowl out of sight.

She shoots me a smile, the corners of her eyes crinkling. "Let's see, this one says..." *You're my biggest dream. Will you marry me?* "Coop."

Tatum stares at the note, eyes glistening. I caress her cheek, guiding her to look at me.

"I love you, T. Because of you, my future became clear." I slide the ring box out from its hiding spot, placing it in front of her. My eyes bounce between hers and I smile. "The clearest part of it has always been you by my side."

"Oh my god," she whispers thickly.

Clutching the note, she launches at me, squeezing me tight. I could ride the biggest, most perfect wave and the exhilarating feeling wouldn't come close to what it's like kissing her like this. I taste the joy on her tongue.

The ring sits forgotten while she reads the proposal again. It's not important. She's holding the piece of this she'll cherish more than any jewelry I could buy her.

I chuckle, resting my forehead against hers. "Is that a yes? You didn't answer."

"Yes!" She cups my face with both hands. "Yes, I can't wait to marry you. Like, I kind of want to be wild and go down to the court house now."

I draw her in for a kiss and murmur against her lips. "I love it when you're spontaneous."

* * *

Thank you so much for reading THE DEVIL YOU KNOW! If you can't get enough swoony South Bay players, enjoy Jackson and Simone's story THE PLAYER YOU NEED for free.
Download a free bonus story: bit.ly/vebonuscontent

Need more new adult romance packed with angst? Meet the bad boys of Ridgeview in SINNERS AND SAINTS: THE COMPLETE SERIES. Enjoy the interconnected standalones of the Sinners and Saints series in any order. Also available in a complete boxset in ebook/audio with bonus content.

Start Book 1: WICKED SAINT now!
Complete Series Boxset

ACKNOWLEDGMENTS

Readers, I'm endlessly grateful for you! Thanks for reading this book. It means the world to me that you supported my work. I wouldn't be here at all without you! I love all of the comments and messages you send and live for your excitement for my characters!

Thanks to my husband for being you! He doesn't read these, but he's my biggest supporter. He keeps me fed and watered while I'm in the writer cave, and doesn't complain when I fling myself out of bed at odd hours with an idea to frantically scribble down.

Thank you always to Becca, Ramzi, Sara, Kat, Jade, Sarah, Mia, Bre, Heather, Katie, Erica, and Jennifer for the supportive chats and keeping me on track until the end! And to my beta queens for reading my raw words and offering your time, attention to detail, and consideration of the characters and storyline in my books! With every book I write my little tribe grows and I'm so thankful to have each of you as friends to lean on and share my book creation process with!

To my lovely PA Heather, thank you for taking things off my plate and allowing me to disappear into the writing cave without having to worry. And for letting me infodump at you, because that's my love language hahaha! You rock and I'm so glad to have you on my team!

To my street team and reader group, y'all are the best babes around! Huge thanks to my street team for being the best hype girls! To see you guys get as excited as I do seriously makes my day. I'm endlessly grateful you love my characters and words! Thank you for your help in sharing my books and for your support of my work!

To Shauna and Wildfire Marketing Solutions, thank you so much for all your hard work and being so awesome! I appreciate everything that you do!

To the bloggers and bookstagrammers, thank you for being the most wonderful community! Your creativity and beautiful edits, reviews, and videos are something I come back to visit again and again to brighten my day. Thank you for trying out my books. You guys are incredible and blow me away with your passion for romance!

ABOUT THE AUTHOR
STAY UP ALL NIGHT FALLING IN LOVE

Veronica Eden is a USA Today & international bestselling author of addictive romances that keep you up all night falling in love with spitfire heroines, irresistible heroes, and edgy twists.

She loves exploring complicated feelings, magical worlds, epic adventures, and the bond of characters that embrace *us against the world*. She has always been drawn to gruff bad boys, clever villains, and the twisty-turns of a morally gray character. She is a sucker for a deliciously swoony hero with a devastating smirk. When not writing, she can be found soaking up sunshine at the beach, snuggling in a pile with her untamed pack of animals (her husband, dog and cats), and surrounding herself with as many plants as she can get her hands on.

* * *

CONTACT + FOLLOW
Email: veronicaedenauthor@gmail.com
Website: http://veronicaedenauthor.com
FB Reader Group: bit.ly/veronicafbgroup
Amazon: amazon.com/author/veronicaeden

facebook.com/veronicaedenauthor

instagram.com/veronicaedenauthor

pinterest.com/veronicaedenauthor

bookbub.com/profile/veronica-eden

goodreads.com/veronicaedenauthor

ALSO BY VERONICA EDEN

Sign up for the mailing list to get first access and ARC opportunities!
Follow Veronica on BookBub for new release alerts!

New Adult Romance

Sinners and Saints Series

Wicked Saint

Tempting Devil

Ruthless Bishop

Savage Wilder

Sinners and Saints: The Complete Series

Crowned Crows Series

Crowned Crows of Thorne Point

Loyalty in the Shadows

A Fractured Reign

Standalone

The Devil You Know

Unmasked Heart

Devil on the Lake

Jingle Wars

Haze

Reverse Harem Romance

Standalone

Hell Gate

CPSIA information can be obtained
at www.ICGtesting.com
Printed in the USA
BVHW041119050822
643874BV00005B/51